I0598806

Published by Griffyn Ink

www.griffynink.com

For ordering information or special discounts for bulk purchases, please contact Griffyn Ink at Mail@GriffynInk.com.

SAVANNAH KADE

CATCHING
Fire

WILDFIRE HEARTS #2

CHAPTER ONE

Seline Marchand was punching her finger at her phone, irritated and running late, when the floor dropped out from below her.

Her mouth opened to scream, but the screeching sound wasn't her own voice, but the squeal of brakes on metal, grinding the falling box to a stop.

Her ankle turned as her heels didn't take the sudden drop and jolt very well, and she dropped her phone as her heartrate cranked up high enough to make her think it would burst out of her chest. Her breathing was heavy from being startled and her hand had instinctually grasped at the handrail, even though it was basically useless.

"Are you okay?" The tall, dark-skinned man beside her was reaching out, but she waved him away.

With two steadying breaths, she assured herself the elevator had come to a stop. She reached down to scoop up her phone, grateful the face hadn't cracked and that it appeared intact.

She tapped at the screen.

No service.

Seline wanted to laugh—the hysterical kind of laughter, not the happy kind.

She'd been pissed at the way her day was going *before* she stepped into the elevator. Having it drop suddenly, then screech to a grinding halt had been the icing on top.

She was huffing out a breath when she felt her heart lurch again. She noticed her body jerk in response before she even realized the floor was missing and she was falling again.

Her mouth opened, but no sound came out. Her fists clenched, one around the handrail and another on the phone this time as the floor slammed back up at her, the horrifying squeal signaling that the brakes had once again done their job.

But damn if she wasn't going to pass out from being startled to death.

This could not be happening. Not *now!*

Once again, the man made a gesture toward her. He was wearing firefighting flame-retardant pants, his red suspenders hanging loose, his broad capable hands at the ready to help her. He was probably used to people needing his help. But she didn't.

With a deep breath that surely came out more as an irritated sigh, Seline tried to relax her hands, to not make fists and howl at the unfairness. She checked the phone again, hoping to catch a signal and call her department chair and let the woman know that she would likely be late to the first meeting of the semester —for the first meeting Seline was supposed to attend as a tenure-track professor. *Pouah!*

She was mad enough to spit nails and trying not to let the hunky firefighter next to her know it. The signal was still dead. Though she couldn't call out, she could still clearly read the warnings her friend Maggie had texted right before the elevator doors closed.

—I'm still on for our sleepover tonight, but I wanted to warn you. Just got word that the Blue River Killer struck again.

— Clearly, FBI was wrong. Seline, this victim was blond haired and blue eyed! Like you. Please, be careful.

At least she was safe from the killer in here. As long as the hunky firefighter wasn't the killer. She'd only been in Nebraska for five years, but that was long enough to know that, despite being blond-haired and blue-eyed, she didn't really fit the Blue River Killer's profile. He took people from clubs and bars and parties, not universities or chem labs … and certainly not elevators.

"Are you okay?" The strapping firefighter was reaching out a hand as though to steady her again, but she waved him off as politely as she could. Once the hideously old contraption had ground to a halt, she'd been fine.

She felt her jaw clench, and she wanted to pop off, "No, I'm Seline." But instead, she replied, "Yes, I'm fine. I was just startled. What are the chances—"

His radio crackled to life and it figured she'd finally try to be nice and she'd get interrupted. Maybe she'd hear something useful, though.

None of her irritation was from the elevator itself, just the being late part. Elevators she understood. Angry department heads would be harder to fix.

"I'm stuck in shaft number four, East tower, between twelve and thirteen. I have a citizen with me." He said into the black, handheld device. At least he had communication.

"Are they afraid of the elevator falling?" whoever he was talking to answered back.

Seline got even more irritated, though she knew she shouldn't. But why did this have to happen today?

Her tone bore the heavy French accent that seeped back in when she was sad, drinking, or irritated. "Elevators are designed with brake pads made out of materials with high coefficients of dynamic friction. This means that, as the elevator drops faster, the coefficient of friction increases. So, the faster the elevator goes the stickier the brake pads get." She watched as his eyebrows climbed higher and higher, but she was irritated enough to not know when to shut up. "It is virtually impossible for any elevator constructed after 1950 to fall wildly out of control."

He was holding the radio out so the person on the other end of the line could hear her. And he was smiling. "Very good."

"I'm a physical chemist." She shrugged. Even as she said it, she could hear clapping on the other end of his radio. It was more than one person listening in. She should have been embarrassed by her little outburst, but at least they were clapping.

Holding the radio back to his own mouth, he said, "No, she's not afraid of the elevator falling ..."

"I am upset," she added, "because my citizenship is contingent on this professorship. The first meeting of the term with the entire staff of the Chemistry department starts at the Uni in..." She looked at her phone again. *Damn.* "Ten minutes ago."

He had the grace to not point out that she'd been running late well before the elevator ground to a halt.

He winced as though he understood her dilemma but tucked the radio back onto his waistband and said, "Well, I'm glad I'm not stuck in an elevator with someone who's irrationally afraid that they're falling to their death."

She laughed finally, grateful that he'd managed to make her smile. This poor firefighter had managed to get stuck with her when she was at her worst. She decided she could do better.

So she stuck out her hand. "I'm Seline Marchand."

"Kalan Smith. Redemption FD." His hand was larger than hers, his grip warm and reassuring. If she hadn't been such a bitch to him already, she could have liked this guy.

Well, she thought, *her job was the most important thing right now.* Though she'd been at the university for several years. She'd been struggling and finally being offered a tenure track position was a coup, but it didn't guarantee she would make tenure. Missing the first meeting only made her look bad.

She slumped back against the wall and didn't speak, though this Kalan Smith firefighter seemed like he would understand.

They were silent for ten more minutes before she asked, "How long do you think we'll be in here?"

"There's no telling. They could get it fixed and get us moving in the next few minutes or we could be stuck for several hours. We should maybe sit down."

"Oh my Lord," she replied, the words rolling in her mouth like distasteful marbles. She thought about her nice work clothes on the old elevator floor, but sat down anyway.

He offered his own wry grin, for the first time revealing that he, too, was not okay with being stuck here. "I was supposed to be off shift at eight this morning. With this extra assignment, I've been on for twenty-eight straight hours and it's not going to end soon. Once you and I get out of here, the team still has to get the guys in to actually repair these now."

"Are you exhausted?"

This time he shook his head. "I'm used to it."

They talked for a little while and Seline appreciated that his easygoing conversation made thirty minutes pass like nothing. Though he got the occasional message on his radio, nothing had happened. Then, she found herself telling him about one of the students who'd managed to blow up a beaker and make a noxious red smoke in her lab on the very first day of class.

A message popped over his radio even as a knock came at the elevator doors.

"We're here! We're going to get you out."

Seline scrambled to her feet, as did Kalan.

It took over twenty minutes for the firefighters outside to pry the silver doors almost two and a half feet wide. Unfortunately, what Seline and Kalan saw was the workings between floors. Above her, in about a three foot square of space, two heads peered through the opening.

"Hey, Kalan!" one of them said.

Kalan immediately replied, "This is Dr. Seline Marchand with the university. We need to get her back to work today." There were instructions quickly exchanged about how to lift her up and out the small window they'd braced open.

On a normal day Seline would have balked. Instead, she took a deep breath and peeled her shoes one by one. It had been made clear that he would lace his fingers together for a classic boost up and out.

She told herself she could do this, even though she was petrified. Putting her hands on his shoulders, she settled her bare foot into his linked fingers, and she pushed upward.

But before she grabbed the edge of the floor above her head, Seline balked and suddenly jumped back down.

"Are you okay?"

"Yes." Then she immediately shook her head no.

"You said you weren't afraid of the elevator falling."

"No," she said, "I'm not afraid of plummeting to my death. This is a legitimate fear." She pointed at the opening, knowing she sounded crazy, but the words didn't stop. "That is a three-foot gap braced by two by fours. If this elevator falls a mere three feet—as it has done *twice* already—it will snap the braces like twigs. And, even though the edges of the floor and the opening are blunt—" she motioned to both as she spoke, while Kalan and the other firefighters looked on. "—the force of it will chop me in half."

She noticed they hadn't stuck their heads through the opening. They knew this, and no one contradicted her. "It's basic kinematics," she said and watched as he nodded, clearly already aware. "That's what I'm afraid of. If this elevator moves while I am going out of that tiny hole, I will lose limbs and maybe my life."

"Okay."

She was being irrational. There was a whole team of firefighters here. They were not going to let her get chopped in half. They did elevator rescues as part of their job. But she was nervous and couldn't stop spouting the physics. "The changing coefficient and the friction and the brake pads do not work fast enough to stop a three-foot fall."

"I thought you were a chemist," he was grinning at her, but not in a demeaning way.

"Physical chemist. I'm not quite up on my string theory or what FermiLab is up to right now, but I have an excellent amount of physics under my belt."

Kalan only nodded and looked up to the men peering down at them. "Hernandez. Kane. I'm going to boost Seline up, you're going to grab her hands and pull her through as quickly as possible." They nodded and shifted a little bit. Then Kalan turned to her. "Don't grab the edge of the floor. Just aim high and grab their hands. They're going to pull you out as fast as they can. The braces will hold long enough, even if the elevator falls at the exact right moment. You'll be fine."

He was so kind and reassuring that she believed him.

"The other option is waiting until we get this fixed. Right now, everything is turned off." He emphasized the last words, then added, "which means the elevator should not start up again. It shouldn't move at all. This is the safest we're going to be, and I'm coming out after you."

Seline nodded. Damn, he was good at being calm. He was even talking her into this, though she was armed with physics and fear. She nodded.

Once again, she placed her hand on his shoulder and her bare foot into his strong hands. This time, he didn't wait for her. Instead, he said, "One … Two … Three." And he launched Seline and her rapidly beating heart almost through the small window above them. *Almost.*

CHAPTER TWO

K alan jumped backwards as the elevator began to fall again. His arms automatically flew upward to shield his face as the two-by-fours bracing the elevator above him snapped exactly as Seline had said they would.

The good news was that she was already out, her delicate bare feet had slipped through the opening as the power had flickered back on.

"Kalan!" She screamed his name over the squealing of the brakes. The rubbing noise crescendoed to a screech that drowned out her cries as he came to a stop just a few feet below where he'd started.

"I'm fine! I'm fine!" He hollered back up, both for her and the guys.

He was looking to the control panel as the lights immediately flicked back off. Above him, and through the radio, he heard the guys swearing a blue streak and demanding to know who had messed with the breaker.

"Please step away from the elevator shaft." Kalan heard Sebastian talking to Seline and he almost laughed. He appreciated that her stubbornness was turned to him now.

Dr. Seline Marchand was tempting.

"We're coming for you." The chief's voice crackled over the radio but Kalan didn't worry.

The inside doors of the elevator had remained partly open, a massive problem. They would definitely be shutting these down until further inspection, though he figured the top floor guys wouldn't appreciate the climb.

He could see the backs of closed external doors on the floor below at his feet. So if the guys could pry those open, he could get out through the bottom. And even if the elevator turned on and dropped again—which it shouldn't—he would have more than enough time to get through the opening.

Son of a bitch, he thought. He'd tried to convince her not to be afraid of the elevator falling. Not only had she not needed his input but, in the end, she'd been right.

If she'd been halfway through the window when the elevator dropped again, it would have gone exactly as she'd said. *Jesus*, he ran his hand over his face and watched as the doors at his feet pried open and the tops of two helmets came into view.

"Alright, dude, we got you."

Unlike Seline, he knew the drill. There was just enough room for a guy his size to wiggle through, and he slid out feet first. Flipping over midway, he grabbed the edge and lowered himself down in a reverse pull up. He would have done it nice and slow, but after the elevator had already fallen, he wasn't taking another chance.

Pushing back, he jumped away from the elevator shaft and hit the linoleum floor with an ungraceful thud before stumbling back a few feet.

"You good, man?" Luke asked, while behind him a softer prettier voice breathed out in relief. "Oh, Kalan. I'm glad you're okay."

He felt his heart twist at the sound.

Was it okay to ask a woman out after being stuck in an elevator with her?

She very personally threw her arms around his waist, holding onto him tightly. "That was exactly what I was afraid of."

"I know." He hugged her back. "And I feel bad that I told you it wasn't going to happen."

He easily saw over her head because she was quite petite, and he wasn't. Behind her, the others raised eyebrows, silently asking what his relationship with the hot blonde was. But there was nothing between them, though he might wish otherwise. If he was smart, he would change that tomorrow. Today, there was too much work to do and she was late for her meeting.

"I'm glad you're okay," she was repeating it as she ignored a series of dings and bells from her phone.

He looked down at her, still wrapped around him.

Shyly, she seemed to realize where she was, and only pulled out her phone to say, "My messages are blowing up since I got out into the hallway."

As she turned away from him, he realized she seemed so petite because she was barefoot and her shoes were still in the elevator. *Dammit*, he thought, he should have brought them out with him.

"I'll see about getting your shoes." He said it but she was frowning at her phone, paying no attention to him at all.

"Maggie?" she asked, putting the phone to her ear. "What's so important? I was stuck in an elevator with one of your firefighter friends."

Oh, shit. This was Maggie's friend, the chemist she talked about! He hadn't expected to run into her here in Lincoln, and he grinned at how lucky he was that the woman who'd just thrown her arms around him lived in his small hometown.

But as he watched, Seline's face went white.

"He what? ... Do you think I'm in trouble? ... No, no. I'm

safe. I'm here with the firefighters right now. I'm putting you on speaker." Seline looked up at Kalan and the others still standing behind him.

"Hey Maggie," Kalan offered, his concern growing with the fear on Seline's face.

Maggie's voice was nearly frantic. "The FBI just called me and I'm not supposed to tell anyone. But I have to tell Seline, and I guess now I'm telling you. It's been five months that William Treat Sanders has been in the wind. The agents are confident that he's the Blue River killer and they *were* confident he was gone." The words tumbled over each other, coming out too quickly, but all the firefighters knew Maggie. She was their volunteer once a week. So no one interrupted her.

"They just confirmed it to me. The new victim they found this morning, matches his profile. The body is probably three or four days old."

Seline was the one who asked out loud what Kalan was wondering. "Are they sure?"

Kalan wondered if Seline knew just how much she looked like the BRK's victims, but he didn't get a chance to ask. Maggie confirmed his worst fear. "They are certain. The Blue River Killer is back and no one knows where he is."

CHAPTER THREE

Seline stood in her lab at the university. She'd come in today to put in an appearance and let her department chair see that she was here and working. Because she was here, she was running the experiment that might just blow up.

Her home lab couldn't handle it if this one went wrong. Besides, it was the first home she'd ever bought, she loved the view, and the gingerbread trim, and she was determined not to blow it up. But for now, she was in the uni lab, staring at the columns in her lab notebook and tapping her pencil.

She was also trying to decide exactly how worried she should be about the Blue River Killer.

Maggie was concerned and felt bad, which made sense. Maggie had brought Seline up to date on the La Vista Rapist and Blue River Killer information. Some of it Maggie said hadn't been released to the public, but she'd felt the need to tell Seline.

But she'd locked her doors, and she wasn't going to parties or bars ... and she had to get this formula configured. She was close.

Seline quadruple checked. If this blew up, it would not

reflect well on her petition for tenure. But maybe she could spin it ... or maybe just not blow it up.

Firing up her Bunsen burner, she snapped on a pair of gloves and began to line up her chemicals. They were organized alphabetically in a variety of containers depending on whether they reacted to air or absorbed water or such. She pulled a pale-yellow powder from the shelf and her brain veered again.

Maggie told her that the latest victim had been found the night before, about seven miles up the Big Blue River from where it passed by Redemption. The body was partially submerged at the water's edge, just like the others. Whatever the other identifying information was, Maggie hadn't known, but she did say the FBI had confirmed that it was the work of the BRK. This victim had been female, but they'd all been blond haired and most of them blue eyed. *Just like her.*

But—like the other victims—this one had disappeared when she'd been out partying. The last place she'd been seen had been a bar, which she'd left after eleven on Thursday night, Maggie said.

Though Seline understood Maggie's worry that she matched the typecasting perfectly—maybe aside from being French and a little bit older than his usual victims—she certainly didn't exhibit any of the dangerous behaviors the man targeted.

The problem was that he was already stealing her time ... even if he hadn't targeted her at all.

But he wouldn't take her from here. And she had work to do! *Dieu*, she had extra work because she could not afford to miss a deadline now that she'd missed the meeting.

Forcing her attention back to the task at hand, she picked up a beaker and checked it for cleanliness. Though she cleaned them all herself, no one was infallible, and a good chemist always checked when they were done, and before they started.

She measured and diluted her acid and double checked it with litmus paper. She noted the shade of pink and was pretty much able to read it by sight, but still she held it up against the reference strip just to be sure. Moving down on the counter, she turned around and pulled another flask and once again inspected it before setting it and another down on the counter.

She absolutely could not blow up the lab today. She had a date with Kalan tonight.

Her lips pulled into a self-satisfied smile as she grabbed another liquid off of the shelf and a small vial of a pale blue powder. Getting tenure was contingent upon her lab work. And her moving to Redemption had been contingent upon her ability to find a home she could afford to convert into lab space and stock with chemicals so that she could do most of her lab work at home.

Already, that wasn't working out for her.

Luckily, most of her work was polymer based. In the worst case scenario, it would overflow her beakers or test tubes and she'd have to clean the counter. She hoped she'd be able to get back soon, to working from the home lab she'd paid so much for.

Two hours later, she had three pages of notes in her lab book. The mixture had gotten hotter than she expected. Not dangerously so, but it still meant she would have to change her formulas. At least she was done for the day.

She cleaned all her beakers and the counters until everything sparkled. A clean lab worked, the slightest speck could cause problems. When that was finished, she checked her watch and headed down the hall.

If she grabbed her bag and got out before traffic hit, she would make it back to Redemption with plenty of time to get ready. Picking up her pace, she headed down the hall and veered to miss the man coming around the corner.

He looked at her a little oddly, but then headed into the open office on her left. *Merde.* She checked the name on the sign. "Dr. Gilman?"

"Hmmm?" He'd been facing the desk, picking up the coffee mug, but he turned at her voice.

"I'm Dr. Marchand." She shifted her bag and held out her right hand. "I just moved into the lab next to yours." In the hallway where all the tenured professors had labs. "I just wanted to introduce myself to everyone since I missed the meeting. I was stuck in an elevator for some time that morning."

"Oh." He finally shook her hand back. A clammy feeling traced up her arm and she let go quickly. Chemists were not generally known for their warmth.

"I won't take any more of your time." She backed out of his office and picked up her pace again, though this time she was more careful at the corner.

Putting the key into the lock, she opened her office and picked up a stack of papers from her desk. On top sat a cut strip of plain white paper that said Hello in blocky letters. She did not have time for student notes.

But how did it get here? The office was locked, so maybe she'd brought it in with something earlier. Shoving the whole stack of papers down into her bag, she locked everything and headed out to the parking garage.

She hadn't quite made it out before traffic and now she was running a bit late. Should she call Kalan and cancel?

Maybe.

She didn't have time to date. She had a position at the university that needed even more of her time this year. Her house payment was at the upper edge of what she could afford. If the toilet clogged, she was simply going to have to use a different bathroom until she could scrape up enough money to pay for repairs. If the roof leaked, then she was in real trouble.

Her heart raced at the thought. Being a new homeowner was both exhilarating and petrifying. Seline reminded herself that she'd had the place inspected and it was solid. The roof wasn't going to fall in or leak or blow away.

By the time she pulled into her own driveway, she was worked up. She'd not cancelled her date—even busy women deserved some fun! Besides, when would she find a guy like Kalan again? She would go on this date if it killed her.

She practically bounced along the stones to the back porch and put her key in the lock. Did it turn too easily?

CHAPTER FOUR

K alan was nervous.
    So nervous that he'd mis-buttoned the front of his shirt and wound up looking as twitchy as he was. He was still looking in the mirror, feeling like an idiot.

Why was he so nervous? It was just a first date. He had done this hundreds of times—or at least too many times.

With a sigh, he undid the buttons and tried again. Clearly, he couldn't be trusted to properly button himself without watching in the mirror.

He wondered if his twitchiness was because Seline was Maggie's friend. If things went wrong, he could wind up in hot water. The better possibility was that he wasn't just going on a regular first date.

This one felt special for a reason he couldn't quite put his finger on. Despite her adorable surliness, Seline Marchand had been enchanting. He'd heard about her from Maggie—friendly, funny, fun, thoughtful—but Maggie hadn't warned him that something about her friend would give him a visceral reaction.

There was also the possibility that this was the first time in a long time where he'd really felt that kind of spark. He didn't need three or four dates to know if he liked her. He did.

Kalan also ascribed to the old adage of *if you want to know who someone really is, put them in front of a slow computer.* A falling elevator on a day when she was already late for her first big meeting probably qualified. Despite being surly, and apologizing for being at her worst, Seline had been nothing of the sort.

She'd been alternately irritated, petrified, and bored, but also captivating and hopeful, and offered him that shy grin thanking him simply for being there.

With the buttons now properly in alignment, he picked up three neckties off the dresser. Holding each one up, he frowned. None seemed right. The fourth answer, of course, was no tie. But what kind of woman was she?

She was a chemist. She'd been in professional clothing in the elevator, but that was because she'd been going to a work meeting. This was a date and he didn't wear suits to work ... not that kind anyway.

Tossing the ties back onto the dresser, he opted for the middle ground. He was in a dress shirt, nice slacks, and he was taking her dancing. He undid the top two buttons, too.

Of course, right then his phone beeped with a reminder and he realized he was running late. He was not going to be late for Seline, hence all the reminders he'd set. This one told him to head into the kitchen. He tossed together a peanut butter sandwich. If he didn't eat something now, his stomach would growl, and she'd wonder what kind of sasquatch she'd agreed to go out with.

Kalan scarfed it down, brushed his teeth again, and headed out the door on time.

The apartment he left behind was small and spare. Not ugly, but not pretty either. Nothing like what Sebastian and his mother had done up. Instead, Kalan had taken a small apartment with small utility bills. A place that only needed small amounts of furniture. His intent had been to keep the rest of the money for a nicer car.

But, even as he climbed in and strapped on his seat belt, he wondered if Seline would judge his choice. She probably out-earned him. Firefighting was like that: You did the job because you loved it. The promotions were more effort than they paid out in cash and, unless you became chief, you might not hit the point where you could support a family on only your salary.

There wasn't much room for more than the basics unless he picked up second jobs. He'd have to keep picking up second jobs if he was going to continue to date Seline.

Slow down, cowboy, he told himself. He had to make it through the first date before he pulled the trigger on anything else.

When he pulled up to her driveway a few moments later, her front door opened and she stepped out. His heart stuttered. A first date shouldn't do this to him. But she did.

Seline wore a pale blue, floaty dress that offered a nod to the last day of summer. His gaze scanned down to her feet, noticing that while she wore heels, they looked relatively solid for dancing. He hadn't quite told her where he was taking her, only offered hints.

Unsure what to do now, he fell back on the normal pleasantries. Holding out one hand, he whispered, "You look beautiful."

"Thank you." She held on as she made her way down the front steps, obviously not needing anything from him. "You look very nice yourself."

He handed her into the passenger seat and closed the door, not knowing what else to say. She didn't need any of the coddling, but he believed in starting off chivalrous until she told him otherwise.

Conversation had come easy when they were trapped in an

elevator together, but now he was nervous how to start. Luckily, she fastened her seat belt and turned slightly toward him, her hands on her knees. "You have not told me where we are going."

He noticed she didn't use contractions and wondered if that meant she was nervous, because she'd used them in the elevator when she was calmer. In fact, the accent had almost disappeared entirely when he'd seen her on her way out of the building after retrieving her shoes. But it was back again now.

Interesting. He enjoyed finding out these little things about Seline Marchand.

"Do you want me to tell you or do you want it to be a surprise?"

She thought for a moment, then grinned and said, "Tell me."

"It's a place down in Beatrice."

She grinned at the name, probably thinking the locals were very backwards, because the town wasn't *Be*-atrice, like the normal pronunciation of the name. Nope, whoever had founded the place, put the stress on the second syllable. But Kalan kept going. "It's actually two places right next to each other. They decided they were better with an open area between them. One is a wonderful Italian restaurant and the second place is a dance club."

"A club?" she asked, her voice climbing, probably thinking he was taking her to a rave.

"Well, not quite like a *club* club. Like an old-school dance club. They teach swing classes on Friday nights." He watched as her eyes lit up, and he realized he'd hit the nail on the head. *Thank God.* "Is Italian okay?"

"I love Italian food!"

He breathed easier then wondering if he'd made a mistake taking a French woman to a Nebraska trattoria. But then again, what French restaurant could he have taken her to around here that would be up to her standards?

So far, so good. He wanted to ask her everything, but

something about her wide smile stopped him. He was going to have to keep an eye on her. He didn't want to make her nervous, but he couldn't help thinking he was taking her to a dance club when she looked like the perfect victim for the Blue River Killer.

CHAPTER FIVE

S eline put her hand to her stomach, stuffed beyond full. She'd tried not to over-eat, but it was delicious and the decadent ravioli in cream sauce had done her in.

Kalan stood and held out his hand.

"You want to dance?" she asked almost incredulously. "I'm not sure I can move."

He smiled that wide heart-stopping grin of his. "Me either. But if we don't exercise some of this off before the tiramisu, we'll never be able to leave."

"Oh, my God. There's tiramisu?"

He just grinned as though pleased with himself. He still stood there with his hand out, waiting. This time she accepted, sliding her fingers into his warm grip.

As he pulled her onto the dance floor, he suggested, "Let's start with a slow dance. I can't do any of the moves we learned in class! They're too fast for right after dinner."

Though she laughed and agreed, Seline asked herself, *What was she even doing?*

She didn't have the time to date anyone. But as his arms slid slowly around her waist, she realized she didn't want to date *anyone*, she wanted to date *him*. The timing was crappy on all fronts, but his hand slid along her waist and down to her hip, and she decided she should at least give tonight a chance.

With his other hand, he traced her forearm bringing her movement along with his until his fingers interlocked with hers.

Seline sighed and settled against him, such an easy thing to do. Could she do this? Her house was requiring every penny she made and every moment that she had. Her job had needed so much, and she had to get tenure to keep the house. It had been tight before she missed the staff meeting.

She simply didn't have time for this modernly beautiful man and his classically seductive moves. But as he pulled her in close, she could feel every cell catch fire.

It stunned her. This was the kind of attraction she felt for a man after time, maybe after she'd nursed a crush. But this flared to life, hot and consuming, and he hadn't even kissed her yet.

Breathing in the scent of him and leaning against his chest, she let one slow dance turn into three. He turned them slowly around the floor, pressed together in a way that made it clear why the waltz had always been a favorite.

When the song ended and began to fade into the next, Seline unlaced her arms from around his neck and stepped back, almost on principle. *What if they burst into flame right here?*

"I'm going to— …" she didn't know what she was going to do. She should have thought this out a little better. "… head to the ladies room."

She needed to catch her breath; she needed space between them. Though she'd let go of him, Kalan hadn't quite let go of her. His fingers trailed down her arm, across her palms, and out to her fingertips almost like a scene from a classic film.

As she slipped away, she fought the delicious shudder that would have let everyone on the dance floor know what she was feeling … if they hadn't already figured it out. Her breath hitched and she looked away as though that would break the spell.

She made her way across the restaurant toward the back corner where they tucked the restrooms, trying to shake the heady cloud of lust. But her knees threatened to buckle, even though Kalan was no longer near her.

She was falling for this guy, hard and fast—the kind of fall that would have her hitting the pavement at a deadly rate.

Seline hit something alright. Not watching where she was going and being dreamy eyed over her date, she'd smacked into someone coming out of the restroom hallways. She wasn't sure if she made the noise or he did. His drink sloshed and he scrambled to right it.

"*Oh, mon dieu. Je suis vraimont desole,*" she scrambled, the words falling out in French. She tried a second time. "I'm so sorry."

"No problem," but he wasn't looking at her. When he did, he jolted back and said, "Dr. Marchand?"

Seline took a good look then. She saw the short brown hair bordering on red, the neatly trimmed beard, and the kind green eyes. And she didn't recognize him at all. Then again, she'd run into students in the past and not recognized them. She stood at the front of the room and they all knew who she was. This one looked a little old to be a—

"I was in Introductory Chemical Analysis last spring."

She nodded, unsure what to say. She didn't remember him.

He caught the awkward silence, but instead of filling in his name for her, said, "I'm so sorry. I didn't mean to run into you."

When she didn't say anything again, just offered a half smile —*what else could she do?* he added, "Funny us running into each other *here.*"

Something about the way he said it held a slight edge. But that would be ridiculous. Unless he'd failed the class? Students with bad grades often felt that was the professor's fault.

"Are you on a date?" he asked with a softer tone.

The haze of lust that Kalan had left her in twisted to

wariness. Just because he supposedly knew her didn't mean he had any right to ask such personal questions.

She didn't want to be mean to a student, that was not the reputation she wanted. And there was a good possibility that he was slightly inebriated ... or more than slightly. She wasn't dressed professionally either. She was, in fact, here on a date, but she wouldn't say so.

"I'm here with a friend." She offered another half-smile. She'd have to explain to Kalan later in case he heard that and thought she was brushing him off.

"I was on a date. Or I *thought* I was," he said with a tip of his drink for emphasis. "Got stood up."

Her heart sank. No wonder he was being overly forward. He'd likely been sitting at the bar and drinking. "I'm so sorry." But before the awkward pause could bloom this time, she pointed toward the back and said, "I'm on my way to the ladies room. Good luck."

That was a dumb thing to say, but she didn't want to be around him any longer.

When she emerged, he was gone and Kalan was waiting at the table with a stunningly large square of tiramisu. He handed her a fork.

"I can't eat all of this," she protested, though she loved tiramisu.

"Do your best." He dug into the other side of it.

It was close to midnight by the time he dropped her off. Just as gentlemanly as he'd started the evening, he hopped around the car and opened her door. When he offered to help her out of the low-slung sports car, he didn't let go as he led her up the front steps and to the door.

Kalan stepped in close. He smelled of tiramisu and something deeper. "I am not ready for this evening to end." Though the words were low and melodious, he immediately stepped back, eyes wide. "Oh shit. I just meant how I feel. I wasn't trying to invite myself in. I realize—"

She'd already grabbed his shirt and pulled him closer. His words cut short as his mouth covered hers and she discovered that he tasted like tiramisu, too.

His hands were in her hair. The sweater she'd thrown over her arm slipped to the porch, followed quickly by the thud of her purse as the kiss caught fire. Her mouth opened and his tongue invaded. Her back arched and she pressed herself to the solid wall that was Kalan Smith. Her fingers ran down the small, flat buttons of his shirt and it was all she could do to stop from unbuttoning him right there.

As he pulled back for a moment, he looked into her eyes and she saw him grab at the edge of his sleeve.

What?

With his hand covered by the cuff of his nice shirt, he reached up and loosened the porch bulb, plunging them into darkness. She couldn't see him, but Seline felt the air shift as he moved closer, his lips softly stalking her mouth by feel.

Her fingers clutched at his belt, while his hands roamed freely now, no longer concerned what the neighbors might see. This kiss was far, far too hot for a first date. They probably lit the place up the way their touches blazed.

She traced his jaw with her mouth, then his lower lip, then realized she was pushed back against the wall of the porch. Her leg was up over his hip, her skirt rucked up. With a quick glance down, she saw only the dark-on-light play of his large hand against her pale thigh. She both watched and felt as his fingers clenched.

They kissed and touched and tried to absorb each other until she ran out of oxygen. With her hands clutching the fabric of his shirt, and her fists bracing into his chest, she took a gulp of air. But when she pulled him back, he was rigid. No longer melting into her, he stayed put.

Damn, the light would have been handy now. She couldn't even see his expression, but she felt the cool night air rush between them as he abruptly stepped back.

All he said was, "I'm sorry," as he jammed his hands into his pockets and turned away. At the bottom of the steps he didn't turn to look back or he would have seen the stunned expression on her face before he drove away.

CHAPTER SIX

Seline moved down the street briskly enough to rival a marching band. Her brain was cycling from foggy and dreamy to irritated and tense.

He'd broken that insanely steamy kiss and walked off with a half-uttered "sorry." *Had she done something? Had he?*

It didn't help that she'd planned to get some work done after she got home. It had been so late when he'd finally dropped her off that wasn't going to happen. Then she was too confused and frustrated to do anything resembling an experiment or even attempting to balance her reaction equations.

She didn't have time to be out for her walk this morning either, but nothing could happen if she didn't get her brain in gear. Seline was smart enough to know that she had to exercise off some of this tension.

As she trekked the neighborhood with her probably sour expression, her mind wandered as much as her feet did. She was three blocks over before she even looked up to see if any of her neighbors were out on a Saturday morning. She passed a young mom and a couple. The older man was clearly maintaining a much younger body than his thinning white hair would have her believe. He didn't acknowledge her as his head was down and he had earbuds in.

They were on a collision course, but there were no waves or greetings. Seline wound up giving him a dirty side eye as she sidestepped to keep him from barreling into her. *What was it with people running into her?*

Then again, maybe it was her.

"Oh, sorry!" he called as he turned around and jogged a few steps backwards, waving in apology. That was hardly the "Nebraska nice" she'd come to expect. But she nodded and continued on her way.

She should simply make a U turn here on the sidewalk and head home. But despite everything on her to-do list, her head still wasn't clear and she didn't want to look like she was following him. So she used her one brain cell that wasn't thinking about Kalan, and turned left on the next block. She walked a short loop and eventually made it back home—not that she'd paid attention along the way. Hell, she might have barreled into some of her neighbors and not known it. She'd barely looked around.

At home, she took a quick shower, though she would have liked to have lingered. By the time she emerged, it was already ten. When her phone dinged from the other room, she pulled the fluffy white terry cloth from her head and followed the sound of her ringtone.

The phone sat in the middle of the bed. Had she left it there? She didn't remember, but that didn't matter, it was ringing.

The number was unknown, but she couldn't afford to alienate anyone from the university. So she hit the button with a frown on her face. "Hello?"

"Is this Seline Marchand? This is FBI agent Melissa Watson."

Seline blinked. "It is."

Was there anything else she could say? Maggie had warned her that the FBI would let her know if something came up. But

Seline had thought it was a ridiculous concern that Maggie had because of her own trouble. Then again, maybe her friend wasn't over-reacting. The FBI was on the phone.

Wasn't Watson one of the agents that had worked Maggie's case?

"What is this regarding?" Seline blurted out.

"We'd like to come and meet with you. We'll explain everything."

Dear God, she thought, followed by a quick sigh. There would be no catching up on work today.

"Dr. Marchand?"

She must have paused for too long. "When?"

"As soon as possible."

Merde. "I need thirty minutes. Where shall we meet?"

"We can be at your place then. Thank you." Agent Watson hung up before she could protest.

As Seline stared at the now silent device in her hand, she realized she'd not given them her address. Of course, they already knew it. They were the FBI. Her nerves were overtaking her and she reminded herself that she didn't have to dress up for them. It was Saturday, after all.

She wound up in jeans and a button-down white shirt, her hair still damp as she opened the door to them. She'd swallowed the last few bites of oatmeal just a moment before she'd seen them pull up.

Letting them in, she checked each of their badges as they introduced themselves. It was good to have names to put with the faces, she thought, though the whole thing was making her uneasy. Watson at least tried to help her stay calm, but there wasn't much she could do.

Seline sat on the couch, trying to relax, but that wasn't going to happen.

"Do you know why we're here?" Decker asked.

Seline found her attention pulled to the man for just a moment. "I'm assuming it's because of my friend Maggie Willis.

She messaged me and told me she was worried because the Blue River Killer victims look like me."

When both agents nodded, Seline continued with what she learned, hoping they would stop her. They didn't. "He takes both men and women, but always blonde hair and usually blue eyes, almost always with a slight build." No one had corrected her yet, so she kept going. "He takes them at night, often on the weekends, from clubs and parties and bars."

The two agents only stared at her as if to ask what she was doing to protect her blond-haired, blue-eyed self.

"I don't do that."

"We're aware of that," Watson replied calmly, once again concerning Seline with the knowledge that they already had about her.

"Is this visit because of the incident with Maggie Willis?"

"Which one?" Decker again.

But Seline shrugged. She had no idea how they had categorized what happened to Maggie.

"We got Merrit Geller. He is confirmed as the La Vista Rapist and he is now deceased. However, in that incident, he took Magdalyn Willis to William Sanders' safehouse. We found copious evidence that the cabin was where Sanders tortured and killed his victims. So he now has to find a new place to carry out his plans and, so far, we haven't found him."

Seline nodded, but none of that made her more likely to become a victim.

"We're concerned that he wants revenge on Ms. Willis. And that he might try to get it through you."

"*Serieusement?*" The word tumbled out of her mouth and she went cold, for the first time considering that Maggie's warning may have been more than just unfounded worry. "You truly think this?"

"We don't know. We can't find Sanders and aren't able to predict where he'll turn up. But it's a possibility that we must consider. We want to be sure you know everything to look for."

Placing her now clammy palms on her knees, Seline sat very still and nodded.

"His name is William Treat Sanders. No one's seen him for over a month—not anyone who can identify him."

Seline gulped. *His victim had seen him ...*

"In fact, Maggie Willis was the last." There was a pause and Seline wondered if they were waiting for something from her, but Watson pulled out a tablet and tapped it a few times. Holding up a picture, she said, "Let's start with what he looks like. Have you seen him?"

She shook her head. The man in the photograph looked entirely unfamiliar.

"What about this?" Quickly, Watson turned the tablet to herself and clicked another picture, before flipping back to Seline.

"That's the same man," Seline pointed out. They'd given him a different haircut and facial hair, different eye color, but it was clearly the same person.

"It is. But have you seen him?" Watson moved the tablet a little farther toward Seline as though the problem might be her eyesight.

Realizing they were trying to show her what he might look like now, she took a closer look, but ... "No."

They went through three more versions of the photograph before Watson brought up the one with thinning white hair and pale, pasty skin.

Seline's back straightened involuntarily. Watson and Decker didn't miss her reaction.

"You've seen him." Decker stated. It wasn't a question.

"Not only have I seen him ..." Seline breathed the words out, fighting not to revert to French. "I just passed him on my walk about an hour ago."

CHAPTER SEVEN

"Go!" Watson told Decker, and he was out the door before Seline could quite process what was going on.

Watson had her gun drawn, and had turned to look out the window, while Seline still hadn't managed to move from where she sat. Gripping her knees tightly with her fingers, she realized that Maggie was right. This was *real*.

Whether or not he was even after her, a serial killer was likely in her neighborhood.

"Maybe it wasn't him," she squeaked the words out. Surely, she was wrong. Or all old men just looked alike? But that wasn't true, and Watson wasn't having any of her denial.

"It's far too coincidental. Do you know the man you saw? Do you know his name? Or where he lives?"

Dread filled her as she shook her head *no* to all of it. "I'm new here."

They would know that, too. Right?

Watson offered a short nod as she continued to scan the street. Her words carried over her shoulder. "Did you see anyone else who seemed to know who he was?"

Seline shook her head, unable to form words. Still stunned at how fast things had changed from 'just a precaution' to one of the agents running out the door with his gun drawn. She realized Watson couldn't see her answer and she pushed the word out between her lips. "No."

Again, she was granted a short nod as Watson stood to the side of the large pane of glass, her gaze still aimed outside. The street was now busy for Redemption, but not like a big city.

This weekend had gone to shit on all fronts. She was getting no work done. She'd decided to give things a try with dating Kalan even though she didn't really have the time … and he'd walked away. He'd not messaged today or anything. And now, she was supposed to be working and catching up on what she'd missed and instead she was petrified in her own living room because she might have bumped into the most notorious serial killer in middle America less than an hour ago.

Mon dieu.

"Two of you might be able to look faster," Seline offered.

"One of us has to stay here with you," was all Watson said, but it was enough to make Seline's already cold blood turn icy.

She hadn't thought of that, but she was grateful for the protection.

For fifteen minutes, she stayed away from the windows as she and agent Watson waited for Decker to return. Eventually, he opened the front door, and Seline looked up anxiously. He only shook his head. "Nothing."

Watson raised an eyebrow and Decker gave them both a full run-down. "I asked everyone I saw if they saw him, but no one had. I showed the picture and knocked on doors along the street where she said she saw him and no one even recognized him. Strange for a small town like this."

Seline agreed. She'd come to Redemption in the hope that she would know her neighbors. Though Lincoln wasn't huge by any standards, she'd been lonely in her apartment there. And the thing about "Nebraska Nice" was real, but it was for passing people in the hallway, and not for making real friends.

She and Maggie had become close within two weeks of her moving here and had confirmed she'd made the right move. But, though she adored Maggie, it seemed her new friend had brought a serial killer to her doorstep. Seline's heart was beating far too fast. While it was understandable that she might not yet recognize someone who lived in Redemption, it wasn't reasonable that no one down the whole street did.

He wasn't from here. So what was he doing on her street? And at exactly the right time to bump into her?

"Deep breaths," Agent Watson told her calmly, realizing she was starting to hyperventilate even before she did.

Seline forcibly slowed her breathing. Though she still couldn't talk, she stood up and rearranged the furniture for something to do … ridiculous though the action was.

"All noted and recorded," Decker told his partner as he motioned them all to sit back down. Watson still had two more versions of pictures to show Seline.

"They all look like ordinary people. This one looks like the student who bumped into me at the club last night."

"Do you remember this student?" Watson asked.

"No, but I don't remember all of my students, and…" Seline almost laughed as she pointed at the last picture.

"What?" Watson pressed, frowning at the odd reaction.

"That one looks exactly like one of the professors at my school."

"But you're certain it's a professor?"

"Yes, it's Dr. Gilman," Seline said, and when they continued to stare at her, she added, "He was in his office. And he's been tenured there long before I was even in the department."

At that, the two agents shrugged and tipped their heads, giving up on that avenue, though they still asked her all kinds of other questions.

"Can you think of anything weird or strange that has happened to you recently?"

She couldn't honestly say anything had.

"We have a problem," Watson said then, as though Seline could help solve it.

But all Seline could think was, how could there possibly be something worse? Hadn't the things she'd already encountered been problem enough? But she didn't ask.

Instead, Watson smacked her upside the head with something worse. "We have another body ... It's confirmed to bear the same signature as BRK. This is why we know that William Treat Sanders is still alive and in the area."

"You're confident it's not a copycat?" Seline asked, having watched enough late-night forensics tv-shows to have an opinion. One that was probably ill informed and laughable, but she'd already asked.

"Yes, there are things about the bodies that have not been released to the public. Something a copycat is unlikely to get correct. However, there was something *new* on this one."

Seline tried to stay calm, but her breathing wasn't steady at all.

"This is a gruesome picture," Watson warned, pulling a printed page out of her bag.

Mon dieu.

She sucked in a breath but nodded *okay* and gripped her knees a little bit tighter if that were possible.

The picture that Watson handed over was cropped, not a picture of the full body, just the torso. Naked. One word was carved into it.

Seline's breathing shallowed as her eyes involuntarily pulled away. She was looking at the wall as Watson took the photo from her outstretched hand.

Once again, it was difficult to breathe. Her nerves constricted, and she felt as if everything were buzzing.

"I'm sorry that you had to see that," Decker apologized. "But clearly he has taken notice of you. He might even be stalking you. We weren't sure if this would mean anything to you. We had to ask."

The words blurred together. Seline was hyperventilating again. Or was she not breathing at all? Her brain rolled.

"Seline."

"*Seline?*"

It was her own name, and she heard it, but the ice forming in her veins didn't let her respond.

"*Seline!*"

Agent Watson grabbed her shoulders and shook her slightly, finally breaking her out of the spell.

"I got a note this week!" Seline realized as she blurted out the words that it sounds stupid. No one cared about a note when there was a dead body. She tried to explain. "It was left on my desk at school, or with papers I picked up after class ... I don't know."

"Where at the school would this be?"

It took a moment to think it through. "I first saw it in my office, which was locked while I was in the lab. But the note was on top of a stack of papers I picked up after my class, so I might have gotten it then ..."

It was terrifying now not knowing where the note had come from, how he'd gotten it to her. Because—after seeing the body —there was no doubt that it had come from the Blue River Killer. She had to tell the agents what it meant. They were still looking at her oddly because she'd almost vomited over a 'note.'

"If the note is important, why didn't you tell us before?" Decker was leaning forward now, though Seline got the impression that he had eyes in the back of his head. That he was watching the street and her porch as well as focusing on her. His words might have sounded accusatory, but his tone didn't.

"It wasn't important, not until you showed me the picture. It was just a little slip of paper that said *hello*. How was I supposed to know he'd carve that into ..."

She couldn't finish the words, just watched as both Watson's and Decker's eyes flicked toward her bag as though they could see inside.

Decker put a hand out. "Let's not jump to conclusions. So, you got a note that said *hello*. Nothing else?"

"No, but it's the same word and it's written the exact same way. With—" she almost gulped, "—*slashes* for the letters. It's in my bag. I'll get it for you

Watson and Decker looked at each other again.

This time it was Watson who gently held out a hand to stop her frantic movement and asked, "When exactly did you get the note?"

"Three days ago."

They looked at each other again, this time not questioning that the two were related and knowing something that they didn't tell her. They waited, though it had probably been less than half a beat of time.

Seline couldn't take the silence and she almost shouted. "*What?*"

"We only found the body this morning."

CHAPTER EIGHT

K alan's phone beeped and his eyes darted toward it, but it wasn't Seline. Just an email coming in.

And why would it be Seline? It was almost two a.m. Most of the guys had gone to bed, but he hadn't been able to sleep. In the past he'd learned it was better not to force it. If the alarm came, he'd want to be able to jump up, ready to go. For twenty-four hours, his job was to be ready.

Only Ronan Kelly was still in the main area, making one of his endless pots of coffee. A-shift always had the best, and it was because of whatever kitchen-witchery Ronan did. Though why he needed fresh brew at two in the morning, no one asked.

Kalan had parked himself in one of the recliners in front of the tv, though the screen was blank. He was staring at his phone.

Could he message her in the middle of the night?

It wouldn't wake her up, would it?

He tapped out, — I'm sorry.

Because he was. He'd been sorry about how he'd handled it from the moment she'd pushed him away.

His only excuse was just how startled he'd been by the

whole thing. He'd been two breaths from taking advantage of her on the front porch, and on the first date. That was something *Thinking Kalan* would never have done. But he was so attracted to her that he'd somehow become *Caveman Kalan*. He'd never done that before, so he had no clue how to stop himself.

He'd completely overstepped and didn't know how to deal with it.

His insides swirled around in ways they weren't meant to. As soon as he'd tapped his apology into the window, he erased it.

He could apologize in the morning. Right now—if she was sleeping—the last thing he wanted to do was wake her.

He'd been a Class A idiot all the way around, being more of one wouldn't help. If he was going to get another chance, he had work to do.

There was no question that one date was not going to be enough. Seline was worth it. It was only a question of whether or not he could convince her of that.

Just then, his chair swayed slightly, and he jolted alert, flipping his phone over. As he cranked his neck around to see who was standing behind him.

Of course it was Sebastian. And of course he'd seen the message to Seline.

His friend nodded. "So you haven't contacted her since the date?"

He sat down on the arm of the adjacent recliner, a mug of hot coffee already cradled in his hands. He'd really not been paying attention if Sebastian had come in, poured coffee, and *still* surprised him.

"I screwed up," Kalan admitted as his friend chuckled.

"I thought you were so smooth."

"I usually am." Kalan frowned. He was, *wasn't he?* Regardless of what he usually was, this time, he'd fucked up.

He was opening his mouth to explain, when Sebastian told

him, "Well, I got an earful from Maggie. And Seline is not pleased."

"Really?" Kalan asked sarcastically, but Sebastian missed it.

"Of course, she's not."

Heaving a bone-weary sigh, Kalan voiced his fear. "Maybe it would be better if I just leave her alone."

"No," Sebastian said, with a tone sharper than Kalan would have expected. Leaning forward, he slowly took a sip from his coffee and made Kalan wait. "She's royally pissed that you haven't called. So I don't know what you're doing dicking around, but you need to contact her."

Well, shit. Maybe she had found a way to forgive him.

He picked up the phone and tapped out the same message again. Only this time, it was Sebastian who put a hand up and pushed the phone downward.

"In the morning, dipshit." At least he said it with a wry grin. "Don't wake her up for this."

Kalan nodded and forced himself to put the phone in his pocket where he couldn't waste time staring at it. Just when he was ready to ask another question, Sebastian interrupted his thoughts again. "Maggie got more information yesterday, and now the FBI is watching Seline."

"Seriously?" Kalan's gut tightened at the thought. Hadn't he just told himself she was safe?

His friend just shrugged at him. "You and I are like little crows, gossiping on the sidelines of this thing."

"What does that even mean?"

"It means," Sebastian said, as he rolled his eyes at his own words. "The FBI isn't talking to me directly, so I only know what I hear from Maggie. But apparently Seline told Maggie that ... Jesus, I sound like the old men at the hardware store!" But that didn't stop him from sharing the news. "Seline told Maggie that the FBI agents visited her—"

"For what?"

At least Sebastian didn't take offense at the interruption. "Another body. It appears, the BRK got into her office at the university—"

"Seline's office?" Kalan was on the edge of his seat. His heart rate kicked hard. The last he'd heard officially, the agents and the Redemption PD were confident that Sanders was in the wind, long gone from the area. Then they'd found the body. This was getting far too close.

And Kalan was too dumb to even be talking to her. He had to remedy that right away.

Sebastian took another sip of the coffee, while waiting to see if Kalan's minor personal crisis had passed. "He left a note in her office."

Holy shit. Kalan pulled his phone from his pocket without even thinking.

"Wait until morning, dude. She doesn't need you waking her up," Sebastian told him, once again, putting his hand out to block the message Kalan had already started writing. Somehow, Sebastian, who had been off his rocker about Maggie just weeks earlier, had become the sage old man in the steady relationship. Once they'd settled in, it was clear that Sebastian and Maggie were meant for each other.

Maybe it wouldn't hurt to take his advice. Sebastian had done something right after all.

Kalan was still trying to absorb the shock of the news when they both heard the faint sound of the phone ringing in the chief's office. TV shows tended to get it wrong—it wasn't usually the alarm that warned firefighters to a potential alert— the phone rang in the chief's office first.

Ronan, Sebastian, and Kalan all looked toward the sound as though moving as one unit already.

Soft noises told them that Patrick Kelly, who was on as interim Captain tonight, had shuffled from the attached bedroom into his office. The conversation came through muffled, but the tone and the street name were clear. The three of them nodded knowingly to each other, already standing and moving toward their lockers as the alarm went off.

"Fully involved house fire!" Patrick yelled out as he emerged from his office already gathering his things. He rattled off the address and by then everyone was in the main room, moving toward the bay and the truck.

But as he heard the address, Luke Hernandez caught everyone's attention by stopping dead and asking, "Are you sure?"

CHAPTER NINE

Seline adjusted her position again on the puffy, pale blue sofa. Her brain refused to fully process what she'd learned the day before. She was missing more work and getting further behind.

But no matter how much she moved, she couldn't sit still and just breathe. She loved this couch; she'd picked it out so she could lean back and sink into it and read. She loved to be enveloped in the cloud of cushions and read her books.

It reminded her of one her mother had picked out. Though he'd always hated it, her father kept it after her mother had passed, just because it reminded him of her. He complained it was too hard to get out of a couch this soft, but Seline chose it because it reminded her of her mother, too.

Right now, though, her butt was barely on the edge of the cushions, her feet firmly on the floor. Her hands clasped in front of her as she leaned forward, the pad of one thumb running across the nail of the other as though it were a worry stone. She was doing everything she could to *not* sink into her couch and disappear.

In her ideal world, she would have gone back to the uni and

worked in her lab and been seen by the department chair. Or she could have emailed and reported results from home. Being seen as a good worker would get her in a better position. Dr. Morales had not been happy about the missed meeting.

But the FBI agents thought it unwise to go back to the place where the BRK clearly had access to her.

In fact, Watson and Decker were at her office right now without her, scouring the place. That made her nervous enough to recount her sins.

Left to her own devices, she still would have been late to the first meeting. But that would have been a forgivable sin. Instead, she'd been stuck in an elevator and missed the entire thing. She'd not been there when she was introduced, and it was clear to everyone that she was absent.

She'd missed all the personal introductions with everyone higher up the chain. She knew them, but there'd been an informal welcome lunch after the meeting—which she'd only found out about later. Seline was mad enough to spit nails. But at least the elevator was one of those things that just happened.

This was not.

Having the FBI in her office wouldn't earn her any favors with the department. Tenure was security, but Seline didn't have it yet. Her status was not secure and could be revoked at any minute.

She should be working right now. But instead, she was sitting on her couch, facing away from the window and the curtains she'd kept drawn since Decker and Watson had left earlier, and worrying.

She built the lab in her home so she could work while she was here. But she was not in any shape to be handling dangerous chemicals right now.

The doorbell rang and Seline jolted from her pity party. She hadn't heard anyone come up the walk.

Her heart kicked up a notch, nervous energy fueling her, but at least answering the door was something to do. Surely, Sanders wouldn't come here and take her out of her own home?

The FBI agents were confident that his communication with her effectively took her off of his kill list. Then again they'd also been confident that he was long gone, but she'd seen him just down the street. So she wasn't putting a lot of faith in their predictions these days.

As she approached the door, she berated herself for not having a weapon handy. Watson had told her a weapon was more likely to get used against her than help her, but the agent hadn't given Seline a chance to explain that her father had trained her from a very young age. Right now, she wanted a gun.

With a deep breath, she pushed up on her tiptoes because the peephole was way too high for any normal-sized person. Through the warped view, she spotted Kalan on the other side. *Just what she needed.*

But she threw the door open, grateful for the human contact even if it was him. He grinned slightly but made no motion to come forward.

"Come in." She swung her arm motioning him toward the living room. She was not being the gracious hostess her mother would have wanted her to be, but none of this had been on her mother's etiquette lists.

Kalan nodded, strangely silent until he was standing in her living room. She felt like she should sit or offer him tea but that seemed inappropriate for a man who'd had her pushed up against her house the other night and unscrewed the light bulb so the neighbors couldn't see.

As she turned around to face him, she saw him visibly take a deep breath to steady himself. "Seline, I just wanted to say how sorry I am about the way I acted the other night."

Her eyebrows popped up. *Oh, good,* she thought, *at least he was addressing it.* "Thank you."

"I can promise you it won't happen again."

Her initial response was to be snarky and say it damn well wouldn't if she never kissed him again. But that wasn't an outcome she actually wanted. If there was some good reason for his behavior ... well, she wanted there to be one, so she asked, "Why did you go three days without communication?"

He nodded slowly, as though the words were hard to find.

They shouldn't be.

Despite his opening apology he didn't seem prepared to explain and the conversation was still stilted. "You could have messaged me."

Even as he said it, she felt her face react. Her arms crossed and one eyebrow popped up as if to say *"oh, really?"* Managing to just barely check herself, she spoke as calmly as she could. "I'm not the one who walked away without a word."

"That's fair." He paused, and if he'd had a hat, he would have been worrying the brim between his hands. He looked like a repentant orphan, but Seline had dealt with men who were sorry before. Without a good explanation all they were was sorry.

"Like I said," he continued, "none of it will happen again."

She smiled and nodded. She was going to ask what he meant by *none of it*, when he began blurting out, "I heard the FBI was here. That the Blue River Killer contacted you ... Did you see him?"

"No," she replied just as quickly as he'd changed the topic. But when she thought about it, "Well, yes, but—"

"Are you okay?" Even as he interrupted, he reached out and took her hands in his. Warm and solid, the touch countered her racing heart and helped her breathe easier.

Seline told him everything ... About the jogger she almost bumped into on the street. The altered picture the FBI agents showed her. She babbled on about the note and how she'd found it.

"I must have seen him!" she almost wailed, finally admitting to herself what had her so upset. "He got that note to me, so I must have passed him, taken a paper from him, I don't know!"

"It's okay," he used his soft firefighter-on-the-scene voice. She knew it, probably the one he used on old people having heart attacks, or the kid he'd told her about who'd gotten bitten by a rattlesnake in a cornfield.

But she didn't fully relax. Instead, she stepped away and paced, the movement making her feel as if she was accomplishing something. She grabbed her phone, pulled up the pictures Watson had sent her and shoved it at him. "Here."

This was all probably proprietary information. But Seline didn't care.

"Look at the torso!" she told him, showing him the picture of the carved up body with no warning. Then she snatched the phone back and pulled up the picture of her note. "Now look at this!" She shoved it back toward him again.

"Look. They are the same!" Her french accent was coming out again. She was scared shitless.

"That does look the same …" He let the words trail off as though he wasn't fully convinced, though.

Seline grabbed the phone again and flipped through more pictures, this time pointing to the mockup of the older man with white hair. "This is the jogger I saw. And honestly—" *even she was starting to doubt*. But the doubt made her heart race just as much as the certainty did. "He looked a lot like this but not perfectly. And this one," she tapped to another one, "I mean, they all look like people I know or people I see around!"

"But the people you know aren't the Blue River Killer …" he was looking at her sideways now, not following. "That doesn't work. They know the killer is William Treat Sanders."

"Right!" that's what she'd been saying. Clearly, she'd been saying it poorly.

Kalan nodded along at her logic. His agreement at least

made her feel better. "Well then, it just means he looks like this, but isn't one of the people you already know."

She nodded, finally breathing a little easier. But whether or not she recognized him didn't really make a difference, because she'd been sitting on her couch, worrying her fingerprints down to nothing for a reason.

"Here's the problem, Kalan …"

He looked like he was about to say everything was okay, but Seline wasn't having it. She headed to the small scalloped-edge table just inside the door, where she set her mail each time when she brought it in.

With one finger, she pushed one of today's bills aside. Kalan was right behind her, his curiosity getting the better of him.

They both watched as she revealed a quarter sheet of plain, white paper—just like before—with the initials S A M on it.

Seline blinked, trying to hold back the tears that threatened.

"What is that?" he asked, though he couldn't have missed that it was her initials.

This time she broke. Her voice cracked and the pressure at the back of her eyes mounted. "I think it means he's killed again. But the FBI hasn't called to tell me that they found a body."

CHAPTER TEN

"I am so glad you're here," Kalan let the words gush out as he opened the door for Maggie and Sebastian. Normally he issued a polite welcome, but this time, it was desperate. He practically grabbed Sebastian's arm and dragged him bodily into the house.

They had to do something to get Seline out of her funk … even if it was a rightful one. Luckily, Maggie's house was only just down the street and the two of them had arrived quickly.

Seline was more than shaken by the new note.

He hoped having friends here would help her breathe easier.

As much as he'd wanted to apologize, Kalan understood that this was neither the time nor the place. She was dealing with something far more concerning than him.

She'd stayed perched on the front edge of the couch, looking as though she might slide off at any moment. But now, as she stood and greeted her friends, she looked falsely bright and cheerful.

"Hello! Thank you for coming over." She was even more formal than he'd been, and there was something in her tone that wasn't quite right. Kalan didn't know what to do about it. But Maggie did.

Rushing across the room, she enveloped her friend in an unprovoked bear hug. It was clear that Maggie was taking charge of things. "I'm so sorry." Maggie was practically in tears. "I'm sorry that I brought this to your doorstep."

Seline seemed to be holding on for dear life. He wished he could do what Maggie was doing, but Seline had taken no comfort from him. That was his own damn fault. So, instead of being her rock, he watched from the sidelines as her cover cracked and she began to cry.

"It's okay Seline," Maggie said. "I understand. I'm so sorry."

But Seline pushed Maggie away. "No, it is not that. It is not about me. He has killed someone else. That's what I cry about."

Maggie took a step back, her entire body going ramrod straight. Slowly she turned to look at him. "Is this right? You *know* this?"

Her tone demanded to know if it was a fact or a guess. Kalan shrugged, it was somewhere in between. Trying to take as much of the burden off Seline as he could, he explained about the second note, assuming that Maggie and Sebastian already knew about the first.

Maggie turned back to her friend, but Seline had dropped onto the couch again, though this time she curled herself into the corner. "Are we targeted because we're new in town? Because we don't know our way around? Don't have a big family network here to support us?"

Something about the way she said "big family network" told Kalan it came from a place of yearning in her. He thought about it. "Maybe. It does make you an easier target."

Maggie sat next to her friend. "I was targeted because I inherited that house. Because I moved in, I started digging through it and it … activated all this old stuff. You're targeted because you're my friend."

Seline nodded stiffly and sniffled. She said the words as though she'd just remembered. "You do have a network here."

Maggie put her arms around her friend. "I don't think it's because we're new here. I think it's bad luck."

With a quick hug, Seline pulled herself together and Maggie followed suit. No longer being the comforting friend but the practical leader, she asked, "Did you call the FBI?"

"We did," Kalan told her. "We called you right after we called them. We took pictures—tried not to touch it."

"It's still here?" Sebastian asked. He'd been lingering in the background, staying near the doorway, but now he was all action.

"Right behind you," Kalan told him with a dark look, motioning to the small, pretty table where it appeared Seline parked her purse and mail each day. That was the kind of fact he wanted to know about her, but the Blue River Killer was stealing that from him, too.

Seline might be softly crying, but Kalan wasn't that far from it himself. If he wanted to be more to her, he couldn't afford any more fuck-ups.

He'd already gone through the whole *It's not your fault* scenario and taken the brunt of her anger for it.

"I know it's not my fault! I'm not a murderer and I'm not provoking him! But it doesn't change the fact that he killed someone else. Or that he saw fit to notify *me* of his murder before anyone else."

Kalan wanted to put his arm around her and draw her close, but Maggie was already there. As much as he wanted it to be him comforting her, the most important thing was that Seline feel better. The tight knot in his chest could unfurl later.

Now that everyone was up to speed, he aimed back toward his original goal: normalcy. "The agents will be here in a while. I thought we would eat dinner together and talk about something else … anything else."

It was Sebastian who nodded along. "Should we order pizza?"

"Or Chinese food?" Maggie looked up at him.

Kalan was watching and, though Seline hadn't perked at the offer of pizza, she'd given a slight nod at Maggie's suggestion.

"Let's order it," he said, glad for something to do. He took only a few moments to quiz everyone on what they liked and then ordered too much food rather than get into a discussion. He found himself irritated that he didn't already know Seline's preferences.

Kalan consoled himself that he would soon. At least ordering food had turned the conversation like he wanted but, as soon as that was done, Seline and Maggie went right back to talking about the Blue River killer.

It was Maggie who didn't seem to understand. "He's mad at *me*. So why is he sending these things to *you*?"

Seline shrugged. "Has he sent you anything?"

"No." Maggie still seemed perplexed.

"But he told you …" Seline was thinking as she climbed her way out of the deep couch. Her French accent deepened, tilting the words softly as she put pieces together, "—that he prefers blondes."

She announced the last part almost like a revelation. Even Sebastian snapped his head at that. But he looked confused.

It was only then that Kalan caught on, though he wasn't sure that he agreed. "Watson and Decker were very clear that they don't think you're in danger."

But Seline's blue eyes were growing wider and more frightened with every churn of her brilliant brain. She had believed the FBI until now. With a deep breath and an expression that told him she was holding everything back, she shook her head.

"It's these notes … If he wanted Maggie, he would have given

53

them to her. Instead, he is messing with *me* because *I* fit his profile. Because he enjoys torturing his victims."

The three of them stood in a small ring around her as Seline offered her horrible predictions. It was clear none of them liked what she was saying, but they all listened.

"The FBI agents are right," Seline told them, "I'm not his next victim … because he's going to toy with me as long as he can, and *then* he's going to kill me."

CHAPTER ELEVEN

No one told her she was wrong.

As Seline's eyes darted between three other pairs of eyes, she looked for rebuttal. There was none in Kalan's big dark brown eyes nor Maggie's moss green or even in Sebastian's pale denim.

Mierde.

Maggie was right. If Sanders was mad at her friend, he would have given her the notes. Unless ... Seline offered up her new thoughts. "Unless his goal is to get at *you* through *me*."

"Sending you the notes doesn't do anything to me ..." Maggie shook her head as they all stayed standing in the tight circle. Almost like circling their wagons, they could pretend it kept them safer. It didn't.

"It doesn't do anything unless he knows we are friends. And he does know that."

They all nodded at her. Not only did everyone in town know that Maggie and Seline were friends, everyone knew that both had moved here recently. And Merrit Geller had repeatedly broken into Maggie's home and tried to steal back the evidence

SAVANNAH KADE

of his La Vista Rapist crimes. Geller and Sanders talked, so they must both know about the friendship.

"If he's trying to get to Maggie," Seline knew she was repeating herself. She heard her accent thicken and she knew the others understood her distress, but she needed to say it to work out what was nagging at the back of her brain. "Then it doesn't work unless Maggie knows I'm torn up about the letters."

Just then, Seline's eyes snapped to Kalan's. Why couldn't he have stayed after their first date? Why couldn't he have called and made all this easier?

Mierde!

Giving Seline the clues didn't make any difference unless she shared them with Maggie. It wasn't enough that he knew they were already friends, he had to follow up ... She could only whisper it, "He has to be watching."

Kalan nodded, having already figured it out, but Maggie and Sebastian both looked surprised.

"Right now?" Sebastian asked, his gaze darting subtly toward the window.

Seline shrugged. "Maybe all the time. Certainly, enough to know that I've passed the information on to Maggie. It only works if I tell Maggie."

She watched as Maggie blinked away her own tears. Then her friend put her hands on her hips, tipped her head back, and walked in a tight circle.

But still no one disagreed with her.

"*Salaud*," she whispered to herself.

She wanted to believe the FBI was right, that she was safe, that his taunting her meant that she was a toy and not a target. But she was growing more convinced that she would ultimately become a target. She fit his profile too well to not be. The problem was she didn't know where on his list she would wind up.

Would there be ten or fifteen bodies between her and the end or would she be next? Would he toy with her until he just decided one day he was done, or did he maybe already have some grand plan?

Right then, the doorbell rang. Adrenaline shot through her system at the sound and she watched as her friends also snapped around. She couldn't live in this state of fear.

It was Kalan who laughed first at their over-reaction. "It's the Chinese food."

His muttered words made her friends breathe a little easier. But Seline didn't feel better. It might be a small town but even the restaurant wasn't going to be that fast.

"Be careful," she whispered, but he was already on his way to the door.

Seline couldn't see around the wall that separated her foyer from the living area, but she heard Kalan say, "Agents."

She felt her rapid heartbeat begin to calm even before Watson and Decker came around the corner. Wanting to rush and tell them everything, Seline instead fought to hold back. She wanted to hear everything they had to say about her new note.

"It's there." She pointed to the table.

It was Kalan who gave them further instructions and watched diligently as they photographed it, pulled out tweezers and evidence bags, and noted the time.

Everyone stayed silent, watching as the agents did their work. Decker held the bag as Watson turned back to Seline. "Thank you. We'll analyze it and let you know if we find out anything that's helpful."

Seline nodded along, but wondered, *Had they not figured out what the note meant?*

She blurted out her theory and felt every muscle tighten as Watson and Decker stayed silent. They both stood still and nodded along.

Why would no one tell her she was wrong? Why couldn't she be wrong about this!?

Instead, Watson nodded one last time, and said, "We agree. We've come to the same conclusions that you did. With the second note, it becomes clear that he is targeting you. I don't know what his long game is, but you're involved."

Seline felt like a wall, crumbling brick by brick. It was bad enough to know she'd come into contact with him. It was worse that she hadn't even known at the time. Evil had passed her and she'd smiled and said hello.

Swallowing her fear, Seline asked her hardest question yet. "Do you think there's another body out there? One that goes with this new note."

"Probably," Decker at least said it with the utmost concern. Not only that there had likely been another life lost but that Seline was dealing with it.

It took more than a moment to absorb that the FBI agreed with her—that she was the intended victim of a prolific serial killer. If she didn't handle everything just right, she would become one of those bodies.

Watson placed her hands together in front of her and looked at Seline and each of her three friends in turn. For once, Seline was grateful for everything Maggie had been through, that she understood. That they already knew these agents and trusted them.

"We have a plan," Watson announced softly. "There are already agents watching your home. And, between ten and twenty minutes from now, there's going to be a knock at your door …"

CHAPTER TWELVE

The knock at the front door made Seline's tension ratchet tighter, even though she'd known it was coming.

She popped up, but Kalan put his hand out, a large, warm stop sign suggesting she let him get the door.

It logically made sense for her to not answer it, but it was emotionally tumultuous. She couldn't see who had shown up. What if it was *him*? What if Kalan didn't recognize him?

She heard Kalan's voice and the whispered crinkle of plastic bags. "Thank you, man!"

The tension inside her popped like a water balloon. It was just the food delivery. Her breath rushed out and she almost folded over. She should not be that tense about every knock or ring of the doorbell, or she'd die of a heart attack before William Treat Sanders even took a shot at her.

Wouldn't that just serve him right?

On shaky legs, she trailed the others into her own dining room. Her small square table looked exactly like what it was: the kind of table that came in a box. She'd assembled it herself. It wasn't a beautiful antique like Maggie's. At least she'd managed to get a tablecloth on it. Homekeeping was not her forte.

For a moment, the thought flashed through Seline's mind that she might die and this stupid, cheap dining room furniture would be what she left behind. The table was a stupid thing to worry about, but her mortality was a thing she had to consider when a killer was leaving her notes.

The others were already laying out the food and corralling her into a chair. Maggie handed her a fork and a drink and insisted that she eat.

Normally, Seline loved Chinese food, but tonight she hardly tasted it. The fork was halfway to her mouth when the doorbell rang again and her tension went back through the roof.

This time it was Sebastian who jumped up. Kalan's thought that they should invite the others over and have safety in numbers had been a good one. She was grateful that she wasn't in charge of anything right now, but how long would this drag on?

They couldn't live with her.

Her thoughts were tumbling in a melancholy cycle that was broken by Sebastian's exclamation of "Holy shit!"

He came into her view, backstepping into the living room as though someone was pushing him. Before she realized she'd done it, she was on her feet, ready to defend her friend, though he didn't even look like he needed it.

It was a relief to see that Kalan and Maggie had popped to his defense as well, but by that point Sebastian was almost laughing.

A blonde woman walked into the room as though she owned it. Seline felt her spine stiffen at the intrusion. The new woman was just a little too tall to be petite, but her icy blue eyes looked familiar. Though she tried, Seline couldn't place them.

Her confusion only compounded itself, but she watched as Sebastian closed the door behind the stranger, an impressed look upon his face. At least he seemed to know her.

The woman opened her mouth and grinned as though they should recognize her. "Hello."

It was the voice that pinged Seline's memory. Next to her, she saw the small movements that told her Kalan and Maggie had caught on, too.

"Oh my god!" Kalan laughed. "You look great."

"She does," Sebastian replied, almost admirably.

Beside her, Maggie's eyebrows climbed to her hairline, as if to ask, *Does she now?*

Seline was so confused until Kalan turned and whispered, "Marina and Maggie's boy here went out a few years ago."

As Seline felt her shock at that, both Sebastian and Marina turned to glare at Kalan. But he did not take the hint. "Y'all were hot and heavy for a while. I'm just saying."

"I'm standing right here." Maggie glared at him now, arms crossed and Seline wondered how he was going to get out of this. Maybe his crap wasn't about her. Maybe he just didn't really get what he should and shouldn't say. It made her reconsider the last weekend in a new light at least.

Even as she thought that, Kalan looked Maggie in the eyes and said. "Your boy has a past. It is what it is, but he loves you more than anything."

"That's true."

The words came at the same time from both the newly blonde Marina and Sebastian, which made them laugh in tandem which made Maggie throw her hands up in the air.

Marina, at least, knew when to change the subject. "Do I pass?"

"Did you dye it?" Seline asked. The normally dark-haired officer was now an ashy blonde.

"Yes," she replied as she flipped it over her shoulder.

"Your eyes?" Seline asked, thinking that Marina hadn't copied her per se, but it felt odd to see someone she knew who suddenly had her same coloring. Even her clothing could have come from Seline's own closet.

"Contacts."

"They look real." Kalan was in her face, though Marina was handling getting inspected pretty well.

"They have to." She looked at the four of them, the conversation turning away from her and Sebastian's past, from hair dye and colored contact lenses. "I'm the bait. If he figures out it's contact lenses, I don't know what he'll do."

Seline's heart pounded in her chest. "That can't be safe! We've all seen what he's done."

There was nothing okay about this.

Marina offered a soothing hand, as though just touching her arm could calm her down. Oddly enough, it did. "I can't tell you everything, but it's a joint venture with the FBI. I'm being tracked, so you don't have to worry about me."

But Seline did. It was bad enough that he was killing random people in association with what he was doing to her. If he hurt someone she knew, that would be too much.

"I'm Wendy Buck. I'm your new best friend." She looked to Maggie. "Yours, too. We are going to do a handful of things together over the next few days, and then become good friends."

It felt odd to have her friendships dictated, but nothing about this was normal.

Marina continued. "You're dating Kalan."

It was just a pronouncement, and that was it, the Redemption PD and the FBI had decided her love life. Before she could protest, Marina added more.

"It doesn't matter if you really date or not, but we are going out on a triple date this weekend. My boyfriend will be another cop. We're all friends."

They were all nodding along. Something about having a plan felt better. Seline was a chemist, not a criminal investigator. Give her a formula and she could balance it. Give her a classroom and she'd make them love the periodic table. But pitting her against a serial killer was out of her *millieu*.

"I'm moving in across the street. The Gutierrez family—" She pointed toward the window as though Seline would know them. "—is out of town for at least the next six weeks."

Dieu! Six weeks?

But she could handle it. She wasn't even playing the role of "bait." So she nodded and tried to listen.

"They've agreed to let me sublet their home."

Now Marina walked up to Seline directly and looked her in the eye. "I'm not just your new best friend. I'm part of your protection detail. And I'm your decoy."

Seline looked the woman up and down. She'd made quite the transformation and she was putting herself at risk. All to catch a killer that *needed* to be caught.

She couldn't say no.

But she looked back and forth between her friends. They caught each other's eyes for a moment as everyone scrambled to keep up and make the right decision.

So Seline turned back to the officer who was offering to take the biggest risk. She asked, "Do you think it will work?"

CHAPTER THIRTEEN

"I think I'm going to have a heart attack," the woman announced as Kalan and Luke arrived at her front porch.

She was small, white-haired, frail, and ornery. She was smoking a cigarette while a nasal canula snaked it's clear plastic tubing to nose prongs. She was sitting on the step, next to an oxygen tank on its own little dolly. Kalan went on high alert as he and Luke stopped dead halfway up the sidewalk.

Putting his hand up to motion 'stop', Kalan said, "Ma'am, I'm sorry. We're gonna need you to put out that cigarette." He said it as calmly as he could, thinking that a heart attack would be the least of her problems if she blew herself up first. The tank said "no open flame" on the huge warning sticker he could see from where he stood.

This was supposed to be a medical call, not fire.

She took two more drags on the cigarette as she looked between the two men. Then finally said, "Fine!" and stubbed the thing out on the step beside her. "Better now?"

Though she asked it to be sarcastic, Luke answered honestly. "Yes, it is."

Kalan felt his too-rapid heartbeat begin to slow. Hell, she

could have blown them all up and, chances were, she did this every day in her own living room. As Luke approached her, Kalan stepped to the side and hit his comm to tell the chief what he'd seen. They could note that this address had O2 tanks for future safety reference.

Luke approached her, staying calm. In his most soothing voice he said, "Ma'am, we'll need to take your vital signs."

She balked again. "I don't need you to take my blood pressure! I need you to take me to the hospital. I'm fixing to have a heart attack."

Kalan looked to Luke who looked back at him as if to say, "this is new to me too."

"We can do that, ma'am," he told her. "But first we need your vital signs."

Again, she sighed heavily, sounding incredibly put out. She pushed up one heavy sweater sleeve, revealing a frail arm.

Luke was the paramedic here. Though they were all trained for medical calls, Luke was the ranking officer now. So Kalan followed along and acted as his assistant.

In no time at all, they had ascertained that her vital signs looked incredibly normal. And Luke told her so.

"I don't care!" She was full-steam angry with them now. "I need to go to the hospital."

Luke nodded. "We can do that ma'am. But if there's nothing wrong with you, the bill is going to be very expensive."

"Well, there is something wrong. I told you, I'm fixing to have a heart attack." She said for what was likely the third time.

"But I don't see anything wrong with your signs." Luke again tried to calm her down, though it clearly wasn't working.

Even her blood glucose was fully normal. Kalan had expected that number to be off when everything else came up good. But the more Luke suggested that she was not going to have a heart attack right this moment, the more she insisted she was.

He didn't want to be here. Kalan wanted to be back with Seline. He still hadn't fully apologized, and he still didn't know how to explain that he'd lost control while he was kissing her. How did he tell her that and not scare the crap out of her?

He'd taken her out on two dates—as per the FBI's instructions that they appear as boyfriend and girlfriend in public. But he'd dicked that up, too. Each time he'd felt the conversation pull him under, each time he'd touched her and felt that kick, he'd had to pull himself out of it. He was there to keep her safe, not kiss her while the BRK walked right by.

But he'd kissed her goodnight each time, soft and sweet— not the growling creature she'd had to push off herself the first time. And he kept it all to himself because, if she told him to leave, she'd be a bodyguard shy. The whole thing was turning into a clusterfuck. And he couldn't even figure a way out of it because he had to keep his mind on this stubborn old woman who wanted a ride to the hospital for no good reason.

Kalan turned away from her and whispered to Luke, "She's going to give herself a heart attack from being so mad at us. Then where will we be?"

The first part of the job was keeping people safe. But the second part—and Kalan appreciated working for a chief who made this one much lower down the list—was not getting sued.

Eventually, they relented.

Luke got the stretcher and wheeled it up her bumpy front walk. It had shock absorbers and was as padded as it could be, but it wasn't going to be a pleasant ride from her front door to the street.

Luckily, that distance was short. This neighborhood was not one for big yards or grand houses. Which is why she was wheeling around a tank of O2, rather than using one of the newer over-the-shoulder machines.

Once they had her loaded and locked, Kalan drove while

Luke stayed in the back with their patient, who continued to insist she was going to have a heart attack. Kalan rolled his eyes.

They left her at the hospital with two orderlies and a nurse who were as confused as they were about her fully normal vitals. Once they'd signed all the paperwork, Luke and Kalan were grateful she was out of their hands. At least she was demanding treatment for her pending heart attack to the hospital staff now.

They climbed back into their rig, put everything to rights and got ready for another run. But, when their comms stayed quiet, Kalan called in and asked anybody if they wanted anything from the sandwich shop. Might as well get lunch while it was calm.

He laughed as Sebastian rattled off an order, and over his shoulder he heard Ronan with another. One by one, everyone announced that they needed a sandwich, and soup, and chips and ... Until the chief got on and picked up the tab.

That was kind, but he looked to Luke. "Getting a to go order this big is almost a guarantee of getting a call as soon as they bring it out."

Kalan expected Luke to agree, but instead he looked out the window while they sat in the parking lot waiting for one of the employees to bring it out. The truck was unusually quiet. He and Luke got along. Luke was a bit of a talker, not like being on a run with Patrick or Ronan.

So when Luke turned to Kalan with an expectant expression, Kalan grew concerned.

"The house fire the other night ..." Luke let the words trail off.

His friend had looked worried. Something about it had bothered him all along, so he was glad Luke was finally talking.

"That's the house my mother and brothers lived in right after I moved out."

"Your brothers aren't that much younger than you, are they?" Kalan asked.

Luke shook his head. "We're all close in age. Mario and Carlos were there for three and four years after I moved out. Tiago is barely eleven months older than me."

Kalan had wondered what that must have been like for their mother. Four boys, all under five years old at once. His own mother had raised him and two younger sisters alone, but his sisters were a bit younger than him. As far as he knew, Luke's father had abandoned the family when the boys were young. But Kalan still wasn't quite sure what to say, so he asked, "Is it a nostalgia thing?"

He wondered how he'd feel if his own childhood home had burned. But his childhood home had been a high-rise apartment in Chicago, and he was certain he would feel differently about watching that burn than watching Luke's small, quaint, slightly rundown house go up in flames.

"It's not that." Luke looked down for a moment as Kalan waited. "These fires …"

Kalan knew exactly what he was talking about. Redemption was a small town. Firefighting was as much about checking smoke detectors, picking up medical cases, and getting people out of their cars or pulled from a flood as it was about fires. So he knew exactly what "these fires" meant.

"They've all been places that I've known. I told the chief at the second one that we were in my old neighborhood. But we're up to four now."

Though Kalan hadn't seen the official report, he could make a deduction. "So this was arson, too?"

"But they've all been started by different methods," Luke told him, clearly frustrated. "The more cases we see, the less likely it is that it's a separate arsonist. And that means someone knows a lot of ways to get away with setting fires."

Kalan absorbed that. It didn't go down well, and Luke wasn't finished.

"The fires had all been in places I'm familiar with, but it's a small town. What area don't I know? But this time it's a home that my family once lived in." Luke looked him dead in the eyes, as if to ask if Kalan was as concerned as he was. Suddenly Kalan was.

Jesus, he thought, he'd spent his whole shift worrying about getting back to Seline to play pretend boyfriend. And now, Luke was suggesting that their arson wasn't random.

What was going on in his little town?

His attention was pulled by the sandwiches arriving in large paper bags rolled tightly at the top. The shop guy handed them through the side window to Luke who traded cash for the wonderful smell.

Kalan's stomach growled just as the radio crackled. His stomach dropped and he looked at his partner as if to say, "I called it."

"At least we have the sandwiches," Luke grinned.

Kalan tapped his comm. "Yes Chief?"

"Don't eat all the sandwiches." It might not be an emergency after all … The chief's voice carried through the cab. "The hospital just called."

Kalan's heart sank.

"That woman you brought in? Five minutes after arrival, she had a *massive* heart attack. They would not have been able to save her had she not already been *inside* the ER."

"Holy shit!" Luke's mouth gaped open.

The chief told them to hurry up with the food and as the comm line went dead, Luke and Kalan let themselves have a slightly hysterical laugh. *The old bat had known what she was talking about!*

But even though the truck now smelled like sandwiches, and

they did manage to save the woman's life, Kalan thought of Seline.

She was at the university today.

Too far away, he thought and the sinking sensation in the center of his chest wouldn't loosen.

CHAPTER FOURTEEN

S eline swore a blue streak. She only did it because she was in her lab all by herself and she was swearing in French.

The day had been a disaster. Everything had to be done twice because she was either interrupted or someone called and wanted the exact same information she'd already given them. She shouldn't have answered the phone.

Then the experiment had gone poorly, the results not at all what she'd expected. This was a big setback in her work to produce a biodegradable, but sturdy, food safe foam. This was the project that was supposed to clinch her for tenure.

Seline swore again even as she mentally reminded herself that negative results were good and often led to breakthroughs. But she hadn't seen the breakthrough, only the disappointment. Missing the meeting, bringing a serial killer to the school, and now failing at her design was almost sure to keep her out of getting tenure. That would mean she couldn't afford her house and she'd have to move. She almost put her hand to her face to cry. The only thing that stopped her was her training never to touch her face in the lab.

So she took her time cleaning up and closing the lab down,

just as she made her grad students do. Her lab was and always would be immaculate, even if she was going to lose her damn job. When she was done, she dropped her lab coat in the laundry with another near-tears sigh and angrily shoved her notebooks down into her bag.

Though she tried to smile at her colleagues and passing students in the hallway, she wasn't quite sure she achieved it. *If her office had another damn note* … she couldn't handle anything from Sanders right now.

It had taken five days for the FBI to locate the next body, even though they knew to check the local rivers' edges and tributaries. And the medical examiner had placed the time of death right around the time Seline had received her note. But the woman had never been listed as missing.

The thought still made Seline shudder. When she hadn't shown up at work for three days straight, the restaurant manager had just marked her as "fired." No one had checked on her. The newspapers reported that her friends said they thought she was "being moody" when she didn't return messages.

Though Seline still struggled to process that, it was harder that the body had the initials S A M carved into the torso. It was disturbing that the Blue River killer now had a new modus operandi, matching the bodies to the notes. By the time she received the second note, she'd understood that the slashes that made up the letters were actually cuts into human flesh somewhere.

But it was far scarier that the thing he'd carved into the last body had been *her own initials*.

It was equally concerning that the note had arrived in her mailbox with no envelope or stamp—so someone had put it there. No one had spotted anyone near her mailbox, except the mailman and a boy scout. The scout had only left her the Snickers bar she'd paid for in their fund drive a week earlier.

At dinner the night before, Maggie had pointed out that it

was illegal in the US to leave things in any mailbox. Sebastian had replied that, in Redemption, no one was going to prosecute the Boy Scouts for leaving candy. But Seline had almost jumped up and yelled.

"I care! I care when a *child* is putting things into a box that also contains notes from a serial killer."

That had stopped the conversation dead.

Way to lose your only friends, she'd thought to herself as they all stared at each other over fish and vegetables. It was Kalan who'd reached out and taken her hand in his own and she thought about that now as she headed toward her office. It had been a week and a half that they'd been playing best friends with Marina Balero.

The three couples had gone out to dinner twice and had their meal once at Maggie's home ... with the dining room curtains wide open.

Officer Juan Gomez played "Wendy's" boyfriend. The cover story was that he and "Wendy" had been online dating for a while, and she was taking the rental to be near him and see how their relationship progressed.

While Seline agreed that if William Treat Sanders wanted to torture Maggie and Seline, taking their new best friend—the blond-haired, icy-blue-eyed one—was a surefire way to do it. But so far, Marina hadn't even been followed.

Her phone rang then and she pulled it from her purse. "Hello?"

"Watching..." the voice said just the one word. It was scratchy but Seline wasn't fully awake and wasn't sure she understood.

"Yes?"

"Watching." Then the line went dead.

With a deep breath, Seline realized that she was not paying attention to her surroundings. Though she felt relatively safe walking around the university, the weird call was a reminder that the BRK had already breached the safety here once.

She needed to slow down; she'd already run into one senior Professor barreling around this turn. She was thinking about the fact that she needed to call the agents again and let them know about the weird call.

Seline knew she should be scared, but she was angry. BRK hadn't ever called her. And she didn't want give any of her energy to the idea that it was him. So she told herself it was probably a student and she had too much to do to play games. If it was BRK, then screw him. She wasn't going to be afraid. She barreled down the hallway and noticed that the door to Dr. Gilman's office was open. As she passed, the man inside looked up and Seline came to a dead stop.

That was not the same man.

This man was taller than the other, broader shouldered. His clothes were all wrong. This man wore an Argyle vest over a button-down shirt, and corduroy slacks. He probably had a jacket with patches on the elbows, he could not have looked more like the quintessential American Professor than he already did.

"You're not Dr. Gilman." She was confronting him before she realized what she was doing.

His eyebrows went up, but he didn't move from his seat at the desk where he sipped from the same mug the other man had held. "I assure you, I am Dr. Gilman."

His calm nature made Seline's blood boil. She'd had enough of this shit. She was opening her mouth when he asked, "Are you a student? Did you see my TA in here? And you thought it was me?"

Her head snapped back as though she'd been slapped. *He had no clue.* "I'm a professor, Dr. Seline Marchand. My lab is down the hall."

"Oh, yes," he said almost nobly. "You missed the meeting."

Jesu! She'd known that would haunt her.

He at least turned a little more professional after his jab. He waved a hand around the small office. "I've been here this semester, but was on sabbatical for the last two years."

That explained why she didn't already recognize him. But ...

Still standing in the hallway—still not willing to get inside a small, enclosed space with this man—she said, "Almost two weeks ago, I ran into Dr. Gilman in this office."

He took another sip from the mug, his smile condescending. "I assure you, you did not."

"I did. He came into *this* office. I had bumped into him coming around the corner. He came in here, and I introduced myself. He said he was Dr. Fred Gilman."

At last, Gilman seemed to take her seriously. His brows pulled together. "But I assure you I am the actual Doctor Gilman. And I never go by Fred." He waved his hands around to indicate the walls. "That's my degree, and my other degree, and my other degree."

Seline tipped her head at him as if to say *now who was being stupid?* The name was written in calligraphy so beautifully it was almost difficult to read, but it didn't prove anything. He nodded a single conciliatory time and said, "These are my family pictures."

Sure enough, she remembered the pictures had been on the desk before, but she hadn't looked. Now she could see that he was in almost half of them. *Arrogant bastard,* she thought, but the face in the pictures was that of the man in front of her. Not the man who'd been here before.

"We should go see Dr. Morales." Seline offered cautiously.

"Absolutely." He agreed as though he were clearly going to have the upper hand here. He set down the mug and stood sharply upright.

Her stomach churned. His willingness meant that Morales

would recognize him. This was the real Dr. Gilman. *So who had been here before?*

She was certain she already knew. And she had to tell her boss what she'd brought to the school.

Opening the door to the main office, she found the department secretary smiling. He ushered them into Morales' inner office. Though he'd agreed to come with her, Gilman now looked as though he didn't have the time to be bothered with this.

Seline offered him a harsh expression as if to say *you will sit and you will wait.* She knew what was at stake even if he didn't.

It didn't take long for Gilman to have worked up a good head of steam over the fact that Seline was making him visit the boss. Sonia Morales finally looked up at them and greeted them by level of seniority. "Dr. Gilman. Dr. Marchand."

Seline felt her heart sink. BRK had been in Dr. Gilman's office. She'd shaken his hand.

Now the only question was: *How many other times had she encountered the killer?*

CHAPTER FIFTEEN

Seline had driven home exhausted from both the meeting and the outcome. She'd spent too long on the phone with Agent Decker after that relaying information about the strange call and the single word, "watching."

"I don't think it's BRK..." Decker had replied. "I mean not off the top of my head, because it would be a strange change in M.O. But we'll look into it."

That made Seline feel marginally better, that and the promise to fully investigate the call. But she'd not returned Kalan's calls or messages all day.

The bad feeling in her gut persisted, though now it was not only because William Treat Sanders had actually been on her campus and interacted with her, but because her department chair had asked her not to come to campus anymore. She was allowed to show up and teach classes, where the school would place security guards in the hallway, but she couldn't visit her own office or interact with faculty or students aside from fielding questions immediately after class. She needed to begin calling roll in each class and learning faces, so she could report anyone unusual.

She hadn't lost her job per se, but she had been severely downgraded.

If she called Maggie, her friend would understand. While Seline desperately wanted to stay alive—and keep BRK's future victims alive, too—she was livid that her life was slowly getting stolen from her. It was all necessary for her safety and the safety of those around her—she understood that. But, through no fault of her own, she was the one who bore the brunt of the ramifications. And she was pissed.

Seline had sat in Morales' office with a senior professor and listened to her department chair call the FBI. Agents had shown up. Ones Seline didn't already know.

Didn't that say everything? She now knew FBI agents personally.

They'd pulled fingerprints and suggested a sketch artist. But Seline had unfortunately been able to say, "He looked like the enhanced picture that Agent Watson showed me almost two weeks ago."

That hurt.

She'd had to then explain why she'd seen someone who looked just like a version of the Blue River Killer and brushed it off. The upside was that Seline didn't have to sit for an hour for a sketch. The downside was that Morales had scolded the FBI for not putting those images on the nightly news so everyone at the school could recognize him.

Dr. Morales had asked her point blank. "Why did you think it was Dr. Gilman?"

"Because he was in Gilman's office." Seline realized that was a slim excuse now. "He sat in Gilman's chair and was shuffling through the papers on the desk. He drank from Gilman's mug."

Though the real Gilman was now visibly disturbed by this knowledge, it was the FBI agent standing over all of them who swore and said, "That was probably right after he got into your office."

The agent then suggested Sanders may have talked some

staff member into unlocking the doors for him. That he was bold enough to impersonate a professor and get access to what he wanted.

But where was he now?

Seline fought to keep her attention on the road. It seemed everywhere she'd ever been was a possible place for William Treat Sanders to have made contact. She was now certain she'd seen him twice. Both times—despite knowing that Sanders was around and would try to get to her—she'd interacted willingly.

What a fucking idiot she was.

Surely, that meant that he had delivered her Chinese food or showed up as one of her students or had come to her door as a parent selling donuts with the Scouts or something.

Seline wasn't dumb enough to think she'd figured out all the times he'd brushed by her or said hello. She'd known she couldn't trust anybody she didn't recognize, but now she also couldn't trust anybody she did.

Pulling into the driveway, she drove slowly on the narrow path toward the back of the house before she remembered she wasn't supposed to park in back anymore. The FBI had discussed why she should keep her car out front and, damn, but she'd forgotten. So Seline put the car in reverse, mad that she couldn't remember anything today, and backed up.

Once the car was far enough in front of the house that her friendly local FBI surveillance could see her, she got out. She might have had a lapse, but she wasn't about to let herself get kidnapped by a crazed serial killer from her own yard.

Seline looked around, knowing she appeared paranoid, but she couldn't help it. She *was* paranoid and with damn good reason. Let Sanders see her scan the street. It was better that he knew he wasn't getting away with his shit anymore.

She turned the knob on the front door and set everything down on the entryway table. Then she pulled her nine-millimeter gun from her purse.

Though Watson and Decker had warned her against weapons, they'd not let her get a word in edgeways to explain that she actually knew what she was doing.

She should have felt more relaxed now that she was in her own home, and Seline was pissed that she didn't. So she kept the gun firmly in her grip as she paced the house, clearing it room by room. She stayed close to the walls, like her father had taught her, alert for anyone to pop up or for anything that was out of place.

By the time she finished the search and found nothing—not even in the closets or the cabinets, her heart was beating hard enough to escape her chest. As she let out a breath, she admitted she was disappointed. She had a fantasy of finding the man and laying him out cold.

She also knew that was a fantasy. The stats didn't support people shooting intruders. And it wasn't that she wanted to kill someone; it was that she wanted to end this. She felt so alone.

She'd seen Maggie go through it, but now that it was on her, she knew why her friend had been so anxious to go after a predator she wasn't quite qualified to face. Maggie's anger had driven her, and Seline understood on a gut level now.

Normally, she would have ejected the magazine and put the gun in the safe, but she debated whether to put it back in her purse or keep it closer at hand …

She'd already rearranged her living room furniture. The couch no longer sat in the middle of the room facing away from the window. Now it was pushed up against the wall so no one could pop up behind her and string a garrote around her neck.

She needed to stop watching late night crime shows.

Before she just burst into tears of emotional exhaustion, she plopped into the fluffy hug of the couch—certainly more comfortable with the wall at her back—and she called Kalan.

This was not what she had wanted from him. She wanted to

either date him or let him go. But the situation was what it was. "Can you come over?"

She didn't know enough people in town to just ask anyone. Some of her old friends—acquaintances, really—were in Lincoln, too far away to pop by. And Kalan was the one that she could invite without it looking strange to anyone watching her house. She wondered if Sanders was watching now.

"I'll be there in a minute," Kalan told her, though it was more like four or five. He arrived with a bag in hand, exactly the way a boyfriend would if he was staying over. Seline almost laughed that Sanders might think she was so forward as to let a man she'd barely begun to date stay over like this.

But if Sanders had been watching, he would have seen the horrible end to their first outing—the steamy hot kiss on the porch and the moment it had all ended with Kalan walking away.

Aside from his apology, nothing more had happened—the Blue River Killer had taken over her life.

Closing the door behind him, Seline rolled her eyes at herself. She didn't look through the peephole anymore when people came to the door. She'd seen enough shows where the assassin took someone out that way. She had her gun in hand when Kalan arrived, and she wasn't quite sure that she'd fully hidden it from him as she slipped it back into her purse.

Still, Kalan's broad shoulders filling the doorway lifted some of the weight from her own smaller frame. She didn't say "Thank God you're here," but he smiled as though he understood. He seemed to know better than to talk or to press her for information, and they ate dinner together in relative silence.

Her exhaustion had almost taken over when they passed time on the couch watching tv. But each time, as she faded and leaned softly into Kalan, he relaxed around her for a moment before straightening and pulling away. Each time she was tugged back into focus by the feeling of rejection.

Clearly, he was her *fake* boyfriend only. His apology had only been meant to say he was sorry, and not that he wanted anything more. She'd been stupid to think that his forward manner of speaking might mean he meant more than he'd said. If she spent any more time mooning over the man, she could wind up dead.

Still, she'd nearly passed out once more. This time, he'd actively pushed her off his shoulder and suggested she go up to her own bed. Only, when she'd gotten there her eyes had been wide and her brain and stomach actively churning.

By the time Seline was finally falling asleep, midnight had passed. Still, she felt much safer with Kalan in the room across from her. He was great protection even if he didn't want her. She was feeling deep sleep finally take hold when the phone rang. With sleepy fingers, she reached out and picked it up without thinking.

But her phone didn't light up. There was an odd echo and the ringtone was coming from somewhere else. Had that been the BRK?

That at least startled her enough to wake up. When she listened, she heard the echo stop and Kalan's confused voice say, "Hello?"

Either he'd gotten a call in the middle of the night at the same minute she did, or someone was calling them both.

Now she scrambled to hit the button on her phone. "Hello?"

She connected into the three-way call and Agent Watson was already speaking. Seline's breath hitched though she lied and told herself there was no reason to be concerned. The BRK had called her, but clearly the FBI was on top of it.

"Seline." Watson said only her name as a greeting, and there was an edge to it that Seline didn't like. Without waiting, Watson asked, "Is Balero in the house with you?"

Seline was on her feet, rushing to the bedroom door. She threw it open wide to see Kalan standing there in just his boxer briefs, but the expression on his face was as disturbed as she felt.

She looked to him as if to ask, *Why would Marina be here?*

But the impact of the question only hit her as Kalan answered for the both of them. "No, she's not here."

CHAPTER SIXTEEN

K alan looked to Seline, but she only stared back at him. *Where was Marina and why was the FBI asking them if she was here?*

Kalan found his voice before she did and offered a quick, "We'll check."

If Marina Balero was in the house, they didn't already know it—which was problematic in the first place. He was starting to put a few of the pieces together and none of the answers were good.

"Hold on." Kalan switched his phone to speaker and used the clip on the back to attach it to his underwear. There was no time to put on clothes. Even Seline was in her drawstring pajama pants and a small top. At any other time, he would have made a move or told her she looked amazing. Right now, she looked afraid and determined at the same time.

She ducked back into her room and emerged with a nine-millimeter in her hand. He would have asked if she knew how to use it, but it was clear by the way she held it that she did.

He ducked back into his own room for his own firearm

thinking, *Well, doesn't that just say it all? We got a middle of the night phone call from the FBI and we both reached for our guns …*

"Start upstairs," Seline told him, her self-assurance radiating through the hallway. Before he could respond, she'd ducked back into her own room, calling first, "Clear!" then "Closet—clear," reminding him that he had to check every available space. In his room, he also looked under the bed for good measure. When he emerged into the hallway, he found that Seline had already checked the other room up here.

Together, they headed down the stairs, quietly treading the steps in their bare feet, as if they hadn't already alerted anyone in the house by yelling.

"Marina?" he called out, then changed to "Wendy?"

He continued to call out as Seline reported to Agent Watson, "She's not upstairs. We're heading to the lower floor. We'll let you know as we go."

In that moment, Kalan's respect for her grew exponentially. He'd understood she was something special but from the determined look on her face to the way she walked and held the gun aimed downward and ready she was ready to face all comers. She was trained and rational. In contrast, he was just a dude with some firearm training.

Downstairs, she cleared twice as many rooms as he did. Watching her, he picked up tips or was reminded of tactics that he already knew. She entered each room by standing at the side of the doorway and leading with the barrel of the gun. Seline did a quick glance with one eye to see into the room without becoming a target for a shooter on the other side.

He had not expected this of the chemist. Tonight, she looked like a soldier.

"She's not here," Seline announced to the phone as the two of them met back up in the living room. Smart as always, she'd not turned on the lights.

"Is there access under the house?" Agent Watson asked.

Kalan remembered that Maggie had trouble with a cellar but he looked to Seline for answers about her own house.

She spoke loudly for both him and Agent Watson still coming over the speaker now at his hip. "There is a crawl space. I have to go outside to get to it. Do you need me to check?"

Kalan was impressed with her cold responses. They'd both been afraid when they first realized what the call was about, but now Seline had been switched to *on*.

"No, *do not* leave the house. Our agents are already on the way." Watson made it clear that she thought 'outside' might be dangerous. Did she think Sanders was still around? "Can you show them how to get into the crawlspace when they get there?"

"Absolutely."

Even as she said it, Kalan heard the knock on the front door and the low but projected voice. "FBI."

Seline moved her head to see out the front window, her gun still in hand, still aimed to the floor. She shrugged at him. Someone she didn't recognize?

With a nod, he moved toward the door and slowly opened it. He didn't recognize them either. "Agents?"

Both women, fully in FBI gear, whipped out leather wallets with badge and ID. Though they seemed a little frustrated at the checkpoint, he was not letting anyone worm their way in. Sanders already made personal contact with Seline at least twice.

He motioned to Seline. Neither of these women could possibly be the BRK and that made him feel better. When she said, "Hello," he opened the door full width, but it was Seline who motioned them inside.

"Thank you," the shorter curvier one said without looking at him. Her dark hair was pulled back in a ponytail that was too bouncy for the mood. Giulia Rossi if he remembered correctly.

The blond was Amy Verner and she immediately pulled out a detector that looked almost like a handheld vacuum but clearly was much higher tech. They traced an odd path around the room, their serious expressions letting Seline and him know how concerning the situation was.

"Metal detector?" he asked, curious.

The first agent was already through the living room and was in the kitchen, waving her machine back and forth. Rossi answered as she headed the other direction down the hallway. "We followed the transmitter to this general area via laptop, but this finds it to the inch."

"Transmitter?" Seline asked as though she didn't understand the word.

Kalan caught on, because the agent had heard the French accent and was going to explain the meaning of "transmitter," but Seline's grasp of English was probably the best in the room. So he quickly said, "Remember, Balero was wearing a tracker."

Verner emerged from the kitchen, motioning to Rossi the detector lax at her side. But she said, "No. She wasn't wearing it. It's in her."

Oh dear God, Kalan felt everything in him go still for a moment.

They hadn't found Marina Balero. They hadn't seen or heard her. No one had answered, though they had called out her name a few times.

Was her body here at Seline's house?

CHAPTER SEVENTEEN

S eline watched as both agents converged at the back of the house in her lab. They'd had to move around a little to pinpoint the tracker, but they'd been led here.

She stood back but watched as both agents slowly knelt toward the floor, placing the devices directly on the hard wood. Simultaneously, they looked up at her, two ponytails bobbing with the motion.

"Under the house?" Seline asked cautiously. She could see the small screen stating the tracker was about four feet directly below them.

Neither answered her directly, but Rossi asked "Can you show us?"

Seline nodded quickly. She could do this even if it meant finding her new friend's body stashed under her house ... Maybe she kept it together because she just couldn't believe that could happen. Luckily, her lab was the room that led to the back porch and thus the yard.

Stepping to the glass paneled door, she threw the bolts rapidly, even as she realized they were completely useless.

Someone could simply bust out a pane of glass and reach in and flip the locks to open. But there was no time to contemplate the errors in her home security.

"Follow me." She was barefoot but didn't care as she tread through the gravel that covered the flowerbeds ringing the house.

She carefully cut between two of the pruned bushes and reached out to touch the trellis that skirted the house. In the dark it was hard to find the exact spot she needed. But she grabbed her phone and used the light to locate the handle and pulled the door open, allowing access.

She watched as the two agents quickly ducked into the dark space. She used the light again, shining it into the dark before thinking maybe she shouldn't.

"Turn it out, please."

Seline couldn't tell which of the two had called back, but she quickly shut it off. At least she hadn't seen Marina's corpse shoved under the house. Then again, she hadn't had time to get a good look. Her stomach churned for a moment, but she forced herself to keep it together.

The agents pulled out their own maglites, lighting the place up like day.

"There is no body here." They reported to someone, probably not to Seline.

Kalan had waited on the porch, and she looked up to find him scanning the yard for intruders or evidence or something. She shrugged at him and shook her head. He seemed to have heard the verdict, too.

Still, she wasn't certain they were in the clear. Sure enough, it came too soon.

"Fuck," she heard one of the agents mutter, then again, "Fuck!"

Seline ducked down automatically and looked inside. There

was enough light to see Verner grabbing the phone at her waist. She spoke into it. "We have the tracker … No. Just the tracker."

"Son of a bitch." Seline heard it faintly through the line the agents both had open.

Confused and still standing in the flower bed, the gravel poking at her bare feet, the cool night air making her wish she'd put on a sweater, Seline stood back upright and held the trellis. She turned her brain off, a handy skill when she didn't like what she was learning.

But the agents weren't ready to get out from under the house. Instead, they duck-walked the entire space, checking every corner and around each support beam. Their flashlights shined ovals on the ground, and Seline told herself not to look.

At last, they must have declared themselves finished because they emerged with their knees dirty from crawling. Hands and faces were smudged.

"No," Verner said into her phone. "There's nothing else here. Just the tracker."

"What does it look like?" Seline heard Watson over the line and thought what an odd question that was. *Why wouldn't she know what the tracker looked like?*

But Rossi's answer cleared that up. "It's bloody."

Bon sang! Seline thought. The FBI had embedded a tracker in Marina Balero and the Blue River Killer had physically removed it.

"Why is it here?" Seline fought and failed to keep the tremor out of her voice.

"My guess is that he's leading us to your house because it was fully believable that Marina Balero came to your home of her own volition several hours ago." Rossi looked to Verner who nodded as the three of them stood in the cold air of the backyard. She motioned Seline up the porch steps and inside the house, the agents trailing behind.

Verner added, "When it arrived here, no one thought

anything of it. But when it failed to move for several hours, the system pinged us."

Seline felt her shoulders slump. Her hand went slack, nearly dropping the gun she still held—the one the agents hadn't asked her to set aside. That might be the most telling thing of the evening.

They headed into the living room where she saw Kalan, now standing guard. She let go of a little of the tension. Would she feel this way each time she saw one of her friends was safe? Or was this reserved just for him?

But even as that layer of tension went away, it revealed the violation that Maggie must have felt when Merrit Geller had repeatedly entered her home. "He was here," she told Kalan, then jumped when Watson replied over the still open phone line.

"Maybe, maybe not. He was close enough—or someone was —to get the tracker into the crawlspace under your home," the agent explained, though Seline wasn't sure whether it was what Watson actually thought or just typical law enforcement refusal to speculate on anything that didn't have full evidence behind it.

"However," Watson kept going. "It appears the tracker was placed relatively in the center of the footprint of the home. So my guess is that yes, someone entered the crawlspace to get it there."

"When?"

Watson had said they believed Marina had arrived earlier in the evening. "Just before nine-thirty pm."

Seline would have swallowed hard if not for the constriction of her chest. She and Kalan had been sitting on the couch watching a television show at nine-thirty. She'd heard nothing, had no idea that someone—probably Sanders himself—had shown up and placed a device he'd pulled from Marina's skin under her home.

She was not squeamish, but she wanted to vomit.

Only then did her stunned brain put the pieces together. "The tracker is here. But where is Marina?"

"That's the problem," Watson replied, and Seline could almost hear the agent grinding her teeth. "He has her. And we only know where *not* to look."

CHAPTER EIGHTEEN

"We should eat something," Maggie announced, though there was no gusto behind it. Clearly, none of them were actually hungry, Maggie was just tending to a need.

Seline agreed, if only for the fact that she wouldn't help Marina by passing out.

The sun had come up almost an hour ago. She had gotten dressed in the middle of the night in a warm sweater, despite the disturbingly sunny day. She still felt cold down to her bones.

Kalan had been smart enough to call Maggie and Sebastian at 4am. Neither had balked. But they'd come and they'd sat on the couch and, aside from a few bursts of frantic conversation, the four had mostly stared at each other.

Wendy Buck may have been their fake best friend, but Seline had really liked Marina the more that she'd gotten to know her. It seemed that even given her past with Sebastian, Maggie liked her too.

"At least you haven't gotten another note." Maggie's soft commentary interrupted Seline's thoughts, but not in a good way.

Maggie stood and walked into the kitchen leaving Seline as

every muscle in her body clenched with the thought of what would happen if and when she did get another note. What if he sent her a message with the letters he'd carved into Marina's torso?

Seline almost bolted for the bathroom as her stomach revolted at the thought, but she managed to hold it back. Almost without her own thoughts, Seline wandered woodenly into the kitchen, following Maggie. As Maggie pulled out eggs, she shook her head at her friend.

"No, I can't."

Maggie merely put the eggs back without a word and turned to the pantry. "Oatmeal?"

Seline could agree to that. It was instant, easy to digest, and she would need the sugar to keep her system going today.

Agents Rossi and Verner came back inside as Maggie pulled a kettle out. Seline was grateful right then for friends who would not only just head into her kitchen and make food, but who already knew where everything was. She, on the other hand, wanted to sit down in the middle of the pretty hardwood flooring and pretend it was just a normal day.

But she couldn't. Leaving Maggie behind, she bolted past Sebastian and Kalan to question the agents. "Did you find anything?"

"Nothing that we didn't already find last night." Rossi was clearly frustrated by that fact. They'd gone out at three am with high intensity flashlights and found what they believed were plausibly footprints in the grass. They'd said it was possible that he'd cut into the yard from the side, where he would have stayed out of sight. The bent and trampled grass and disturbed gravel in the flower bed made their best guess that he had thrown the tracker through the trellis or wiggled a hand through, to toss it toward the middle of the home.

This morning everything looked the same.

Seline couldn't tell if that made her happier or more upset.

Just then Verner's phone crackled to life. "Send it over," she said, heading across the living room to where she'd stashed her bag by the side of the couch.

The two agents had conferred with Watson and Decker, who'd begun their search at the Gutierrez home as soon as there was word about the tracker. So far, they'd found blood and evidence that Sanders had pulled the tracker from Marina's arm there, then taken her elsewhere.

None of this was good. Sanders had bypassed every measure the Bureau had put in place to keep Marina safe. Seline wished she could feel something, but the numbness was probably protecting her.

She watched blankly as Rossi and Verner set up in her living room, looking like command central.

Now, all Rossi had to do was park herself at the card table Seline had put in front of the couch for them and open her laptop. Rossi quickly powered it on, then leaned in to watch something. Only a minute later, she motioned to Verner. "Come look at this."

Though she wasn't invited, Seline moved closer, too.

"This is the map of where the tracker went and when," Rossi told Verner, but included Seline as well.

"So we can see earlier in the day, she's in her home."

The Gutierrez home, Seline realized, and watched as the dot moved quickly through the house. Eventually, it paused in one room of the blueprint that Rossi had expanded on the screen and stayed, unmoving, in the corner of the room. "What happened?"

Rossi offered a small grin. "She probably took a nap. This is why it doesn't ping just because it doesn't move for a while. It would ping us all night when she was asleep. Honestly, the tracker itself is very invasive. See?" She pointed as the dot began moving on the screen again and headed down the hallway to a small room. It took Seline a moment to see that the small space was a bathroom and that, yes, being tracked everywhere allowed no privacy. But Marina had agreed because she wanted Sanders caught.

"Go back." Verner pointed at the screen. "There."

"What?" Rossi asked what Seline wanted to.

"See how it stops moving so much?"

"Maybe she just sat down?"

Seline was trying to keep up with the rapid back and forth.

"But why would she just sit in the middle of the back room? Play it in real time." They'd been watching a speeded version so they could get to the point where the tracker arrived at Seline's house.

Rossi clicked at the keys and touched the screen and the dot jumped back to the other side of the house. Seline watched as the dot moved through the home. This tracker was specific enough to pinpoint Marina's location to the inch, prompting Seline to ask, "Where was the tracker on her?"

"Under the skin near the bend of her elbow," Verner answered almost without thinking. Her own eyes were glued to the screen.

Seline wasn't surprised by the response, she'd thought she might be seeing Marina swing her arm as she walked.

"There! It jerks back."

It was a small movement, and Seline wouldn't have noticed on her own.

"Nine fifteen. I'm guessing that's when he got the tracker out of her. She didn't have time to activate her emergency call."

"What?" Seline asked. "Emergency call?"

"She also had a necklace that looked like jewelry but she could activate it and let us know she was in trouble."

"She didn't activate it," Seline murmured, but neither of the agents answered her.

They watched through what they now believed was Sanders restraining Marina and removing the tracker.

"Look, here." The tracker moved down the street at nearly nine-thirty p.m. toward Seline's home. It tracked the property line between the neighbor's home and hers and then headed toward the side of her home. Next, it jumped under the house.

"Looks like he threw it." Verner commented softly.

Seline wondered if anyone had noticed the odd movement at the time. She couldn't hold her tongue. "What did you think of this when you saw it last night?"

"We didn't see it until now." Rossi tipped her head up as though to look her in the eyes and let her know that she, at least, had not missed this and let her friend go missing. "Another team of agents was watching the tracker in live time. It's a shitty, boring job, and they are only supposed to check it every minute or so."

So they might have missed the odd little movements that were the only clues. *Merde.*

Verner kept her eyes on the screen but added, "We were in our car down the street, watching in real time. He—or whoever —came in from the other side of the property, like he knew we were watching and what car we were in ..."

Seline was only more confused. "But if you were watching from the car, did they not tell you that she was on her way over?"

She shouldn't have asked. She shouldn't have put the agents on the spot or suggest that they had failed.

"We weren't watching the tracker. The people watching the tracker probably thought we'd see Marina. She came here on other nights and visited just fine. There was no protocol for them to alert us." Verner looked up from where she was watching the video again.

"I'm sorry I asked."

"You were right to ask." But Verner was looking at the next thing, her attention clearly not on soothing Seline's wounded and worried nerves.

Rossi stood up and walked around the room as if she would find the clues she needed here. She looked out the window, checking up and down the street, just as she had every fifteen minutes since she'd arrived. She pulled out her phone and texted someone, while Verner took over her seat at the folding table and watched the video again and again.

Maggie had served steaming bowls of oatmeal to the guys while Seline watched the dot move on the screen. Her own bowl was waiting and it was a relief to sit down and do something normal, but it only lasted for five minutes—just long enough for Seline to realize she wouldn't be eating the whole thing anyway.

"Giulia, come here." Verner motioned to the other agent. "Quickly."

Rossi crossed the room and watched whatever Verner was pointing at. "Holy shit."

"Yeah," the other agent replied, snapping Seline's attention back to them once more.

"What?" She abandoned the food and her friends who'd sat silently by.

Though she stood and confronted them, the two agents looked to each other, as if deciding whether or not they would tell the residents in the room what they had seen.

CHAPTER NINETEEN

"Here, look ... and here." The murmured responses from his friends finally made him leave the table.

Kalan was the last one still sitting there, finishing the double sized portion of oatmeal that Maggie had made.

He'd wanted to stay out of the way. The FBI was doing all they could. He figured he would make it his job to help Seline. But now, that seemed to mean getting involved with whatever was happening on the couch.

Scooping his last bite, he stood up. Oatmeal wasn't his favorite, but he'd eaten far worse when Ronan was in his first year at the Firehouse. The new guy did most of the cooking. It had taken Patrick's son about six months to figure it out.

His belly full for the moment, Kalan joined the others crowded around the couch, watching as Verner showed them a video. Kalan had to lean way over the side to see what was on the screen.

His arm brushed Seline's for a moment, but he pulled back. The last thing he wanted to do was crowd her. None of the things he wanted to say or do fit into this scenario in the slightest. Verner kept forwarding and reversing the video, speeding up and slowing down the moving dot.

"Here," she told the group, not bothering to bring him up to speed. "Watch it in real time."

He was still huddled close enough to Seline to smell her shampoo. Leaning in close to Seline again, he whispered, "What am I supposed to see?"

On the one hand, he was trying not to bother the others, who were coming to some very serious conclusions. On the other hand, it was a good excuse to get closer to Seline where he could.

"The dot is Marina's tracker," Seline whispered back, her breath brushing the skin of his neck. "What Verner is pointing out is an unusual motion, where the dot went forward and then suddenly jerked backwards."

Verner overheard them. "I think this is where Sanders attacked her. Because after this, we can see that the tracker moves to the center of the room in an odd and slightly jerky pattern. Then it remains in that one spot—though with some movement—in the center of the room for several hours."

She muttered something and no one asked her to elaborate, but Kalan was fairly certain she'd said, "Why did no one notice this when it was happening?"

"Do you think she was tied to a chair?" Seline's voice was shaky.

Kalan didn't really want to know if his friend was tied to a chair by a serial killer. It was clear Seline already felt guilty.

He asked another question. "What's the timestamp?"

"Seven-oh-seven." Verner had clearly already looked for herself.

If Sanders had caught her in her own home—her own borrowed home—at just after seven, then Marina had been in BRK's clutches for just over twelve hours.

Everyone came to the same conclusion.

No one said anything.

Kalan wanted to ask how long Sanders tended to keep his victims alive after he took them, but he wasn't even sure if Verner and Rossi could answer that.

A sharp sound cut the air and even Kalan jumped. He brushed Seline's breast and was in the awkward spot of apologizing—yet again—or dealing with whatever the hell that noise was.

"Ring tone." Rossi waved her phone at them as it lit up with the incoming call, then headed through the kitchen toward the back of the house to answer it. Clearly, she didn't want to be overheard and his curiosity was piqued.

Verner—unfazed by the obnoxiously loud ringtone or her partner's absence—kept rolling the video, watching the dot move from one location in the digital house layout to another. Kalan didn't learn anything new, though Verner apparently did with each time she watched it.

When Rossi came back, she flicked a hand in front of her partner to get her attention. "We've been called out."

"What?" Seline jumped to her feet, seemingly involuntarily.

Verner didn't even question the order. She simply began powering down the laptop and closing everything up. She had her bag zipped before Rossi was able to tell Seline, "You'll still have agents on you. But it's important that it looks like you've been left alone."

Jesus, Kalan thought. *Seline should appear to be alone?*

Despite the fact that baiting Sanders had worked, everything had gone wrong. Balero wasn't supposed to be taken, nor her tracker dug out of her arm. Now the FBI was leaving.

As Verner and Rossi headed out the door, he looked to the others and realized that they'd just decided to use Seline as bait.

CHAPTER TWENTY

"I have to do *something*," Seline announced. She could still hear the fear in her own voice even though she'd tried to quell it.

She lasted all of twenty minutes after the agents had left.

The four of them had been told to stay put and go about their normal days. Sebastian and Kalan were off duty today, Maggie didn't have clients, and Seline had been told to only come into the university for classes ...

"Can you do something here?" Kalan asked. "You look really worried."

No shit, Sherlock!

It was one of her favorite English phrases and she bit her tongue not to yell it in anger now.

"I *am* worried! My new friend put herself out as bait to save me and now he has her and we don't know where she is or if she's even alive!" Once she started speaking her stomach clenched. Maggie and Sebastian were looking at her as if they couldn't look away. She was yelling, but she couldn't stop. "I bought this house at the upper limit of my buying ability, but I did it because I am on a tenure track. I could make tenure in two years! But now ..."

"I don't understand ..." Kalan reached out, his expression mimicking his words. "Why is tenure so important?"

She lashed out. "Do you have any idea how hard it is to get a job in academia? I have student loans up to here!" She motioned over her head. "Tenure is job security. Tenure is the best promotion I can get besides becoming department chair or a dean. *And I don't want those things!*"

A tenured position at an American university had been her dream. She was so close and the BRK was stealing it from her. She turned to her friend though she was still breathing heavily, still on the verge of tears thinking about what she might lose just because her genetics put her in Sanders' crosshairs. "I'm so sorry. I thought you were crazy to go after Geller the way you did. But I understand now. This bastard has flipped my whole life upside down."

Maggie was nodding along in sympathy, maybe the only one who truly understood. She'd taken Seline's hands in her own to calm her but Seline still couldn't stop the runaway train that was her voice.

"First Sanders and now the FBI and the school are slowly stripping away everything I've worked for. If this lasts any longer, I won't have any life left to fight for!" That was wrong. She knew that. Nothing had been truly lost yet, but *everything* was in jeopardy. Not to mention her very life if Sanders did get her.

She couldn't process it all.

"Take some deep breaths." She felt Kalan's hand on her back, and it was all she could do not to shrug him off and yell at him not to use his 'soothing unruly victims' bullshit on her.

After her outburst finally faded away, they all managed to take seats around the living room. Seline sat on the front edge of her once-comfy couch again. It seemed as if they would have a meeting, talk this all out. Only no one was talking.

Finally she asked, "Where are Watson and Decker?"

"They're out looking for Marina," Maggie told her, as she reached out to put her hand on Seline's arm. But then, at the last moment, she pulled it back. Maybe she realized Seline couldn't be calmed.

"We have to do *something*," she repeated her initial plea. "At least, *I* do."

"We're supposed to stay put," Sebastian told her, but she wasn't having any of it.

She understood: he and Kalan were firefighters. Their lives depended on following protocol and doing what the ranking officer told them to do. Hers might depend on breaking the rules.

Up until now, it had been easy to be motivated by her fear of losing tenure. Everything in her life was fragile, set up like dominoes. If she lost her chance at tenure, she would lose her salary, maybe even her position. But just a simple salary cut meant not making her mortgage. Her house would be foreclosed on. She could handle one major crisis, but not this many at once.

She could lose it all. But in a blink, her worries disappeared. What if she just considered it all gone already, what was left? Marina's life. Her own life. The lives of every other future victim of the Blue River Killer.

Screw tenure. This was much more important.

"Where do we go first?" she asked the room. When no one answered, she turned to Maggie. "Where did Geller take you?"

She knew but only in a vague sense, that Merrit Geller had taken Maggie to Sanders' cabin in the National Park.

"He won't go back to the cabin," Maggie answered calmly. "The FBI knows exactly where it is."

Something had nagged at Seline, and she hadn't asked before

because she truly didn't want the answer. But with Marina's life on the line right now, if she wasn't already dead, Seline didn't have the luxury of ignoring what she didn't want to hear. "How do they know he took his victims there?"

Maggie looked to Sebastian, the two of them exchanging a glance that spoke volumes. The look that passed between them clearly said they didn't want to tell her. But Seline took half a step forward, planted her feet and glared.

Maggie answered her. "They found blood. They matched it to at least eight of his victims."

Merde! she thought.

"So he first went to a place that his family owned ... Where would he go now? What was his second-choice option?"

Around her, all three of them motioned that they didn't know.

Pacing the room now, she found the motion of her feet helped quell the churning of her brain. She asked another question. "How long does it usually take from when the person goes missing until the body turns up?"

No one had the answer to this either. She would have to figure it all out.

She stopped moving, looked up at her ceiling and did some quick math in her head. "There have been two recent bodies. The one they found before Geller was killed and the one associated with my 'hello' note."

Pushing back on the churn in her stomach that she had a second note and no body, Seline kept working her way forward.

"What about before that?" Sebastian asked, popping to his own feet as he thought.

"It doesn't matter before that. Before that he was taking at least some of them to the cabin, we need to know where he's taking them after that, so probably only the two most recent cases matter."

"Gotcha," he replied but didn't look at her. Maggie and Kalan remained seated, but she could see from the way Maggie was almost preternaturally still and the way that Kalan tapped his thumbs together and bounced his knee that both were very much in thought.

She grabbed her phone and started looking up what she could. In a few minutes she had enough news reports to put a little info together.

"It was Friday night that the first victim disappeared. They found her Sunday morning."

"So, thirty-six hours?" Kalan asked.

"Wait." She took a moment, pulled another article up and amended that. "The M.E. declared time of death at least by Saturday night. So that victim had less than twenty-four hours."

Then there was the first note Seline had gotten, the one that said *hello*. She did the math quickly on that one. "The second one was less than fourteen hours from when she went missing to when the autopsy declared she'd been put in the water, still slightly alive."

That made Seline shudder. Sanders was a pro—if a serial killer could be called such a thing. But he'd missed with that one. Before that, he'd always put the bodies into the water already dead … this one had water in her lungs. She'd breathed it in *after* being left to be found. Seline didn't mention how she'd come to the number but reiterated, "Fourteen hours was the longest he could have had her."

"What about the one with the second note, the third body from this cycle?" Maggie's voice was tentative. No one had wanted to bring it up.

The one with my initials.

But Maggie's question triggered her thoughts and the pieces pulled together into a single picture. "It took a long time to find that body. Could he have kept her alive longer?"

"Or—" Kalan's voice was concerningly serious. "—maybe he gave you the note before he had someone."

Seline looked to Kalan. "Like mind games? That just by leaving the note for me, he made all of us afraid? He was making the FBI look for a body that didn't even exist yet?"

"It's a good ploy," Maggie conceded with a heavy sigh. "The FBI said he wants to torment us. That works."

It was all a good way to torture her, Seline thought. But she went back to the one thing she now knew. "The one time window I know is fourteen hours. So ..."

She pulled out her own laptop now and settled herself where Verner had been the center of attention. Now she was the one clicking keys and pulling up images.

"His cabin was here." She pointed to her screen. "Almost two hours away."

"Three by water," Maggie added softly, having made that trip herself, though she said she didn't remember most of it.

"So a long round trip isn't out of the question for him. It doesn't have to be a location nearby." She thought it through. "Fourteen hours means it could be seven hours out and seven hours back. That gives us a very big radius from where he takes them."

But Kalan was shaking his head at her as he sank onto the couch next to her. His arm brushed hers, his leg and hip pressed against hers, but if he noticed he didn't show it. At least he didn't? visibly pull away in front of her friends. Seline reminded herself she didn't have time to pine over a man who was only pretending to date her.

"I hate to be the bearer of really shitty news, but there's evidence that he tortures them—for quite some time. So he needs a minimum of four to six hours with his victims at this location."

Seline couldn't help it. She was glad for the information, not because of what Sanders was probably doing to Marina right now but because it gave them a much better timeframe.

"You're right. Fourteen hours minus six is eight. A trip out and back gives us a four-hour radius from here." She'd narrowed the map a little from her initial too-big radius around Redemption and Lincoln. The new one was still too big though. "What we need to know now, is if Sanders owns any other land within this circle."

The others were nodding along. Sebastian was shaking one finger. "He needs to own the place or at least have unfettered access to it! For what he's doing, if it's not a place he owns or controls, someone will find it and figure him out. He's too smart for that."

"But where can we find out what land he owns?"

Even as Seline asked the question, she watched Maggie's face brighten.

CHAPTER TWENTY-ONE

Seline marched through the double front doors of the Redemption Public Library as soon as the librarian opened them.

The woman's bright blue eyes had flown wide to see four people on her doorstep waiting. Probably not the norm in the tiny town.

Seline was quick to assess that the woman's hair was a caramel color and not what she would call blonde. *Thank God. Not a target.*

"Maggie!" the woman exclaimed, her surprise turning to a smile.

Maggie grinned back and motioned to the prim looking young woman in her shell pink sweater set. She told the others, "This is Ivy Dean, librarian extraordinaire."

Seline must have frowned, because Maggie answered the question she hadn't quite asked. "I'm in here all the time. I handle property with wills and disputes, so I'm always checking records and looking up county ordinances. Ivy is a genius with all things document."

Ivy seemed apologetic, or maybe humble. "The newer

county records are at the county seat, not here. We only have the older ones ... On microfiche!" She added the last bit with a wry look.

"That's okay." Seline liked Ivy Dean already. "We're really looking for broader information. Land records, probably older ones."

"All right, then." Looking around to see if she had another rush coming at library opening on a Thursday, she let the door fall closed behind them. "Follow me."

She almost unconsciously tipped up a sign at the front desk as she passed by, and Seline caught that it said "I'll be right back." Ivy moved as though she owned the library herself, as if everything magically appeared beneath her fingertips as she needed it.

With her caramel hair and pink smile and slightly-too-old-for-her-age outfit, Ivy could have been a fairytale princess. If she sang and birds or butterflies brought the books to her, Seline would not have been surprised.

"In here." She led them into one of the small back rooms, whatever tasks she had planned for the opening already pushed aside. Two walls were lined with boxes, dated and marked carefully in a variety of handwritings. One wall held large record books that Seline would guess were filled with neat, slanted script entries. The last wall held a low desk and three machines close enough that the users would bump elbows. One end of the table was lined with neat, round rocks for no apparent reason.

Ivy turned in the center of the room to face them. "What it is that you need to know?"

Seline took a breath and told Ivy her very crazy idea. "So I need to know what kind of property William Treat Sanders might own or have access to within a four hour radius of Redemption."

"Sanders?" Ivy asked, a look of confusion pausing on her

features for only a moment before she clearly placed the name. Everyone in town recognized the name Sanders now.

"I thought he was using a cabin in the national park." The words were out of her mouth before she jerked back, her hand flying to her mouth as though she could swallow them. She must have realized Maggie was the reason he wasn't still using the cabin. She breathed out a hushed apology, "I'm so sorry."

Maggie held up a hand. "I'm fine now. It's not me I'm worried about. Do you know Marina Balero?"

"The officer?"

Seline thought, *of course the town librarian knew their officer friend*. This was why she'd moved to Redemption in the first place—to be someplace where she could have real friends and where she knew her neighbors.

"Yes," Seline said, as Maggie replied with even more information. "Sanders has taken her."

"What?" Ivy's stunned reaction wasn't a surprise, only that the news hadn't traveled faster. "Is no one looking for her?"

"Everyone's looking for her," Seline assured her. "The FBI, the Redemption Police Department, everyone."

Ivy caught on. "Including you guys."

"I couldn't sit at home and wait." Seline felt the muscles of her torso twitching even as she said it. The nervous energy still flowed out, lacking a direction. She hoped Ivy Dean could help her find a way to channel it.

Ivy didn't ask if they'd brought Sanders to her doorstep. She'd simply said, "Okay, show me where he was before. And we'll start looking from there."

Striding the few short steps to one wall, she moved around the edge of one of the industrial metal bookshelves and reached into a bin that held tall cardboard tubes. She looked at a few then picked out one and rolled open a map of eastern Nebraska that spanned almost the whole table. She turned, picked up four of the waiting rocks behind her and weighted the edges of the old map. Redemption Public Library was not high-tech, but Ivy made it work.

The four spaced themselves out around Ivy, putting five sets of eyes on the map. Ivy looked up first. "Geller was a resident at Sabbie's boarding house for some time, correct?"

"Yes," Maggie answered.

Seline filled in more. "My thinking was that maybe there's something else from his family. Some property that came to him with little or no fanfare. Something he can use ..."

She didn't say for what.

No one asked if this even mattered. The FBI had to be looking into every possibility. The four of them surely weren't better than the feds at this, but Seline had to *do* something. And if they did get anything that helped, then it would be worth every minute.

Even as Seline thought this, Ivy asked, "I know his cabin was in the park, but where?"

"Here," Sebastian immediately put his finger on the map. It was probably forever burned into his brain from when he'd run to save Maggie's life. He'd pinpointed a small batch of mostly abandoned cabins in the middle of a swath of green. "And it was listed as being owned by one of his great uncles. He'd passed about a decade ago."

"The uncle's last name was also Sanders?" Ivy asked.

Maggie and Sebastian both nodded and Seline was grateful. She hadn't known that.

Ivy looked at all of them expectantly. "Has anyone looked under his mother's maiden name?"

CHAPTER TWENTY-TWO

"Those are in a different room," Ivy told them. "Follow me."

Maggie and Seline were immediately on their feet, tagging along behind the petite librarian as if she were the Pied Piper.

But Kalan put his hand on Sebastian's arm and held him back. He waited until the room cleared but didn't wait for his friend to ask what he wanted.

"We're on shift in less than twenty-four hours. If there's no word about Balero ..." He left the question hanging in the air between them. *What should they do about Maggie and Seline?*

Sebastian pressed his lips together. "I've been thinking about that, too. We passed Marina's fourteen-hour mark while we were here."

Kalan felt that settle heavily into his heart. Though he too had noted when the time had passed, he hadn't commented. He hadn't wanted to bring up the time frame that they knew the Blue River Killer dispatched his victims in. Though the FBI hadn't called to tell them anything, Marina Balero was most likely dead.

"Even if we find anything," Sebastian said, "We're probably saving the next person, not Balero."

That was hard to come to terms with. He'd managed to push the twist in his gut away enough that it hadn't quite dug its claws in until Sebastian confirmed it just now.

They'd all ridden Seline's coattails of anxiety earlier. When she'd demanded that she had to do something, they'd all agreed. Doing something had certainly felt much better than sitting and waiting as the FBI had instructed. In fact, if Sanders was watching, what they were doing now was an appropriate response for four friends—two couples—given the news that their friend had disappeared.

He didn't know if the women had noticed that they were in the other room by themselves, though it would have been hard enough to miss. They were probably just quietly giving him his space.

Ivy had been on her feet all morning, popping up and down as she answered the phone or the door or helped another patron. At ten, a volunteer had come in and the librarian had finally been able to fully lend them her full focus. It was making a difference.

Just maybe not enough of one.

"There's also the issue of that strange call Seline got." Kalan kept his voice quiet, not knowing what might be happening on the other side of the slightly ajar door.

"The FBI hasn't found anything from the call." Seline shrugged. "They thought it was a prank, too."

"But what if it wasn't?" he asked. Did it mean there was another murder?

Sebastian didn't need to answer. In Blue River Killer shorthand the single word could mean that there was another body out there waiting to be found. But no one had found a body—yet.

Frustrated, Kalan rubbed the palm of his hand over his short, curly hair, the texture of it soothing in some way. "Sanders likes his bodies to be found."

Luckily, Sebastian didn't need the full explanation of how he'd gotten there. "That's true."

"So why did it take so long to find the body with the second note?" Sanders didn't hide his victims. He posed them with the intent that they be found and terrorize everyone who knew about them. He offered up something that had been bugging him, something he hadn't wanted to share with Seline.

"It wasn't properly anchored," Maggie replied.

"Was it a real accident or has he gotten sloppy?" Kalan asked the group. But no one knew the answer.

"That's exactly the problem." Sebastian was arguing back. "If we understood his methods, or even particularly his goals, he would have been caught long before now. He's been operating for ... *What?* Twenty-plus years and they've only within the last year, found out his name."

That was all true and all disheartening. Kalan sighed, once again running his hand over his hair. "But we *do* know who he is now. So I don't understand why they can't find him. We even know he's here, locally. He's taunting Seline. She's interacted with him twice and had a conversation with him!"

His voice was rising as his irritation at his inability to do anything got the better of him. He had specific training as a firefighter on how to handle de-escalating a tense situation. It was fine when it was someone else's problem. But this was Seline. His training had apparently gone out the window. Though he took a deep breath, he was still frustrated and unable to fully calm down. Kalan tried looping back to his original question. "When we go back tomorrow ... What then?"

"The FBI is watching," Sebastian tried to assure him, though Kalan was having none of it.

"Marina had a tracker in her arm, and Sanders still got her. They have no idea where she is or if she's even alive." He watched as his friend's eyes darted down toward the tabletop, and then off toward the floor. But Kalan couldn't hold back. "And if—as we both clearly believe—he's already killed her, then there's no reason not to come back for Seline or someone else. What happens to them if we're not there?"

That at least brought Sebastian's eyes back toward his. "Honestly, I think Maggie should stay with Seline. She'll keep Seline safe."

He was talking it through, but Sebastian was laughing at him. "Seline is better trained with that gun than either you or I are."

Kalan had to concede that note. Though he wasn't quite committed to the "Kalan and Sebastian just go back to work as usual" plan, he didn't have an alternative.

He didn't have long to think one up.

Even as he got frustrated again, this time with the time crunch, Seline came through the door at full speed. "I think we found it!"

CHAPTER TWENTY-THREE

Seline stared at Maggie across the breakfast table, this time over a bowl of cereal.

It was just the two of them now. They'd shoved the men out the door at seven-thirty, insisting they were fine and they could take care of themselves.

All of it was a lie.

They *could* probably take care of themselves, but they weren't fine. None of them were.

She'd watched at the window until Kalan's sleek little sports car turned at the end of the street. Then she'd stepped back into the living room and called Watson. She'd checked up on everything they'd figured out the day before.

Ivy had found Sanders' mother's maiden name. Not surprisingly it was Treat, but that hadn't been a guess they could bank on. Then Ivy had been excited to announce that she'd found his grandmothers' maiden names, too. One had been Bland and the other Holden.

Despite the information dump Seline provided, Watson had had nothing to add. Marina had not been located. No notes had appeared at Seline's house or at the school.

She didn't have classes to teach on Friday, so she wouldn't be back on campus until next Monday. It sucked more than ever that she'd been instructed to stay away. What if he'd left something and Watson and Decker missed it? They didn't know her office or even the campus like she did.

Apparently, Sanders knew it better than even the FBI agents …

Seline swallowed one more bite of cereal before she gave up. Her stomach was still not ready for eggs or any more serious kind of food. She'd been living on oatmeal and Cheerios since they'd gotten the news about the tracker being under her house.

She'd managed only half the bowl before the rest had gone soggy. Next to her, Maggie was methodically working her way through a bowl of her own as she scrolled through her phone. But Seline couldn't go on with the mundane task of breakfast. She was done pretending everything was okay. At least for right now.

She was convinced her life was about to become a true crime novel. Between planning her lessons for next week and speculating wildly about where her friend might have been taken to be tortured and murdered, she lamented how many hours had passed.

Setting the spoon down with a bit too much of a thunk, she said to Maggie, "If Sanders had a cabin and he was using it with his victims and he was found out …"

That part wasn't an "if," it was literally what had happened. "… wouldn't it be really disturbing if he took Marina to that same cabin? It's the last place anyone would think to look."

"It's an interesting idea," Maggie said. "But the FBI is all over the cabin, aren't they?"

"Do you know that for sure?"

"We can call Watson and ask. I just don't get the feeling that she's invested in our amateur sleuthing."

"We're not amateurs," Seline countered, trying to hold back

her irritation and her fear. *"You're* certainly not. You helped catch Geller!" She waved her hand up and down at Maggie as if to indicate a certified private eye.

"I don't think that qualifies me." Maggie set her own spoon down much more gently, though Seline noticed that her own bowl was still half full, too. Having their friend go missing at the hands of a serial killer wasn't doing anything for anyone's appetite.

For a moment, Seline reined in her thoughts.

The FBI had multiple sets of agents on the case. The Redemption PD was all over it. There was a serial killer Task Force that had assigned agents to the BRK long before they'd known his real name. What could she and Maggie possibly contribute?

But the fact was, she and Maggie were sitting in the epicenter of Geller and Sanders' work. So maybe they could contribute.

"If I were a killer, I would go to where I was least expected. That would be where I previously was—where I'd almost been caught."

Maggie tipped her head, acknowledging that she was thinking about the idea at least. "But I do think they're watching the cabin. Just in case."

"I'm sure you're right. But when Ivy showed us the records, even on the map you can see that there's a cluster of cabins up there. I got the impression that many of them are unused and in disrepair." The ownership was grandfathered in, since the families owned them before the land became national park land. Ivy had told them that the cabins had water pumps and outhouses, but no plumbing or electricity. It was no wonder some families weren't using them.

Seline pressed the idea a litter harder, unsure why she was so attached to it. "Could Sanders get to one of the other cabins and use it? Surely he's familiar with all of them."

"That's an interesting idea," Maggie said. "He'd have to know if he had neighbors nearby when he was bringing a victim up there."

Though she said it with calm certainty, Maggie didn't manage to hide a small shudder than ran up her spine. She'd been brought to the cabin by Gellar in hopes that Sanders would dispose of her.

"How would we even find out though?" Seline was musing through her problem again. She needed to do something to help find Marina. "I don't think it's wise to get in the car and go driving off to some cabins where there might be a serial killer."

"Agreed." Maggie reached for her phone. "However, there was a ranger who helped out when I was missing. Let me see if I can find him."

Maggie stood up and walked through the living room, tapping out a message to someone—probably Sebastian—and leaving her food behind. Seline cleaned up for something to do.

But Maggie was back within just a few minutes, exclaiming, "His name is Leo Evans, and he's with the National Park Service."

Seline emerged from the kitchen, finally excited. "Let's call him now."

Less than fifteen minutes later, they had the Park Ranger on the phone. "Yes, there are other cabins there," he told them, "And yes, there's more than one route into the area. We'll check them out."

"Wait," Seline said, though she hadn't spoken while Maggie ran the phone call. She didn't want to butt in, having not met Evans herself before. "Be aware. William Treat Sanders is possibly in one of the cabins and he may be there with the victim."

"He has another one?" Evans asked, clearly startled by that information.

"A friend of ours … He took her almost thirty-six hours ago."

The words choked in Seline's throat but she managed to get them out. She was grateful that he didn't feel the need to tell her that her friend was most likely already dead.

"I'll go up there with the team myself. I was there when Geller went down. I'd love to see Sanders fry." The conviction in his voice soothed her. "I may pick up on something having been there before."

"Thank you."

Seline felt much better as Maggie hung up the phone. But as soon as she did, Seline's phone rang from the other room.

Her heart perked, her heart rate rising with hope as she ducked to grab the phone. "Hello?"

She hadn't looked at the caller ID! What if it was Sanders?

"I'm looking for Dr. Seline Marchand." The voice was feminine and friendly and immediately calmed her heart.

"This is Dr. Marchand."

"You don't know me, and I don't know what this is about ..." the wary tone in the voice seeped into Seline's blood. She could feel it now. This was not going to be good.

She caught Maggie's own worried glance but couldn't offer her any reassurance.

The voice continued, "I'm supposed to tell you *she's still alive.*"

CHAPTER TWENTY-FOUR

"She is?" Seline practically screamed it. If her pulse was high before, it was spiking into dangerous levels now.

When no answer came, she asked again. "She's really alive?"

"I don't know!" The woman's tone was more irritated than helpful or hopeful, and her next words cleared it up. "Some guy paid me a hundred dollars to call and tell you this."

Seline turned frantically in a circle, her phone pressed to her ear, as she looked for Maggie. She practically ran right into her friend. Of course, Maggie had not missed any of it.

Maggie made a rolling motion with her hand, indicating for Seline to keep the woman on the phone. But for a moment, she simply froze. Her mind blanked. *What should she say? What should she do?*

"Well, there you go, honey. My job is done," the woman said and seemed about to hang up.

That was enough to break whatever awful spell was keeping her silent, and Seline interrupted. "What did he look like?"

"What did who look like?"

"The man you said paid you to call me." Seline tried not to let her frustration through. But who knew what was leaching into her voice? She was ecstatic that Marina might actually still be alive, but didn't want to believe anything that originated from Sanders. His main goal was to toy with them and lying about this would certainly do it.

"Oh, he was just average looking."

Sanders had not chosen the brightest bulb in the box to deliver his message—probably on purpose. Fighting to keep her calm and keep the woman on the phone, she asked more specific questions. "What color hair did he have?"

"Blond. With a little white in it maybe."

"That's great," Seline tried to consciously unclench her fist, but it didn't work. "Did you get his eye color?"

"I don't know that. Maybe blue."

"His height?" They went back and forth, eating up time. But Maggie was still making the motion at her, so Seline kept talking. So far, the description had fit Sanders perfectly.

"He was average tall. I told you that." There was a soul weary sigh from the other end of the line as her caller was getting ready to tap out. "Listen lady, I don't have time for this. I have things to do."

Maggie was still motioning her hand to keep talking, even though it was getting harder to drag this out. At some point, while Seline had frantically been making conversation, Maggie had gotten on the phone herself. She moved away now to talk to whoever she was contacting.

"And he gave you a hundred dollars to call me? He gave you this number?"

"I already said that."

Seline tried another tack. "And where are you calling from?"

"I'm not supposed to tell you."

In the background, Seline heard Maggie utter the words, "phone call … trace … it's something about Marina …"

Seline desperately wanted to give Maggie what little

information she had, but she needed to keep the woman on the phone. She pushed again. "Where did you meet him?"

There was another moment's pause where she thought she was going to get the same answer of *I'm not supposed to tell you.* But the woman replied, "In the parking lot at the store."

Both of them were getting frustrated. "Which store?"

"The grocery store! Look lady, I gotta go."

And with an audible click the line went dead.

Bon Sang!

But right then, Maggie turned around, one hand on the phone but the other giving her a thumbs up sign—whatever that meant.

Had Seline managed to keep the woman on the line long enough to trace the call? Did it mean Watson or Decker had found where the call came from?

Maybe it meant they'd found Marina!

But no. Maggie would have yelled that so the whole neighborhood could hear.

Now Seline was stuck waiting until Maggie's call finished. As she stood there, wondering if she'd ever find a way to live without this soul-twisting feeling in the center of her body, her phone rang again. If she wasn't young and healthy, she would have dropped dead of a heart attack right at that moment.

Flipping the phone to her face, she pressed the button even as she read the words, Redemption Public Library.

"May I speak to Dr. Seline Marchand?" It sounded almost identical to the start of the last call she'd gotten, but this time she recognized the voice.

"Ivy! I'm going to have to call you back."

"Oh, did something happen?"

She wanted to say *yes.* And then *No.* Because what did they really know? Except that they'd gotten a call from a stranger. But surely Sanders had given the strange woman in the parking lot Seline's number. So she settled on, "maybe."

"Well, fingers crossed! But I think I might have found something important, so call back as soon as you can."

"Okay, I will." That at least lifted her heart. Maggie had something good on her call, and Ivy had good news, too. She said goodbye and hung up. Even as she turned it off, she wondered now how quickly it could ring again.

Maggie hung up and told her, "Watson is getting the call traced. She pulled your records and thinks you kept her on the line just long enough to make it happen. She's going to call back."

Another sigh of relief hit her. Maybe Marina was still alive and maybe she would be found. A brief silence descended as she and Maggie stared at each other waiting for phone calls that didn't quite come.

Seline forced herself to move around. She was behind on her work. Even though she had her wonderful lab at home, she wasn't getting anything done. She had good reason to fear that she'd lose her track to tenure. But worse, Marina Balero was in the hands of that madman.

Though Seline hadn't admitted it to herself, when they'd passed the fourteen-hour mark, she'd consoled herself that Marina wasn't in any more pain or terror. Now her friend was possibly still alive. Was that better or worse? Seline didn't know.

It felt like an eon later, though it was barely a minute, that Seline asked, "Do we call Sebastian and Kalan?"

"What are Kalan and Sebastian going to do that we aren't?" Maggie replied after a moment's careful thought. "If they're out on a call, they won't even get the message. If they're in the station, they could decide to leave the shift. But if they leave, then they need to get subbed out first. Two of them getting a sub at the same time is harder than you might think."

Seline understood. If they both left without subs in place, the station would be very short-handed in the face of an emergency.

And the fire station faced real emergencies, while she'd had a concerning phone call.

Seline conceded. It hadn't been her best idea, even if she wanted Kalan here. Even if he didn't feel the same. She'd deal with her feelings when all of this was over.

So they stayed there in the living room, accomplishing nothing but discussing a few pointless options until Maggie's phone rang again. She smiled as soon as she saw who was calling and held the phone out with the speaker button on before she even answered it. "Watson!"

Without even a return greeting, Watson began explaining what they'd found. "I want you to leave Seline's line open in case she gets another call. If someone calls you that you know, answer and hang up immediately. Message them that you'll call back on another line. I want your line as free as possible."

She could do that, but instead of just agreeing, she asked, "What do we know about that call?"

"Well, it's a landline, of all things. We figured out that it came from Stromsburg. Do you have any connection to Stromsburg?"

"No, I don't even know where it is." Seline had come to the US as a graduate student. She'd attended Cornell and, after completing a postdoc for two years in Georgia, she'd quickly landed the position at Lincoln.

It was Maggie who said, "It's another small town. North and West of Lincoln."

Watson continued matter of factly. "The call came from a payphone at Martin's Grocery. It's a mom and pop kind of place. Local chain with about fifteen stores across eastern Nebraska."

After relaying as much of the conversation as she could remember, Seline heard Watson talking to someone near her. "Get footage from the parking lot of that store."

Her heart breathed another sigh of relief. They were doing everything they could. The grocery store answer had been true.

Maybe, so had the rest of it. And the footage they got might just show Sanders—or at least what Sanders looked like now. She added, "Her description of the man who gave her the money was relatively spot on to the real Sanders."

"We're tracking him down. And we're looking in the area," Watson told them before ending the phone call.

Once again, Seline was left pacing her own room. She had no work to do that she could accomplish. She had no way to save Marina, and nothing at her fingertips to even keep herself busy. She turned to Maggie. "Can I borrow your phone for a minute?"

Pulling the number up on her own phone, she dialed it into Maggie's.

"Redemption Public Library."

"Ivy! I'm sorry it took so long but I wanted to call you back. What was the important thing you found?"

CHAPTER TWENTY-FIVE

Kalan could feel everything tensing, even his skin. It had been an hour since Seline had called and asked if he could join her and Maggie—quickly. It had taken most of the hour to find Patrick Kelly to sub for him, then for the man to show up at the station house.

There had been a discussion of pulling both him and Sebastian, but when only the new captain had been available, Sebastian had merely turned and said, "You go. I trust you, man."

Kalan couldn't remember the last time he'd been so relieved. He'd been worried about Seline and Maggie all day. He hoped Marina was dead and gone and out of the hands of the killer who'd gotten her. And he wanted to hold onto Seline and keep her safe.

As Patrick walked through the bay doors, bag in hand, Kalan heard the alarm go off behind him.

Thank you, God, he thought.

He fist-bumped the older man as an unofficial tag-out. The Chief waved him off and Kalan felt odd heading out the back door and climbing into his car as the crew rushed into action behind him. They stepped into pants already draped into boots. And he sat for just a moment with his engine running, waiting for the trucks to pull out in front of him.

He was just an observer as they headed down the street, bouncing rhythmically from the gentle curb at the front of the station. As they turned out of sight, Kalan peeled out of the back lot and headed the other way.

He pulled up to the curb relieved to see Maggie and Seline well and healthy but surprised to find them already sitting in her car.

"Get in!" they both called and waved him over frantically. Everyone had been waiting.

"I can't." *Shit.* "I have to change."

"No, you don't!" Seline protested, the French accent tilting her words again. This time the lilt was not sweet but frantic.

"I have to," he explained. "This is official Redemption Fire Station firefighter gear and it indicates that I'm on the job."

She muttered something that he was relatively certain translated to a swear. What she said that he understood was, "Go." She climbed out of the car and motioned him up the porch steps, her key in hand. Not the warm welcome he'd hoped for. The porch light just above his head mocked him.

Jamming the key into the lock she flipped the bolt then stepped aside to let him and his bag through the door. At least he was a firefighter; he could do quick changes better than anyone.

He was headed back out the front door in moments. Seline waited in the hallway and as he went by, he brushed against her soft skin. She seemed not to notice as she entered a code into the box on the inside of the door, then pulled it shut and locked it behind her with the key. The old Victorian certainly had a high-tech front door.

Kalan still had his bag in hand out of rote habit rather than for any reason. He was sliding into the back seat as Seline started the car. For a moment, they all settled in, but he didn't even know what was going on. He only understood that they had somewhere to be. "Where are we going?"

Seline made the tires squeal just a little as she pulled out onto the main street. "We got a call. A woman told me *she's still alive.* And Watson traced the call to Stromburg. She's right now pulling footage from the grocery store there in hopes that they get a shot of Sanders interacting with this woman."

"That would be amazing." Kalan didn't clarify which part. All of it would. The pieces she'd given him clicked together in his brain. "Maybe they can see which direction he went, and they can follow him. Maybe they can find Marina if she is still alive."

He regretted saying that last part. Clearly, from Seline's excitement, and the way she and Maggie were pedal to the metal, they did believe that Marina could survive. He didn't want to take that away. He figured Sanders would accomplish his own goals soon enough. If that meant keeping Marina alive, he would. If it didn't, it didn't. They clearly weren't in control here. "So, where are we going?"

"Ivy called me. Remember she found all the maiden names in his family?"

"Here," Maggie said, plugging her phone into the car. "Let's call her back."

Kalan watched from the back seat as Seline looked at her friend oddly.

"Have Ivy explain it to him. That way we don't make any mistakes." Seline was starting to nod along as Maggie spoke. Maggie turned around and talked to him this time. "We got on board really fast with this. We're already literally on the road."

She swayed as Seline took a turn at a slightly higher than necessary speed and Kalan grabbed for the door handle even as he automatically checked that it was locked. Maggie was still talking even as she managed to hit buttons on her phone. "Let's make sure we have all of our information double-checked and correct. I think we were so excited the first time we heard it, that we just started making plans!"

He didn't want to burst their bubble, so he didn't say anything. Whatever had happened to Marina, the FBI would stop it, not them. But he was in the backseat and not in charge of this little mystery mission. Maybe he was just the hired muscle.

They were down the road, getting on the interstate, his curiosity well piqued before the library volunteer managed to get Ivy on to the line.

"Oh, hi Mr. Smith!" Her always cheerful voice was comforting when not much else was.

"Please, call me Kalan." The words tumbled out of his mouth, the tone sincere even as he realized *none of that matters right now*. He watched Seline's hyper-focused expression in the rearview mirror—tight lines at the edges of her eyes and mouth, her lips pursed in concentration rather than desire.

He pushed his attention back to the librarian. "Maggie and Seline suggested I get the information from you again so that they can double check and I can learn."

"That's smart," Ivy replied before launching into full-steam-ahead information mode. "I found his mother's mother's maiden name: Bland. And on his father's side, his grandmother was a Holden. After y'all left yesterday, I scoured all our records. I started with the newspapers—all the way back to nineteen hundred."

Kalan watched as Seline nodded along, her blond hair swaying behind her, making him think this wasn't going to be too serious of a mission if she'd left her hair down and that he wanted to run his fingers through it.

Ivy was still going, and he pushed his attention back. There might be a test on this.

"His great-grandfather Holden went through seven wives—"

"What?" The word popped out before he could think it

through. He backpedaled. "I guess for his great-grandfather that might have been a time when people died young and in childbirth."

"But they didn't die in childbirth!" Ivy revealed it as though it were important.

He felt his brows pull together and the corners of his mouth turned down. "That is odd, right?"

"Not only is that odd," Ivy filled in exactly what he was thinking, "—they died in accidents. All of them. Which makes it likely they were murdered."

There was a pause in the conversation, and for a moment the whole car was silent. Kalan reminded himself that Seline and Maggie had heard this before.

"Sanders currently has an uncle on his mother's side in jail for a rape committed twenty years ago."

Again, Kalan felt his face pull together.

But Ivy was still leading him through the info. "Think about how rape cases were prosecuted twenty years ago ... and this man is *still* in jail for this one crime. It must have been horrific."

Seline and Maggie once again nodded from the front seat as the car flew down the interstate. He still didn't know where they were going.

"Tell him about the *great* uncle," Maggie prompted.

"Yes, his great uncle has a long, long record for violent crime. Some strange ones too."

"So it runs in the family?" Kalan asked.

"Given some criminal records from the men on his mother's side, too, it's possible that violent aberrant genes run through *both* sides of his family."

The librarian's words fell heavily into the middle of the car. Kalan felt his shoulder blades pull together at the thought of that. But what did that even mean? They already knew he was a violent serial killer. The fact that it ran in his family was interesting but didn't help them find Marina—which was the one thing he thought this little outing was about. He was opening his mouth to ask, when Ivy filled the gap beautifully.

"From that information and newspaper clippings, I knew where to look and what names to look for. The Holden family owned—and still does—a farm just north of Benedict."

"Where's Benedict?" He asked and was granted an answer from the front seat in stereo.

"Just south of Stromsburg! It's where the call came from, telling us that Marina was still alive." Seline said it with such hope that it made him feel what she was feeling. And *Holy shit!* No wonder they were on the road. Between the call and Ivy's information, they may have actually found Marina Balero. If the caller was right, they might just find her alive.

Ivy was still doling out information and requiring his dedicated attention. "The Holden family farm outside Benedict is a hundred acres that no one has farmed for a generation. At least as far as the records show. The last living Holden died there about fifteen years ago. I'm struggling to find formal records, but it could have easily fallen into Sanders' hands."

Kalan was struggling to keep up with all the bits and pieces that Ivy was now raining down upon them. He was piecing it all together and trying to think if there was anything he should do or say or ask.

"But there's one more thing," Ivy added, her tone suddenly making him worry. It had changed abruptly from information-dump to warning.

"I found this out after I talked to you, Seline."

Kalan watched as the two women in the front seat straightened, ready for whatever the additional news might be.

"The great uncle with the strange criminal record? He's the last one to be listed as an occupant on the farm. He's the one who died there fifteen years ago … and honestly, the death is still listed as *unknown causes*."

"You think he was murdered?" Kalan asked, not liking where any of this was going. He was about to like it even less.

"I don't know. I'm more concerned about the trail of odd charges against him. When I add them up, it appears that he was a serial rapist himself at the least. He was questioned more than once in conjunction with several murders, but never formally charged ..." there was a pause, then the most concerning information of all. "We already know that the La Vista Rapist and the Blue River Killer were friends. If their friendship goes back further, it might go back to Alexander Holden. If he's as horrifying as I suspect, then you need to be prepared. I don't know what kinds of things you'll find at that farm."

CHAPTER TWENTY-SIX

"I don't know where they are," Seline replied to Kalan's inquiry about where Rossi and Verner were.

"Did you not alert them?" His concern carried as he climbed out of the back seat and joined them next to the car.

Oh, my God, she liked this guy, but she turned and gave him her dumbest expression. "Yes, of course, we alerted them. They're on the investigative team, and they said they would be on their way."

He nodded slowly and backed away, probably because of her expression.

But Seline kept going. "Also, if you noticed, there was a blue sedan that trailed us almost all the way here. That would be the officers who were watching my house. They watched us go to the library. They watched us come back. And Rossi and Verner and even Watson and Decker have been in contact with them all along. We're not truly here alone."

This time her erstwhile boyfriend looked contrite. "I apologize."

She grinned at him, she had to. "I'm sorry for being rude. It's a weird situation."

And it was about to get weirder.

She reached into her purse and pulled out her gun and the magazine she packed with it. Pushing the two together until she heard and felt the satisfying click of a loaded gun, she racked the slide.

One in the chamber, she thought.

Though Kalan was looking at her with concern, she reached into her large bag again and pulled out a holster. This one was made to slide onto the waistband of her jeans, but she didn't put the harness strap over the butt of the gun. This was one of those situations where she needed to be ready to draw quickly.

Seline untucked her shirt and pulled the tails over the gun, though she knew she wasn't fooling anyone. Turning to Kalan, she crossed her arms, cocked her hip, and waited until he reached into his own bag and pulled out his own gun, which she knew he'd brought.

Maggie was the only one going in unarmed.

Or so Seline thought. "Maggie? Are you—"

As she turned to her friend, Maggie lifted the edge of her jeans, revealing a hunting knife strapped to her ankle. Seline was impressed.

Maggie had brought down Merrit Geller with a shard of glass. Though her own cuts were healing well, Maggie still had the scars. This time, she was ready.

As Seline watched, Maggie modeled the other ankle as well, and showed off another knife.

Bien!

With the three of them now ready to go, she realized she was going to be disappointed if they didn't find anything. She turned her head a little so the others could hear her over the light wind. "A hundred acres is very large."

"Very," Maggie replied.

Kalan chimed in with, "Most of it looks open."

Though Maggie seemed to agree, she reminded the two

others, "A farm this old could hide all kinds of things. It's been through the ages. The nearly broken down barn—" she pointed, "—could be reinforced and hold something dangerous or be used as a hidden storage. We need to check the ground as we walk. A place like this went through the Cold War. They might have an underground bunker. Something like that might have a manhole cover or it might be accessible under a building."

Her chest heaved with the hit of those ideas as Seline admitted to herself that she'd not been prepared for all the options. "The place is supposed to be abandoned."

That didn't mean it was safe.

"House first," Kalan declared.

They'd driven all the way up and parked just beyond where they would have had they been visiting. The gravel had crunched as it bounced them along and left slight ruts from their passing. If anyone was inside, they'd just watched the three of them arm themselves.

When they hit the front porch, Kalan put a hand out, stopping Seline when she was ready to grab for the knob. He motioned for the others to look around the porch and particularly the edges of the door frame.

He turned his head without taking his eyes off the old-school peephole. His hand now rested lightly on her forearm, the touch both warming and warning. "Seline, you installed your own cameras, you have a better idea what they look like."

Smart. Though she searched carefully, she didn't see any. In fact, the door didn't even look like it might have a serious lock on it. When she motioned to him that she'd found nothing, Kalan looked to Maggie. Once the three of them silently agreed, he turned the knob and headed in.

With one last look around, Seline noted that the agents following them were now nowhere to be seen. Rossi told her that, if the three of them were intent on going in, they should make it look like a home job. Seline figured they were doing damn decent work of looking like amateurs.

She crossed the threshold carefully, worried about rotted flooring, rodents and killers. But the house was empty.

It smelled stale and old. Not even the ancient smells of food-once-cooked lingered. It had been abandoned that long.

They opened every door but found nothing. A few pieces of old furniture were covered in dust, and Maggie stomped on the floor, making an odd pattern in the footprints they'd already left as she tried to brush old carpets aside. One was so old that it crackled as she toed it.

Dust poofed into the air, and all three of them jumped back.

When the rug was finally moved and the dust settled again, there was only hardwood floor and not the cellar or crawlspace entry they had hoped for.

The sun had moved noticeably in the sky in the time it took to inspect the house. They declared the house done and headed back outside.

"Garage," Maggie declared, and the three of them agreed.

Again, Seline looked over her shoulder, still not having seen the agents that had followed them here.

The garage proved just as useless as the house. The old car was rusting under more layers of dust, and the mouse droppings indicated that the only ones who had been here weren't human.

The barn yielded nothing, the hay dry and crackling. When they moved a few old bales aside, again they filled the air with dust and old pollen. Maggie sneezed and Seline coughed, though Kalan seemed somehow immune.

She was starting to lose hope. She looked to Kalan who seemed to understand her distress. Softly, he reached out and took her hand in his. She felt her heart rate steady, and she wished she was anywhere but here. Anywhere but searching for a friend and hoping she wasn't a serial killer's latest victim. "Where do we go next?"

Maggie pulled up her phone. Though cell reception was terrible, she'd been prepared and taken a screenshot earlier. She showed them the picture and pointed. "If you look at the aerial photos, it looks like there's another building out that way."

From where they stood, the building was off in the distance. They'd be getting further from the car, unless they drove it.

Seline shook her head. "I don't think my car can make it over this turf. And I didn't see a tractor we could drive."

They would walk it, even though the sun was low enough now to make her wonder if they'd make it back in time.

It was Kalan who said, "We need drinks."

Though Seline hadn't thought of it herself, her dry throat agreed with him, and they reluctantly walked the other direction back to the car. Within minutes, Kalan had put a cold bottle of a sport drink in each of their hands.

"Drink it as we go," he motioned them onward and the three began trekking across what had once been cornfields.

Seline had learned quickly that while the dry stalks looked like they would crumble beneath her heavy shoes, they poked and tried to push through the sole. She stepped carefully.

When they got to the building, Kalan reached for the door, but this time it was Seline who stopped him.

Pointing toward the corner, she said, "Look."

CHAPTER TWENTY-SEVEN

K alan froze. "Holy shit."

Though he'd told Seline to look for cameras—or anything else digital—by the time they hit the barn, he'd quit looking. The farm appeared truly abandoned. Clearly, he'd expected this small building to be, too.

Thank God Seline had taken the instruction seriously. He would have walked right past the tiny spyware she was now quietly pointing out. Hidden almost completely by a sagging piece of siding, she'd maybe seen it because she was shorter.

He realized then that they'd been discovered. Anyone smart enough to install and mostly camouflage a camera was mostly likely watching or had a motion sensor alerting them to activity. Sanders had probably just watched them find his hardware.

Crap.

But if Sanders was inside, Kalan wasn't going to give him the time to run. With a quick motion, he grabbed for the knob already leaning in to open it before he realized it didn't turn. "It's locked."

"Is there a key?" Maggie and Seline were looking around for plants, checking the top of the door frame, maybe looking for hide-a-key rocks. But anyone with cameras wouldn't leave a spare key around.

Kalan's heart was racing. They didn't have time to find a key. The camera dramatically improved the chances that Marina was here. Kalan considered the possibility that their friend was behind this door.

He wished he had some of their firefighting equipment, but at least he knew that kicking with his heel—just above the doorknob—was his best option for breaking through. He didn't even take the time to speak, just reached out and gently pushed the two women aside, as he gained his balance. With one solid kick, he struck at the door as hard as he could.

The door didn't give.

Had it been reinforced?

It didn't matter. Marina might be in there. Gathering his strength, Kalan kicked again.

It took three tries, but he offered up the kicks in rapid succession, until the frame splintered and the door swung inward.

The room was too dark to see, and he was pulling his gun, only to see that behind him, Seline's was already aimed and Maggie had her blade in hand. *Good.*

The sun was behind them now, casting shadows all throughout the little house. His breathing shallowed out as he waited for Sanders to pop out and stab at him. Or maybe Kalan would just feel the white-hot sear of a bullet passing through his flesh. Still, there was no other option but to go in.

He tensed his shoulders. He'd brought the brute strength, and remembered drinks, but apparently forgotten flashlights. Then again, when he'd gotten in the car he hadn't known he'd be raiding a rural farm for a killer's hiding place.

Without speaking, the three of them crowded into the space, and quickly found the front room empty. Not just without people, but entirely empty. No furniture, no lighting, nothing. Just an empty box with bare walls and wood floors.

The squat little boxy building was designed like a house inside. This was once the living area. To the right was a small kitchen, the olive green tile on the counter dated the work to an era gone by.

Seline put her arm out as if to hold Kalan and Maggie back. Her open palm landed against his stomach and every muscle in his torso clenched. He loved the feeling of her touching him but now was not the place for any of those softer emotions.

She whispered, "It's not dirty ... I wouldn't call it clean, but there's no dust."

They all looked to each other.

Inside the main house, they'd left imprints of every footstep they'd taken. In the barn, they disturbed old hay and pollen. In the garage, rust and rodent droppings had taken over. But here, despite the emptiness, someone had taken the time to maintain it.

Slowly Seline crept forward. The place was quiet as a tomb and Kalan was becoming concerned that's exactly what it was.

Pushing open the door to the bathroom, Seline again lead with her gun. There was nothing inside but a plain while toilet and pedestal sink that had seen better days. The tub had no shower curtain and the faucet looked as if it would spew only brown water, if any. She turned away with a disgusted look on her face.

Whether that was from the state of the building, the fact that they were being watched, or because she hadn't found her friend, Kalan couldn't tell. He was learning how to tell, though. And he could read the determination on her face clear as day as she stepped gingerly past him and turned the knob to open the second door. This was a small room, likely once a bedroom. The little house was apparently an old two-bedrooms/one-bath model. This too looked unoccupied. But not quite empty.

"Wait." He whispered it harshly, stopping the others where they stood. A small table was pressed to one wall. On the opposite side, under the lone window, stood an old-fashioned dresser on high legs. The tops of both were pristine, and clear of all clutter.

Kalan stepped across the space and yanked open the first drawer before he gave himself time to think about it. Items, heavy and metal, jostled. They slid to a stop as he identified them: knives, a wrench, a small saw. They were clean, but disturbing enough that his stomach rolled.

Who kept things like that in a dresser? Spotless and lined up like surgical instruments? He almost vomited in the corner of the room because he was certain he knew the answer to those questions.

Shoving the drawer angrily back into place, he next jerked open the other five drawers. Each, in turn, revealed something similarly distressing.

When he closed the last drawer, still horrified by the clean needle drills, pliers, and glass syringes, he turned to ask what the women thought. But they weren't in the room with him anymore. They'd left him to the dresser and headed back to the hallway and cautiously opened the third door.

No one had screamed.

But as he stepped into the small space, he could see the horrified expressions on their faces.

CHAPTER TWENTY-EIGHT

"I'm pulling off," Seline announced as she abruptly turned her blinker on and changed direction. As she exited the freeway, she could feel her hand shaking even though she was death-gripping the steering wheel. She could hear the demand in her voice.

Maggie calmly answered, "We're supposed to be following the FBI vehicle."

"They'll figure it out!" Seline snapped. Her blood sugar was dropping precariously low.

If she didn't eat, she'd pass out. As the driver, that was dangerous. But those were all critical, logical thoughts. The real problem wasn't her blood sugar. It was the *blood*.

They'd opened the door to the last bedroom in the little house and seen it. *Everywhere*. A harsh wooden chair sat in the center of the room. It had belts, buckled and hanging loose at both of the front legs of the chair. Another pair hung waiting in the back, ready to hold someone where they didn't want to stay.

The blood around the floor—the spatters on the wall— meant that Seline and her friends didn't really have to imagine what had happened. The evidence was everywhere.

Pulling her focus back to the present, Seline looked around the road as she hit the bottom of the exit. She'd seen the signs for restaurants here, but now there were only gas stations. Luckily, she caught a sign for fast food less than half a mile down the road. Making a beeline for the nearest one, she pulled into the drive thru lane with a sigh of relief.

Food was near. Food was normal.

She looked at her two passengers with a question of what they wanted to eat. As though this were any normal highway stop. Quietly, they all ordered burgers, fries, and sodas. And once she had the bag in hand, Seline pulled into one of the parking spaces. She didn't want to go inside or interact with anyone any more than she already had.

"We can eat in the car, okay?"

After a moment, Maggie said, "It will make it easier for the FBI to find us."

Seline couldn't give two shits about being found by the FBI right now. The three of them had stood in that little house, looking at the empty room where presumably their friend had once been. Whether it was Marina Balero who'd been there or not, someone had been. And whoever had been there likely hadn't survived the visit.

It was Seline who had broken the horrified silence and yelled out. Maybe she had thought there might be a room under the floorboards or another building somewhere nearby. So she called, *"Marina! Marina!"* over and over, hoping to hear any response in return.

Instead of hearing her friend cry for help, she'd been brushed aside as the FBI flooded in.

Now she took the first bite of her hamburger because she needed the fuel. Though it had smelled wonderful, she couldn't muster up an appetite. She chewed and swallowed mechanically, just to change her blood sugar. But her thoughts turned back to what she'd seen.

The three of them stayed long enough to watch as the FBI swarmed the place. Rossi and Verner were the first in, but close behind them were techs already in paper suits and face shields. It felt as though Watson and Decker were the last to show, as others pushed by Seline and her friends, telling them to move out of the way, and then move again, and again, until they were back in the empty living area wondering what in the hell they'd just seen.

Seline heard them say 'crime scene' more than once. From where she stood, she could see through the open door as one leaned down with a swab and dipped it into the blood at the foot of the chair. It still wasn't fully dry. He placed the swab into a small plastic test tube with clear liquid, shook it once and looked at the others. He only said, "Human."

Seline had felt her stomach roll but managed not to actually vomit then. Right now, forcing herself to eat a hamburger and fries, she wasn't so sure she could hold it back any longer.

She took a sip of the cola and with a deep breath, attempted to center herself.

Surely the FBI agents that had been escorting them home would notice them missing by now. Surely her phone would ring any minute asking where they were and if they were okay. In the rearview mirror, she didn't see the FBI pulling up, but she saw Kalan polishing off the last of the burger that had been dwarfed by his hand.

"Alright guys," he said, taking control of the conversation since the two women were still attempting to eat. "What do we know?"

Seline thought about that for a moment. It was a good question, and pooling their observations would help. "We know we found a room where a killer worked."

Though Kalan's voice had been forceful opening the discussion, it grew softer with his second question. "Was that enough blood to declare someone dead?"

It was a straightforward, logical question and completely ignored the fact that they believed the blood was from the very woman who was trying to protect Seline. In the end, the three just looked at each other. No one here was in any kind of field to be able to answer a question like that.

But Seline had other things to throw into the ring. She'd been putting pieces together for a while. With about a third of her burger left, she quit. As she set it down into her lap, the waxed paper wrapper crinkled loudly in the silence of the car. "We know that Sanders took Marina. We know that he passed the fourteen-hour mark at which point pretty much all of his victims were dead—"

"All the ones that we know of." Maggie inserted.

"Good point," Kalan added from the back, but Seline kept going.

"We know I was slipped a note with my initials on it, in the same odd print as the first one, indicating that it would be carved into a human body. A body that he would leave for the police or for us."

"And no one's found it ..." Kalan offered, his tone lingering somewhere between a question and a statement.

"As far as I know, they haven't. At least, none of the agents have told me."

"Would they?" Maggie asked.

"I don't know. You might know as well as I do." After all, Maggie had worked with Watson and Decker before Seline had ever met them. But her friend only shrugged. There was no telling what the FBI agents would share or hold back.

Seline took a sip of her soda again. Her mouth going dry, not from speaking, but from what she was thinking. Still, it was better to speak it out loud, as awful as it was.

"He took Marina." The emotion burbled in her voice, coming out even though she fought to keep it back. "He hurt her in her own home."

Her fake own home, Seline thought, but didn't say. "And then he had her and he told us she was alive. Then he led us to this place."

Maggie interrupted again. "He didn't lead us. We found it."

"Do you really think he didn't lead us here?" Seline turned in her seat as best she could, the seat belt still trying to keep her straight.

"It was Ivy who found that information," Maggie countered.

But Seline smacked right back with, "It was Sanders who gave us the phone call. He had to think we'd have it traced." But she had to agree with Maggie, too, and she'd been bitchy in her response. Seline conceded a bit. "I don't know. He did seem ready for us at the farm."

"He definitely had cameras and lookouts," Maggie pointed out between bites of the fries she was still slowly working on.

"So he probably knew we were there—" Kalan chimed in from where he hung forward between the front seats, the last of his food having disappeared, "—when we first entered the property. So while the whole place looked abandoned, he had plenty of time to be working in the back while we were checking the front house."

That made Seline want to vomit again. Once again, she fought the urge down as best she could. *Had Marina been there— had she been alive—when they arrived?*

It might be a question she would never answer.

She filled the space of her grief with knowledge. It was just how she worked. She balanced chemicals and made new products. If she could just balance this equation, she could make something better from it.

As she opened her mouth, the car with the FBI agents who'd been escorting them pulled into the spot beside her. She ignored them. When they didn't get out of their car, and seemed to act as if nothing had gone wrong, Seline began speaking.

"Here's the thing—and no one's mentioned this! Not you guys, not Verner or Rossi—*Why?*"

Both Maggie and Kalan looked at her expectantly. She'd worked herself up before she'd even told them what she was talking about. So she took a deep breath that—even to her—sounded more like a heavy sigh. "The tracker!"

They looked at her as if she was still off her rocker.

"When he got Marina, the first thing he did was take the tracker out of her arm and throw it under my house. He *knew* she had a tracker in her! He *knew* she was an officer."

As Seline watched, Maggie's eyes grew wide. But she kept pushing, because this had been bothering her for a while. She'd wondered if no one was talking about it because it was so obvious and she was the only one missing it. From the look on Maggie's and Kalan's faces, Seline realized that was not the case.

"He knew she was an officer. He knew she had a tracker. There was minimal blood at the Gutierrez house. It was there, but it wasn't much. So he didn't spend time searching her for it," Seline concluded. When her friends didn't speak, she said the words they were all thinking now. "He knew where it was before he started."

CHAPTER TWENTY-NINE

The first one up the next morning, Seline made herself another bowl of instant oatmeal. The two minutes it took the water to boil in the microwave seemed an eternity. She waited a second era while her oatmeal steeped. Cringing at her memories the whole time.

Her hair probably looked a fright, but it didn't matter because her head pounded with each pulse of her blood. Though she'd come home and been grateful to sleep in her own bed last night, she hadn't rested. The few times she did fall asleep, the only reason she knew she hadn't actually screamed herself awake was because no one had rushed to her door.

She was surprised she'd slept at all. The entire day had been a disaster, right up until she'd seen Maggie and Sebastian to their room last night then headed up the stairs. Her adrenaline hadn't worn off ... at least that's what she told herself for the monumentally poor decision making she'd displayed.

Seline had knocked lightly on Kalan's door. Though he'd opened it, he hadn't motioned for her to come inside. He didn't want her, and she'd missed every signal.

Though her reckless fantasy had her sitting next to him on

the bed and her fingers tracing his chest, she hadn't gotten much further than that. So when he'd stood there filling the doorway, far too clothed for her taste, and blocked her way to the bed, she'd lifted onto her toes.

Without a word or a further thought, she'd pressed her mouth to his.

He'd sighed, and she'd taken it to be a cue.

What a fool.

She'd moved closer, letting her breasts brush against his chest through their clothing, he'd stiffened at the motion, and she'd again taken it as a sign for more. Throwing her arms around him, she'd melted into a kiss that lasted all of two seconds.

He'd politely taken her arms away from his neck and stepped back.

The kindness had been the worst part. The soft words, "You should get to bed," still echoed in her throbbing brain this morning.

And she couldn't get away from him. He was still sleeping in the room across the hall from hers. Maggie and Sebastian hadn't even left yet. So they could see the awkward fallout of her stupid actions last night, too.

So Seline sat by herself and listened to the scrape of the spoon on the ceramic bowl as she stirred the oatmeal. Did it matter if she waited for the oatmeal to steep fully? She wasn't going to taste it anyway.

Quietly, she seated herself at the table, looking through the archway into the living area, hopeful she would spot anyone who got up. She was grateful to be alone for a moment. Her home and her life had not been her own for far too long. Maybe at least her friends were getting some sleep. Maybe she could avoid the awful embarrassment for a little while longer.

Probably Kalan would pretend it had never happened.

Probably he and Sebastian had slept like babies, having

learned to fall asleep anywhere, anytime, regardless of what they'd seen. It was a skill Seline did not possess. Certainly not last night when she relived her horrible day and mortifying night.

She ate her food carefully, as though formality needed to be observed, and she managed to choke down half the bowl. When this was over, she might never eat oatmeal again.

"When this was over" was a glorious thought. She clung to the idea that it would, in fact, one day be over and that she would be here to enjoy it. That she wouldn't have to endure with "fake boyfriend Kalan" anymore. She wondered if she could ask the FBI to assign her a new fake boyfriend?

She forced one more bite, knowing that she wasn't eating enough. She was running on shock and terror and that wasn't good. Placing her hands flat on the table on either side of the bowl, Seline closed her eyes and took a deep breath, the way she had always done before a test. She tried for a second inhale but became terrified that William Sanders was standing behind her.

Jolting around, she found only the empty room, glad that none of her friends had seen her making an idiot out of herself. But just as she settled back into the seat, a knock at the door made her jolt again.

She was on her feet and heading toward the front of the house before realizing she was barely passable in her pajama pants and camisole with a robe wrapped around her. Given the circumstances, "barely passable" was more than acceptable. So she padded barefoot to the front door and checked her camera, thinking about how William Sanders must have seen her looking directly into his.

When she spotted Verner and Rossi on the steps she threw the door wide and waved her hand in a sweeping gesture. "Come in, Agents."

As though etiquette had any place here, the agents came in

and settled themselves on the couch. It was impossible to not notice the grim look on their faces.

Seline couldn't breathe. Earlier thoughts of her mortification slid easily away as the truth gripped her in a tight fist. "You found her."

"We did."

That was enough to know that Marina Balero was not alive.

"Tell me," she whispered, but it was a demand. She needed to know.

"She was in the water. Near the dock." Rossi pointed toward the back of the house. "There's a trail that runs behind this street, connecting all of the houses."

Seline nodded because she couldn't speak. They had believed Merrit Geller was accessing Maggie's house from the back via the trail.

Rossi continued, "About a mile down to the west, it connects to another trail that leads to a dock. Her body was found floating face down, anchored at the edge of the water."

Just like the others.

Shockingly, she had no emotional reaction. She just felt cold. Maybe she'd used up all her emotion in the past several days. Her brain took over as though it wasn't her friend who'd been found in the water, as though it were a random case, or a chemical equation to balance. She sank into the chair as her knees gave way.

"She..." Verner started but didn't finish. There was something about the way she said it ...

"She had something carved into her," Seline commented, the realization stunning and meaning that there was almost definitely another note somewhere that had been missed.

"Yes."

Seline glared at Verner. That was not a sufficient answer. She waited, now leaning forward, hands on her knees, ankles pressed together, toes pushing into the floor, as she waited for Verner to supply more.

At last, the agent complied. "It said *'closer'.*"

The chill drove from her head down through her spine like an ice spike.

Closer had so many meanings, and so few, and none of them good.

She was running on such low fuel that she could almost feel the gears clicking in her head. "But I didn't get a note with that word."

"Actually, you did," Rossi said. "It was in your mailbox yesterday."

"No one told me!" Seline protested immediately, as though her knowledge of the note was the most important thing. When no one replied. She asked the obvious question. "Well, who put it there?"

"No one that we can tell," Verner replied softly. At least this time she had the grace to look concerned.

"Somebody had to put it there! You were watching the mailbox. Did your agent screw up?" Seline was angry, hurt, and terrified, ready to sling blame in any direction. Still, she knew as she said it, that it was the wrong thing to suggest.

"No. It went in with your regular mail. The mailman has been questioned. The note was sandwiched inside the stack he delivered yesterday. He pulled the rubber band and placed it in the mailbox, never noticing anything unusual or that there was a slip of paper involved."

Seline slumped backward, her head flopping into the luckily soft cushions. The words tumbled out of her, so much of it too disturbing to process. "So before he took Marina, he knew she was an officer. He knew she wasn't Wendy Buck. He knew she had a tracker and exactly where to find it. And now he can get into the mail with no one seeing him."

Verner and Rossi didn't respond.

He'd done all those things right under the noses of the FBI.

It all added up to one thing, Seline thought. *He can get to me.*

But even as she wallowed in her concern, another fear tugged at the back of her brain. "What other information are you hiding from me?"

CHAPTER THIRTY

"What are you talking about?" Kalan demanded, barely holding back his anger as he watched Seline methodically take apart and clean a gun at her table.

He'd thought it would be a nice calm breakfast between the two of them. Maggie and Sebastian had gone home early this morning. Instead, he'd come downstairs to this. Instead, anger was the only thing he could process. The fear slipped through his hands too fast to hold onto but it lingered in the cold in his blood. Loss ran a finger down the back of his brain, making him want to shudder, so he held tightly to the anger.

The scene before him was more than vaguely disturbing and the intent behind it had nothing vague about it.

"He's going to kill someone else." She spoke with perfect diction as her hands moved with a mind of their own. The cloth rubbed at each part, leaving shiny metal in its wake, the smell of gun oil filled his nostrils and twisted his brain, completely out of place in the box store dining room. Seline's words were full of crisp logic. "He's killing other people trying to get to me. I might as well give him me. Fewer people will die."

"And what happens after he gets you?" Kalan decided to push forward with her model, to show her how crazy it was.

But Seline didn't answer, just rubbed down the piece and put the gun back together with a mechanical proficiency. When she was finished, he thought she'd at least look up and talk to him, but she set the gun aside and shocked him by picking up another.

She had more than one?

Clearly, she did now, he thought. He needed her attention. "What happens after he gets you?"

His heart pounded at the thought that she might have a reasonable answer to this. Seline was smart. She wouldn't run off half-cocked in the figurative or literal sense. That maybe scared him more than anything else.

She had a plan.

"He wins."

"Nobody wins in that case!" With that, he smacked his hands on the table, his anger growing, even though he knew it came from true concern.

He couldn't tell if the things that had happened between them were real or if Seline was just pretending because the FBI told her too. He couldn't tell if she actually liked him or if her adrenaline simply made her think she did. But in the end it didn't matter. To say he was crazy about her was an understatement of epic proportions. Her strength and her vulnerability all pulled at him. He hated that she was ready to go after a killer that outmatched her—he'd outmatched everyone so far. And he hated that part of him understood. Everything hung in the balance for her. If Sanders didn't kill her with a blade, he could just as surely gut her by stripping everything she'd achieved. And Seline couldn't stand to see anyone else die on her watch. Kalan knew that about her. She would willingly be tortured to death if that would end Sanders' reign.

"I'm getting a tracker," she told him with far too calm a tone.

While he wondered which agency would agree to that, he didn't ask. Instead, he said, "What's the point? Sanders knows about them and he'll cut it out."

"I'll swallow them." She'd clearly thought this through and Kalan didn't like the chill that brought on. "He can't get them out of me if I swallow them. But you'll be able to find me."

Kalan stood up, his hands pressed against his forehead as he fought to keep his breathing even. He wanted to yell at her like he yelled at the kids setting off homemade fireworks with kerosene last fourth of July. But he couldn't. She wasn't a kid, and he wasn't in charge here.

Just thinking through her idea made it sound at the same time too crazy to even be plausible and yet strictly reasonable. *If* he didn't consider who it was out there with a tracker and waiting for Sanders to get her. But Seline was already moving on to round two, and Kalan hadn't figured out round one yet.

"If he wins, he'll stop. We know he goes in cycles. I would be number five. He'll quit for a while. And—worst case scenario— they'll have all kinds of evidence from me so they can stop him."

The new gun was already dismembered, the pieces laid out in neat order on the oily towel. Her hands worked methodically, like a soldier who'd done this a thousand times.

"This is not okay," he told her, even though it was a shit argument. "You can't just offer yourself up as a sacrifice on the chance that it will give us enough information to get him."

"It *will* give you information and it *will* buy the FBI time. *And what do I have left?*" She looked up at him, finally, but her bleak expression broke his heart. "I'm pretty sure he's ruined my job."

She motioned with one open palm around the room, but he wasn't sure quite what she was gesturing at. "They won't let me back on campus at all now, not since there's been another body. And it was associated *even more closely* with me than the last two!"

Shit, he thought. "I'll cover your house payment."

He knew she was mortgaged to the hilt.

"It's not that, Kalan. I live and work here *because* I teach at the University. At *this* university. I waited to buy a house until I knew I was staying in one place."

He'd known that her job wasn't like his, that she couldn't just pick up and go somewhere else. She'd built her plan and her life here, away from the continent where she'd grown up. She'd created a home where she had no other. Sanders was chipping away at all of it, methodically stealing more and more from her with each move.

"Kalan," she emphasized his name as though he still wasn't catching on. "Unless the university just forgives this massive misstep, then I'll never get the salary I need to keep my head above water. I'll have to move to any place with a university willing to let a dismissed professor in, and if I'm lucky, they'll let me start over at the bottom. I have to sell the house."

He sighed at that. She loved this house, and she loved the town. And he loved having her here. But she wasn't done.

"I bought this house for *me*. I built a chemistry lab in the back room. Who will pay me what I put into it?" She emphasized each of the last words. "I can't even sell it for what I owe. Not for at least several more years. When I don't have a job, I can't make the payments. The bank will repossess it and I won't be able to buy another home for ... I don't know."

At least seven years, he thought. Though he still disagreed with her plan, she was right: he hadn't understood what was at stake for her.

"I came to Redemption to make a new life for myself. And this asshole *targeted me*." She slammed the body of the gun into the table with her anger. Luckily, it was just the piece, or it might have gone off.

"I'm done being his victim!" She said the words with conviction, though it sounded to him as if "being his victim" was exactly what she intended to do.

When Geller had come after Maggie, Kalan had mentally understood her anguish. But now, caring about Seline, and *feeling* it happen to her rather than just watching it was another circle closer to hell. Still … "You can't do this, Seline."

She didn't answer, but her hands stilled. She glared at him as if to ask *Can't I?*

"What about me?" he asked.

"What about you?"

Ouch. She tossed that back too casually as her hands started cleaning the gun again. She could not have cut him deeper. "I care about you. I want us to be together."

"We only had one real date. You're just my fake boyfriend, Kalan. You're not even physically attracted to me."

"What?" He stilled, then, far across the room to where he'd paced. *"What?"* he asked again, wondering where in the hell she'd gotten such a ridiculous idea. And maybe that was the problem. Maybe she was so mad that she wasn't seeing anything clearly. "I told you I was sorry. We went out, several times. Obviously, it's not easy to date right now, but I'm more physically attracted to you than I have ever been to any woman. What on earth would make you think that I'm not?"

She stood up abruptly, leaving the gun, the oil, and the brushes on the table. The chair slid out behind her in her anger. She stomped her way into the kitchen and washed her hands, though she clearly wasn't finished with the job or with him. When her hands were dried with jerky motions, she grabbed the edge of the counter, as though needing the support. Anger radiated from her.

He could see that she took a calming breath, turned, and placed her hands on the edge behind her, and jumped up to where she sat on the counter. She'd gotten herself back together. "Everything. Everything says that."

Then, one by one, she counted off his faults on her fingers. "When I touch you, you pull away like I've burned you. When we go to a restaurant, I've asked you to sit in the seat next to me and you always refuse. You insist on sitting on completely the other side of the table. You act like I have ... *lice!*"

He knew what she was talking about, and she was reading it all wrong, but she wasn't done. "When I kissed you the other night, you didn't even respond! One chaste, little peck that *you* ended. And it's been that way *every single time* we've kissed."

"Not the first night." He could still feel the heat flare through him like flashover just thinking about the hot kiss on the front porch. He'd lost control.

"Honestly, the first night on the porch is the only reason I still wanted you."

She did?

She waved her finger at him as though she had another fault to go. "The FBI asked you to be my fake boyfriend and, honestly, if you're doing anything other than pretending, I can't tell."

Kalan felt his heart crack in two. He couldn't talk her out of her crazy plan to get Sanders to come after her, but maybe he could talk her out of the ridiculous idea that he didn't have any feelings for her. "Seline, you don't know the half of it."

She just stared at him, as if daring him to speak and say something stupid.

So he took the dare. Let him say something stupid. Not saying stupid things had landed him here. It couldn't be worse, could it? "I can't sit next to you when I'm trying to see the entire restaurant. I positioned you to look one way and me to look the other so Sanders couldn't sneak up on us while we were out on our fake dates."

"So, they were fake." She latched on to the one shitty part.

"Yes! If they were real—if I could make *any of this* real—I would have kissed you the way I wanted to!"

She was still frowning at him when he said, "Like this," and grabbed her face in his hands.

CHAPTER THIRTY-ONE

Seline felt Kalan's lips touch hers and the rest of the world melted away. Their fight about her guns and her plans, her anger at his resistance, all disappeared.

The way she felt about him was all consuming, and though she knew it shouldn't be, his kiss removed all doubt that this was right. Still, she was too smart to dive into something that sounded wrong. She pushed him away. "I don't understand."

They stared at each other for a single hot second, and she could feel the magnetic force pulling her, but she fought it. "If this is how you wanted to kiss me then why were you so cold for the last month?"

His explanation of each little reason didn't add up. It didn't explain why he'd pulled away each time she'd tried to kiss him. Seline couldn't afford to have romances that didn't add up or men who didn't fully show her how they felt, so she waited.

Kalan took a breath, and something crossed his face, maybe shame? She couldn't tell.

"I've always known you were special. I hoped that maybe *we* could be something special, too." He paused, but Seline didn't fill the space for him, even though it was awkward for her not to. "After the way I treated you the first night, I didn't want to push you. I'll wait however long it takes until you know that I'm not that guy."

"What are you even talking about?" Holding out was off the table. She'd gone from resistant to utterly confused in one sentence.

This time he looked at the floor. "I lost control. I've never had that happen before. I don't force myself on women." He snapped his head up and looked her in the eyes for that last line. "I've kept a very tight rein on my actions since then. I don't sit next to you so that I can keep my head in the game and not get too focused on your leg pressing against mine. I don't kiss you like I want to because I don't want to push you too far."

"Push me too far?" *When had he done that?*

But he seemed to understand even though she didn't. "That first kiss, on the front porch?"

She nodded.

"You had to push me off of you … I've never had that happen before. I've never lost it like that be—"

"I didn't push you off." *He thought that?*

"Yes, you did."

"No, I didn't." *Was he crazy?* "I was there, too. I would know."

"You grabbed my jacket—" he mimicked the motion, "—and pushed me backward."

What? Seline shook her head. She didn't remember this at all. What was he— *ooohhhh, she* had *pushed him back.* "Kalan, I needed to breathe. That was all. I took a breath and then I was trying to pull you back to me and you tugged out of my hands and disappeared!"

"What?" His turn to be confused now, she thought. But he'd walked away believing she'd simply shoved him off.

Maybe it was better to show than to tell. Petrified that she was wrong, that he still didn't want her, she tried one more time. Last night had been mortifying and she'd survived. If she didn't survive this, she could throw herself at Sanders, at least.

So Seline reached out and gathered the fabric of his shirt in her fists, much the way she'd held it that first night on the porch. This time, she completed the act of pulling him towards her. She whispered against his mouth, "That kiss was the only reason I was still giving you a chance."

Then she felt their lips touch again and the world caught fire. Their mouths fused but she felt it everywhere. His hands found her hips and slid her along the counter top until she was at the edge, legs wrapped around Kalan's waist. Their bodies pressed closer, his hands roaming until his fingers twined in her hair.

He tipped her head back, the lush feel of his mouth traced her jawline, scrambling every thought except the one that wanted him.

With a mind of their own, her fingers tugged at his shirt, and she had it halfway up his chest before she realized what she was doing. But now she could see enough to know that what she was doing was a really good idea, and she peeled him like a banana with a grin and a kiss as she exposed his mouth.

Kalan paid her back by sliding his hand under her shirt and brushing his thumb across her hardened nipple.

"Dieu!" It fell from her lips, all reason gone with his touch as her body reacted to his. Her skirt was now rucked up between them and she wished she had even less clothing on.

Working together, his hands slid up the side of her ribs and only when her breasts felt the cool air did she realize he'd slid her shirt up. He must have also popped the back of her bra when she wasn't paying attention, because she was completely exposed to him.

She'd gotten her wish to be wearing less clothing, that was for sure. But she was wishing for less than this.

He pulled back, his bare chest heaving with the effort of

restraint. Her breath rushed out, finally feeling his desire after so long believing that he didn't want her. But he didn't lunge back at her even though she could feel the sing of blood in her lips, the surge of her pulse through her breasts, all saying that her body wanted him.

"Seline?"

"Yes?" She didn't have to say it so breathy but she couldn't help it. *Why was he talking instead of kissing her?*

"You have to promise me that you'll stop me before I go too far. I don't know that I have the ability to put the brakes on here. Okay?"

"I promise," she added as she hooked her fingers into the waistband of his jeans and hauled him close again.

It shouldn't have been possible to burn hotter, but they did. Seline tipped her head and let him drive her crazy with his lips and teeth on her earlobe. By the time he'd moved to her neck, she was surprised to learn that she could be that turned on by her ear.

Her hands clutched at him, keeping him close and feeling the heat radiating off him as he worked his way down, a slow, burning path along her skin until he was stopped by her rucked-up shirt, which he quickly dispatched to the kitchen floor. It hit with a soft slap, still tangled with her bra, but the feeling of his skin—finally—fully against hers made her not care. His mouth closing over her nipple had her making sounds she'd not heard from her own vocal cords before.

He moved to the other side, worshiping her other breast even as his hand slowly—too slowly—made its way under her skirt. When he touched her, she fell apart, writhing in his arms, riding out the waves of pleasure he gave her. Her ankles locked behind his hips, her fingers dug into the bold muscles of his shoulders as her own body clenched and released, clenched and released.

As she sank back to earth, Kalan stepped back.

But she had enough wherewithal to know he hadn't finished. Still, she let him have his space for a moment, and watched as his eyes widened when she reached under the edge of her skirt, grabbed at the sides of her panties and slid them down her legs. Seline watched his face the whole time and she could tell the exact moment he realized he was a goner.

When she crooked a finger at him, he pulled his wallet from his back pocket and nearly slapped it onto the counter beside her. She hoped to hell there was a condom in there. But her hands were working the snaps on his jeans and pushing everything away to bare him to her touch.

This time, the groans came from his lips, as she stroked and kissed him. His fingers fumbled with his wallet and produced the condom she'd hoped he had.

Her skirt was still around her waist as he covered himself and pushed inside.

Seline's head slid back, smacking into the cabinet behind her.

"Oh, my God!" he looked up, his body straightening as he asked, "Are you okay?"

"I'm fine," but his movement had put him into some perfect alignment that set her on edge again. Seline grabbed at him and made him stop asking if she was alright. She was more than fine. Her hips acted of their own accord, rolling against him, striving to feel more, to take him deeper.

His voice changed as her movements changed his concern to pleasure. He thrust again and again, his groans getting deeper with each answering call of her own voice until she saw stars and both heard and felt the release in him.

Collapsing into the circle of his arms, she breathed in great gulps until she had enough oxygen to think. She was opening her mouth to comment when he beat her to it.

"Shit."

She blinked and stiffened. *Well, that ended fast.* "Just what every woman wants to hear after mind blowing sex."

But his arms tightened down, not letting her move. He pulled back and looked at her, heavy lidded, still sated. His was not the face of a man who said 'shit' after sex. "You promised to stop me before I went too far."

"Oh," she replied, smiling as she understood. "I will."

CHAPTER THIRTY-TWO

Seline rolled over feeling deliciously warm and sated, the sheets a cool comfort against her heated skin. Though her body had never felt better, her brain had rarely been more confused.

The time between her saying there was nothing between them yesterday and then her screaming his name with literally nothing between them had gone by explosively fast. Just a few hours ago, she'd been convinced that he had absolutely no interest in her, that he was just doing his due diligence and taking care of the community. Then she'd been raking her nails down his back.

Was it one of those *heat of the moment* kind of things?

He'd made it clear he wanted her, he'd said she was special. But did that mean he wanted more than a screw on the kitchen counter?

He'd also made it more than clear he didn't like her plan. But her plan hadn't changed. Though she couldn't say she regretted the interlude, this didn't make Kalan her boyfriend any more than the FBI asking him to watch after her did.

Slowly, she peeled back the covers, letting the warmer air of the upstairs room brush over her skin. She padded the few feet into the bathroom attached to her bedroom.

Her thoughts churned. Were Maggie and Sebastian coming back over tonight? Would Kalan spend the night in her room with her? Or …? Well, any number of things could happen and she didn't have the mental space to deal with any of it right now.

Seline tried to softly close the bathroom door behind her but it was difficult to be quiet in these older homes. The metal knob was smooth in her hand and she was slow in her movements but the door still made an audible click in the silent afternoon.

She looked in the mirror. If she'd had a life changing alteration it didn't show on her face. Not like when she'd looked at herself the first time after she lost her virginity or when she'd walked out of her interview at the University of Nebraska. Not like when she'd lost her mother, or not too long later when she'd lost her father.

If there was a revelatory moment on her skin, it was being covered up by all the accompanying crap she was dealing with these days.

She washed her face and ran a brush through her wickedly tangled hair. Then she stood in the bathroom for a moment, almost trapped there by the naked man asleep in her bed on the other side of the door. When she went into the main room, he would likely be awake. And if he was they would need to have a conversation, one she was quite certainly not prepared for. But she couldn't stay in the bathroom all day.

Taking a deep breath and bracing herself to walk naked into her own room, Seline was forcing herself to reach for the small doorknob when her phone rang from beside the bed. *Well, that decision was made for her.*

She threw open the door, dashed across the room, and grabbed the phone. Watching as Kalan came awake from the noise.

"Seline?" he asked, even as she picked up the phone, double checked that the camera was not on, and answered.

"Agent Watson?"

Watson, her usual cool self, did not mince words. "We have another body."

CHAPTER THIRTY-THREE

Kalan sat next to Seline on the couch, his fingers loosely intertwined with hers, though it didn't quite feel as if she was truly holding his hand.

Watson and Decker sat in the two chairs, facing them—a position he was getting all too familiar with. He could only imagine that Seline had been here twice as often as he had.

"The body was heavily decayed. A fisherman came across it. It appeared the rope used to anchor it had given way and the body had drifted." Decker was running down the details as though talking about a corn harvest and the size of the necessary silo rather than discussing another dead Nebraskan. "The fisherman spotted it stuck in a jam of logs and twigs that had been caught up between some rocks."

"When was this?" Seline asked, ever the practical one.

"The fisherman found it around four a.m. this morning. Our team has been out all day, processing the scene, trying to figure out where the body was originally placed."

Kalan noted that they didn't seem to say where they had found it, only that it had 'drifted'. They didn't say if Sanders had left it for them or not, nor did they say if the new body gave them any evidence to use against Sanders, to find him, or bring him in. But this was the second body it had taken time to find...

Kalan wondered if Watson and Decker were on board with Seline's plan to get a tracker and bring Sanders after her. They asked a few more questions, but not anything that Seline knew the answer to. Watson reached into her bag and even Kalan knew what was coming ... pictures.

He felt his head automatically turn away. But when Watson slid the photos across the coffee table, it was impossible not to notice the word carved into the torso. His stomach rolled but he fought to keep the feeling off of his face.

It was hard to read. Something had taken small bites at the skin around the cuts. He didn't know if that was normal or not, but the agents hadn't said anything about it. With the skin nibbled away there was just enough left to read "watching."

Kalan wasn't sure if the dead body or the cuts in the torso bothered him more than the fact that Sanders had called and spoken to Seline.

"So the phone call that everyone dismissed was the real deal?" he demanded.

"Yes." Watson laced her fingers together and sat still. There was nothing more she could admit to at this point.

Silence fell over the room.

Kalan wondered what it meant. Did the FBI agents have nothing more to do? Were they waiting for Seline to spill secrets that she didn't seem to have?

After a moment of prolonged awkwardness interlaced with somber reverence for whomever this dead body had once been, Decker spoke.

"We wanted to thank you—you and your friends." He nodded briefly to Kalan. "For heading into the farm by Stromberg. It was the perfect way to not have agents raid the place if there was nothing obvious there."

Jesus, Kalan thought, his anger growing. They'd used Maggie and Seline and him as an inexperienced lead team.

At least Seline didn't say *You're welcome*. Instead, she asked, "Now what?"

"Well," Decker said, cutting a quick side eye to Watson. "Now we are at this."

He handed over a mid-sized metallic-looking capsule and Kalan didn't want to believe what he was looking at. *Was this the tracker?*

"Is this for me?" Seline asked far too easily.

"Yes," Watson replied as though they were talking about TV channels. "And that one's active. You should swallow it now."

There was nothing he could have done to stop her. Seline had popped it into her mouth, walked into the kitchen for a glass of water, and returned with an expression that said the deed was done.

Kalan was also on his feet, but for an entirely different reason. He didn't mean to raise his voice, but he didn't mean to sit idly by and watch them track the woman he was ... falling in love with? He didn't know. But his lack of certainty didn't make this plan okay. "You just lost an officer that way! And now you're going to put a private citizen in the *same situation?*"

"No, it's not the same at all," Decker replied far too calmly. They were always far too calm. *But it wasn't their girlfriend on the line now, was it?* But Decker was still having a reasoned conversation. "We weren't openly watching Balero's home. We counted on the tracker and on Sanders not knowing that it was there."

"You counted on too much." Kalan stabbed his finger angrily at the floor because he couldn't jab them physically.

"You're right."

Watson's quick concession deflated his anger balloon, but only just a little. "So why would you do the same thing with Seline?"

"Kalan?" She called from behind him. "I'm fine."

That blew him up. "No, you're not! You just *ate* a tracking device in case a serial killer kidnaps you. *That's not okay!*"

Watson jumped to her feet, too, Decker now the only one remaining seated. His expression looked as though he did it just to maintain some semblance of status quo, so the room didn't break into an all-out melee.

Watson tried to calm Kalan, but he didn't like being *calmed*.

"We only monitored the tracker with Balero, just like Decker said." Watson even used her hand to make a signal as though she were driving and needed to apply the brakes. "This time we're maintaining physical eyes on Seline. We're not going to trust the tracker alone. We're still watching the house, the same as we've always been. We also—if you noticed—changed the type of tracker that we are using."

Oh goody. It was a different brand. That made it all so much better. He quelled the sarcasm that wanted to rise in his head and instead just clenched his jaw.

"This version will make it much harder for Sanders to remove it."

Kalan gritted his teeth against the thought of Sanders removing the tracker he'd just seen Seline swallow. Given what this killer did to his victims, Kalan had no doubt that Sanders would happily cut it out of her if he knew where it was.

Watson offered an odd expression as she turned to Seline and said, "You'll need to swallow a new one every third morning."

Seline almost grinned and offered an odd laugh in the middle of this strange and awful conversation. "Will it go through me that fast?"

"Not usually," Watson replied. "And that's the point. It's better to have you double dosed than have a gap where we can't follow you."

Or losing *her,* Kalan thought again, the anger hard to scrub from his thoughts or his tone.

Just when he thought the morning couldn't get any stranger, or weirder, Decker reached down into the bag at his feet and pulled out another of the small shiny pills. "This one's for you."

"I'm sorry, what?" Kalan asked.

"We'd like to put a tracker in you, too. We know that Sanders is going after the people around Dr. Marchand."

That threw him for a loop. He wanted to believe he didn't fit Sanders' profile at all. He wanted to believe that he was simply too big, too bulky, to let a serial killer haul him into a car, or that he might lose in a fair fight.

But Kalan knew the facts: there would be no fair fight. If he got hit on the head hard enough or drugged, the only challenge he would pose was his heavier weight to drag around.

He practically snatched the pill out of Decker's hand and headed into the kitchen, where he used the same glass Seline had. Given the things they'd just done to each other on this counter then again upstairs, sharing the same glass was not an issue.

Watson had already pulled a tablet out of her bag and was tapping at it with her thumbs, as she almost gleefully replied, "I've got you both!"

Oh, Lord, he thought. Given how well the tracker in Marina's arm had worked, Watson and Decker would know exactly what was going on between him and Seline at every single moment. There would be no more repeats of this morning without an audience, he thought.

Fuck it. Let Watson and Decker know about him and Seline. Let them know he was now sharing her bed, figuratively and— he hoped—literally. He'd already swallowed a damn tracker and the FBI agent in the living room had already pinpointed him. He'd moved past the point of caring about what they saw.

They could be jealous or die mad about it.

The two agents wrapped up the utterly bizarre and painful conversation. Watson put the tablet away and they stood, declaring the whole weird thing over.

"We'll be back," she announced as the agents neared the front door to let themselves out. "We're monitoring you. Rossi and Verner are in their vehicle watching the house right now. The trackers aren't like with Balero. These aren't the only measure we're taking. They're an *added* one."

Seline's voice stopped Watson before she went out the door. "Are you tracking Maggie and Sebastian?"

"Not yet, but they're our next stop."

"Good." Seline obviously relaxed at the thought.

The room felt empty as Watson and Decker left. Kalan turned to look at Seline. He was opening his mouth to say something when it occurred to him that for all the conversation they'd had, and everything he learned, no one seemed to have told the agents that Seline had a bigger plan than just swallowing the tracking pill.

CHAPTER THIRTY-FOUR

Nothing had happened! It had been a week since she swallowed the first tracker. Well, nothing except that Seline slowly got more and more tense.

No bodies were found and she received no more notes. There was some speculation as to whether or not Sanders had finished for the round.

Seline both loved and hated that thought. Sanders tended to kill in clusters of four or five—at least that they knew of. So he might have quit—for now.

While she breathed easier at the thought that no one else would get murdered for a while, she understood it was the last part that was the most important. If they didn't catch him, things only stopped *for a while*.

Which meant they would wait, get complacent, and Sanders could surprise them again. She couldn't have that. She couldn't wait out the rest of the semester, let alone into next year, wondering when she might get her job back or if they would simply let her go.

She'd worked endless hours in her lab at home, filling notebook after notebook with the experiments she'd run. She sent daily copies to Dr. Morales, and she would be ready to publish the results soon. But this wasn't the research she was supposed to be spending her time on. She couldn't pursue that entirely in her home lab. This setup had always been intended as a backup.

Still, she would write up the paper and submit it to journals for peer review in a desperate attempt to prove that she was still useful to the university.

Thankfully, Maggie and Sebastian had come over several times to have dinner. Though they were just friends visiting, those little shots of normalcy were the only thing keeping her from pulling her hair out.

As Watson and Decker had encouraged them to keep going about their lives, Seline had swallowed her third tracker that morning. She stood in the kitchen with her glass of water and stared blankly out the window. She didn't know how much time passed before she heard the footsteps behind her.

Seline didn't turn around, she didn't have the emotional energy. "After Marina's funeral today, I think you should move back to your own place."

She braced for the onslaught. It would feel bad if he put up a fight, and it would feed bad if he didn't.

"Are you serious?" Kalan's voice wasn't flat, but she couldn't tell what it was.

Though she'd worked through a million options and was ready for each, she hadn't been prepared for that question. "Yes. This situation is too strange. You probably have things to do in your own home. I haven't had a moment to myself for weeks." *Ooof*, that was too harsh. She turned around and faced him, braced against the very counter where he'd made her scream his name just a week ago. "I don't know what our relationship really is ..."

He offered a slow nod at that. Then he backed up a step. "Well, I'm sorry you don't know that."

Did he really think this was normal? "How can you figure anything out in a time like this? The *FBI* pushed us together— that is not normal. Things are dangerous and stressful and I don't even know what my own feelings are."

He didn't flinch, but she could see the exact moment her blow landed. She hadn't meant to hurt him. Just to tell the truth. But she scrambled to cover. "I cannot express how grateful I am for you staying here and doing everything to keep me safe."

But, in reality, no actual threats had been made against her. She received notes from a killer. He'd said hello to her several times in passing, but there was never any threat against *her*.

"But you're fine now."

She shrugged. "They think he stopped, at least for a while."

Merde, there were no right words for this.

"So, you don't need me anymore because you believe you're no longer in danger."

The way he said it put a knife through her heart, too. Her throat constricted, and her shoulders ached. She'd put a rift between them and she hadn't meant to. She just wanted … "I don't mean it that way. I don't want this to be over, I just want to know that what happens between us is real. I want to know that you went out with me because you wanted to, and not because the FBI said you needed to."

That at least earned her a little thaw. Not entirely, but his eyes were softer. Still, his mouth stayed pressed in a thin line. She knew what that mouth could do … But she couldn't keep tumbling deeper and deeper into this with a man who might be here for the wrong reasons.

Though she waited for him to respond, to say that he was here because he wanted to be, instead he offered only, "I'll pack." And he left the room.

Pressure gathered at the back of her eyes as she told herself it was for the best. Their relationship, if it could even be called that, was giving her whiplash.

Seline told herself she would feel better sleeping in her own bed alone tonight, rather than with a man whose motives she questioned. She wasn't even sure if he could untangle his feelings for himself. She sure couldn't. And she deserved better.

So did he.

They headed out to the funeral together, but Kalan drove his own car with the intention of leaving in a different direction. His bag was packed and tossed in the back of his car.

Seline thought the fact that he could get everything into the one bag was pretty indicative of the reality of their "relationship." So she tried to take it at face value.

Still, she clutched his hand as they walked into the church and toward the closed casket at the altar. As she headed down the aisle with Kalan at her side, she saw that the entire town had turned out. She wasn't surprised to see the officers from the Redemption PD, and she recognized a small handful of agents from the FBI. There were others Seline suspected possibly belonged to other agencies. Some were here to grieve, but others were scoping the place out. Even she was watching to see if Sanders had come to follow up on his handiwork.

She didn't spot anyone who could be him, but since she'd screwed that up in the past, she kept looking. Marina deserved her attention for this last service ... the last chance that Seline would ever have to interact with her, and Sanders had stolen even that.

Her vision blurred and her jaw clenched even though she fought the sensations that swamped her. Marina was trying to help *her*, trying to save *her*, when she died the most brutal death a person could. Seline owed this woman far more than she could ever repay.

For a moment, the exhaustion and sadness and anger overtook her and she felt the tears rolling down her face. Kalan's arms came around her, holding her in a way she didn't deserve, not after she'd kicked him out so unceremoniously.

She should have been nicer to him—and to herself—she did want a relationship with this man, she just had no idea if this was it. Was she just the object of his clearly protective instincts? Sanders had managed to worm his evil into every aspect of her life, piece by piece picking her apart. Still, she sank deeper into Kalan's embrace.

"We'll get through it," he whispered softly in her ear. No one could hear him. Marina's mother was sobbing openly in the front pew, her sister beside her in near wails. But Seline didn't begrudge them their grief, she was simply grateful they hadn't thrown her out of the service.

Though her heart twisted with her own added layer of guilt, she smiled a sad, watery curve of her lips against Kalan's shoulder. Even in the middle of all of this, she wanted to be in his arms. But she didn't want crumbs or his pity. She didn't want to be the princess his hero complex rescued.

She sat in the funeral with tears rolling down her face, while her throat clenched and every muscle tensed on high alert, and she still had no idea if he actually had real feelings for her.

What if even her own feelings were created from the intensity of the moment? That kind of passion would fade as soon as Sanders did. Kalan's protective vibes would fade, too, as soon as her need for protection did. The third possibility, the one she gave very little voice to, was that there was something real between them.

And that was the real problem with her heart.

It was shattered already. Her friend was tortured and murdered and left in the water. Her friend had a threat for Seline carved into her skin. Though the agents hadn't told her this specifically about Marina, she knew in the past he'd done it when the victim was still alive.

She wanted to vomit each time she thought about it.

She wanted to lean into Kalan and shelter her heart there

from all the things battering it. It was hard to admit that—whatever Kalan felt—she was falling for him *hard*.

She'd kicked him out without being able to form the proper words. Though she'd said she wanted them to keep dating, she'd botched the hell out of the conversation. He'd been mad when he went upstairs to pack.

But right now, despite the fact that they were at a funeral, and not truly together, and that there was a threat of a serial killer looming over their heads, they seemed like any normal couple.

She just had no idea if Kalan actually belonged with her or not.

CHAPTER THIRTY-FIVE

"Of course I've been checking my mail every day!" Seline almost snapped the words out. She'd been irritable for the whole week, but she couldn't seem to stop herself.

"And you haven't seen anything?"

Agent Watson somehow managed to remain calm, but Seline couldn't. "Of course I haven't. I would have told you if I did."

Had she done anything to make the agents think she was hiding evidence? She couldn't imagine what that would be, so they were probably just covering all their bases, but she didn't have the mental wherewithal to figure it out right now.

"Has anything been slid under your door? Have you found anything in your bag? Or in pockets, anything like that?"

Mon Dieu. "How could he have gotten anything in my bag? I'm not allowed on campus anymore." That sucked, but it was the truth.

"But you've gone to the library ..."

She *had.* She'd gone back and talked to Ivy Dean again. This time, Ivy had set her up with true crime books and psychological accounts of the minds of serial killers. Seline had been consuming it like a voracious predator herself. "Yes, I have gone to the library. And yes, I have checked my bag. No, I haven't run into anyone at the library who might possibly have been Sanders."

"Are you sure?"

"*Yes!* I'm sure there were no males older than twenty or younger than sixty that I passed in the library or on the street and the only man that might be Sanders is my mailman and that's Bob and you already investigated him!"

"All right then," Watson still hadn't gotten riled despite Seline taking out much of her frustration on the conversation. "Look, I just wanted to let you know that we are ending the tracking situation."

"What does that mean?" But she was putting it together even as Watson spelled it out.

"The last tracker that you swallowed? That will be the last one. We took the others off their trackers a week ago. Unless we get new evidence that he's still stalking or killing, we won't be able to keep feeding them to you."

Seline paused and pulled back from the phone as though this were the device's fault. Watson must have picked up on that.

"This is incredibly expensive. Between the trackers, the people monitoring them, and so on … I'd keep doing it if I could." She sighed. "It's also incredibly invasive, I know. I'm sure you'll be glad to be done with it, too."

But would she?

Then again, it would be a horrific mistake on the part of the FBI to lose her to Sanders after they decided to stop tracking her. They must be very sure of themselves. That was cold comfort, and she was still bitchy. Her life was still upside down and the FBI was no longer interested in fixing it.

A small pause settled between them and Seline wanted to bite out, "Are we done?" but she was at least smart enough to know not to purposefully antagonize the agents. She might need them again.

Wouldn't that be the ultimate 'fuck you' from Sanders? To leave them all shaking in their shoes for another year or so, when he wasn't even here anymore?

Seline felt her face dip forward into her open hand. Could she survive another year of this? She couldn't, not financially. She would definitely lose her job if she wasn't allowed back on campus.

"What kind of progress are we making?" she asked as though she were part of that process.

"Do you want the honest answer?" Watson asked.

That couldn't be good. But ... "Yes."

"Almost none."

"What about the farmhouse?" Seline had seen the evidence with her own eyes. Surely, that was worth something!

"Yes," Watson replied, but the tone of her voice made it clear that it wasn't good. Her next words clarified, "What was in the farmhouse is what we refer to in the business as an *orgy of evidence*—as in, almost too much. Meaning, it doesn't give us anything really solid. It's staged. If a criminal like Sanders leaves that much behind ..."

"He left it on purpose," Seline filled in.

"Exactly."

"Okay, but what did you find in the farmhouse?" Now, her tone had swung full pendulum to a different angle—needy, but scared of the answer.

"We found Marina Balero's blood."

Seline nodded along though she knew the agent couldn't see her. She'd already known that.

"We also found the blood of the previous two victims. So he was using the farmhouse as a killing location."

Seline fought to keep her breakfast down. The way Watson had said "killing location" as though it were just some kind of place like, say, a grocery store or an office was more than she could handle.

Watson was still talking, unable to see that Seline needed a moment. "We found DNA from Sanders all over the place. Fingerprints and ..." She let the words trail off.

Though Seline had wanted to know, she didn't have the guts to ask what other kind of DNA they might have found from the killer.

"But none of it tells us anything we didn't already know," Watson filled her in. "Once we confirmed that the blood was Marina Balero'sa pretty much everything else was a given."

"You didn't find anything else on the farmland?"

"No." She could almost hear Watson shrugging. "It appears he was accessing the building from a back road and dragging the victims through the woods. So anyone watching the front wouldn't have seen him coming or going. He's either stopped killing because he has nowhere to do it, or else he's setting up a new location."

"Or he's on a break," Seline filled in, thinking that was maybe the dumbest thing she could have ever said, except that it was true. Sanders often went on a "break." It was his standard pattern, enough for Seline to feel confident that it would be a while before they heard from him again. "Do you have any idea where he is?"

"We don't have anything," Watson admitted softly. "We didn't know where he was before this. We saw him when Geller took Maggie Willis and after that we thought Sanders was gone. We were confident he'd left the area at that time ... But now we have four more bodies to tell us how wrong we were."

Yes, Seline thought, *they'd been so very, very wrong*. What she said out loud was, "Well, thank you for your time."

She said it as though the agent had called to see if she wanted home insurance, not as though this woman had been in her house, peering through her drawers and checking her bank account and learning the kinds of things that even her closest friends didn't have access to.

They said polite goodbyes and Seline hung up the phone.

She was running out of options.

It was past time to make her move.

CHAPTER THIRTY-SIX

"Hello?" Kalan had used his key, maybe a little too quietly? So he called out as he pushed open the door tentatively, looking around as he stepped inside.

The problem with these old houses was the foyers—he didn't step directly into the living room, and his sight was still limited by the narrow entryway. So he couldn't see if she was home or not.

"Seline?" Kalan called when she didn't answer his first question.

"I'm in here." Her voice rang back clear. She didn't sound at all worried that she hadn't heard him knock three times.

Not a good sign. She needed to be paying attention.

Then again, the second option was that she *had* heard him knock, or she'd seen him on her camera, and had simply decided to ignore him. When he pushed open the door, she'd no longer been able to keep to that plan.

Taking a deep breath for fortitude, Kalan headed around the corner toward her voice. He had no idea what was going on between them.

She was right that the FBI had pushed them together, but it

hadn't been anything he hadn't wanted in the first place. He would have to come to terms with the idea that maybe she hadn't wanted it.

He intended to come in with a smile and ask her how she was doing. If things went well, he'd ask her out on a *real date*, and let her know the FBI wasn't involved at all. But none of that came out of his mouth. "Are you cleaning your guns again?"

Hadn't she just done that?

Seline looked up from her work, her expression making it clear that he was interrupting and that his question was dumb. She faced him where he stood in the living room, seated with her back to the wall. Was that coincidental or was she positioning herself for safety?

Kalan didn't know, and he had bigger fish to fry. He opened his mouth to say ... anything, but she beat him to it.

"You clean your guns as often as you think you might need to use them." Her hands still moved mechanically, though almost lovingly, through the task.

Crap. He'd had an idea a while ago, one that he hated. Kalan had figured he'd keep it in his back pocket as a last-ditch effort. Now, instead of asking her out, he found himself playing his very last card. "This can't go on, Seline."

Though she smiled, the barking laugh that came out of her mouth was as cynical as it possibly could be. "Thank you for clearing that up for me." She looked back down to the pieces she had laid out on the stained towel.

"I think you need to go back to France." The hated words spewed forth, the idea as distasteful to him as anything. While he wanted her here, he needed her alive. She needed a job— since she wasn't anywhere near letting him pay her bills, or at least trying to help. This was his last resort.

Again she barked the same cynical laugh. "Where in France would I go?"

"Home," he stated the obvious. He knew her mother had

passed when she was young, twelve. His understanding of her loss was that was about the worst possible time in development for a child to lose a parent unexpectedly. So he didn't ask about her mother. "Where's your father?"

Surely, her father would want her home safe with him. And Seline loved her father. Surely, she would want to go home and be with the man, protected under the wing of his army experience she always spoke of. Kalan wondered if the man knew what his daughter was going through. How had her father not turned up on her doorstep yet?

As he wondered all of these things, he saw her cold stare, and his heart turned to stone. He didn't know what was coming, but it couldn't be good.

"Kalan. My father is dead."

He froze. Even after her death glare, he'd not expected that. He'd been ready for a rift between the two of them. Or maybe her father wasn't in France anymore; maybe he was off, traveling the world, teaching Special Forces how to be even more special. At least that's what Kalan imagined, given the way Seline always talked about him.

"When?" he asked, like an idiot who wasn't paying attention.

"When I was seventeen."

Oh hell. he thought. How had he missed all the signs?

Her hands finally stilled, though they still held the gun parts lovingly. She looked over his shoulder, into the distance. Her eyes glazed because Seline was somewhere else, somewhere his stupid questions had sent her. "He didn't see me win state in volleyball my senior year. He even missed my high school graduation. He did encourage me to take science classes and suggested I would like it in college. He was right. I did."

The man had missed every step of the way. All of Seline's big achievements had been made without her mother or her father. Kalan felt his shoulders sag, his back lost some of its rigidity, and his brain turned from what he'd thought was a brilliant last card to feeling like he'd played the biggest Joker of all.

"I'm sorry," he uttered the pointless words. He watched as her expression changed and realized his condolences had bounced right off with no effect at all.

Still, he felt like crap for not knowing, for acting as though he were brilliant when he was mortally stupid. He scrambled for another card to play. *How could he keep her safe?* "Do you have other family there?"

"No," she said. "Sometimes I spend Christmas with a friend in Idaho. She's a cousin of a sort. But my mother and father were both only children. My grandparents have passed. My only ties to France are my memories and the fact that I was born a citizen there."

What did he do now?

Where could she go to be safe? It wasn't here. And it wasn't somewhere alone where Sanders could get to her.

Seline had already kicked him out. She didn't have family to return to. Sanders was stringing them all along, playing his sick game with their lives. But mostly, he was hurting Seline. He'd managed to destroy what she built with several well-placed sweeps of his hand.

And Kalan couldn't think of anywhere to send her where she'd be safe and cared for. His apartment wasn't far enough away. He didn't care that it wasn't big enough for two people, but she would. She would care because she'd lovingly crafted this place to be hers, but she'd never intended it to be a prison.

"Don't worry," she told him, which made him worry a lot.

Her next words made him worry even more. "I have a plan."

When she started to tell him, it wasn't at all what he'd expected.

CHAPTER THIRTY-SEVEN

"Dr. Morales," Seline leaned forward and put one hand softly onto the desk, as though making a case. The fact was she'd been making a case since the moment she arrived. "The FBI believes Sanders has left the area."

Okay, that part wasn't quite true. The Bureau believed he *could have* left the area, so it wasn't an outright lie, only a slight fudge. "He hasn't contacted me or had any interaction with me —" She didn't say *that I know of,* "—in over a month."

The way Dr. Morales was looking at her let Seline know that the department chair was seriously considering her bid and *mon dieu* she needed this. Though she would never forgive herself if she led Sanders back to the school, to her students, or to a fellow professor, the fact was that none of it seemed like any interest of his. And it did seem as though he was gone.

When he'd been taunting her, he'd done something every several days. He'd bumped into her somewhere and she'd find out later that the person that she'd spoken to had actually been Sanders. Even the guy at the restroom at the club had been Sanders, she'd realized later. Of course, she told Watson and

Decker about it and they'd filed that information away, but it didn't solve anything.

For a whole month now there had been no one who even could have been him. And Seline had scrutinized every man between the ages of twenty and sixty that she encountered. She had been quite confident none were the BRK. One man's eyes had been a bright, bright green, so Seline had gotten close enough to be sure he wasn't wearing contacts. Another had a nose far too small; he couldn't possibly have been Sanders. While Sanders could fake a larger nose, he couldn't fake a smaller one.

She'd gotten no notes. The FBI had found no new bodies and no missing persons had matched Sanders' type. Seline was growing more and more confident that the Bureau was right.

"I'm ready to return to the lab and to teaching," she said. As though any of this was about what she was ready for ... but she pushed. "You've been paying for a substitute."

She didn't mention Dr. Wexler by name, not wanting to give the university any reason to feed Wexler into Seline's position. That part sucked, because she truly liked Wexler. The woman was brilliant and deserved a good position, too, but Wexler was two years behind Seline in line. And Seline had worked too hard to put herself on this tenure track to give it up for something that wasn't even her own fault.

"You make a compelling case," Dr. Morales conceded, her fingers interlaced on the desk.

Seline braced for the hit of, *but I just can't do it.*

Morales smiled. "I'm inclined to go ahead but, given the severity of what we're dealing with, I do want to take several days to consider all options."

Seline nodded. She understood it was the right thing for Dr. Morales to do. The problem was she'd never had a very good poker face.

Even as she felt the disappointment coursing through her

system, she could see Dr. Morales picking up on it from where she sat.

"Dr. Marchand," she said it with the proper accent and inflection and Seline appreciated that Morales didn't butcher her name. Though probably the woman did it out of her own understanding. "*I'm* not letting you go."

Seline knew she shouldn't look so surprised, but her head had snapped up, and her expression betrayed her once again.

This time, Dr. Sonia Morales tipped her head and offered a small smile. "Do you have any idea how hard I worked to become department chair?"

"I want to believe I do, but I probably don't," Seline answered, hearing the French tilt her accent just a little more. Her heart raced now, wondering where this conversation was going to go.

"I want good researchers in this position but I also want good teachers. We're here to produce papers and get grants, but we also have the students to consider. You are both." Then Morales glanced somewhere over Seline's shoulder, and for a moment she almost turned her head to see. But the department chair was merely checking her options. "If you repeat this to anyone, I will deny I ever said it. But Wexler is not as good of a teacher as you are."

Poor Wexler, Seline thought even as she felt her heart swell. She'd worked so hard at teaching. It was good to hear that it was paying off. Morales was still talking though and she pushed her attention back to catch anything important.

"I would love to tell you that mine is the only decision that matters for your tenure track. But what I can tell you is that *I* want you here and I'll fight to keep you here, regardless of what William Treat Sanders has done or does in the future. That's not on you, and you don't deserve to be penalized for it."

"Thank you!" Seline fought back tears and figured the meeting was probably coming to an end.

"Again," Dr. Morales reinforced, "it's not solely my decision. So I'm not going to make promises that I can't keep, but I am on your side."

This time, the woman surely saw the wetness gathering at the edges of Seline's eyes, and Morales graciously motioned that she could go.

"Thank you. Thank you so much," Seline gushed.

"How about I get back to you on Friday with the decision? And then, if I get the *go ahead*, we'll have you back in the classroom the following week."

"That will be wonderful," Seline was gathering her bags, fighting to keep the tears from falling. She realized she'd said it as though she had the position back already, but she wasn't going to fumble over explaining herself.

Standing up abruptly, she draped her coat over her arm, her bag clutched tightly in one hand. She held the other out to Dr. Morales for a good firm handshake. "I hope to be back in the classroom and in the lab next week."

Morales nodded at her as though she expected the same, and Seline breathed easier as she left the office. Still, she didn't offer a proper goodbye to the administrative assistant who sat at the desk out front, but instead waved over her shoulder so that one less person would see the tears that were now happily dripping down her face.

She made it through the hallway without any incidences, ducking her head so as not to be caught by the one student walking by. She took the connecting bridge to the parking garage, thinking she would climb into her car, lock the doors, and finally let out her tears there.

She had just taken a deep breath and looked up when she bumped square into the man coming the other way.

CHAPTER THIRTY-EIGHT

Kalan looked at the email on his phone, his heart thudding.

"K, come home quick. Mom had a heart attack. Tried calling but it didn't go through. –Deja"

Again?

He wasn't sure his mother would survive another heart attack. The one three years ago had brought all three kids running. But he sure as hell was running again now. Deja was in Chicago with his Mom, that was the good news. The bad news was obvious.

He'd been on his way to buy a new shirt for his date with Seline tonight. Or the date he hoped she'd say yes to. It was a little last minute, and now it wasn't at all.

As he sat in his car in the parking lot, having not yet gone inside, he felt his breathing constrict to the point that worry became a white-hot poker in his chest. His skin felt clammy at just the thought of losing his mother. He told himself she'd made it through the last time she'd make it this time, too, as he punched awkwardly at the tiny buttons on the screen of his phone.

He needed a flight. He needed to go home and pack! Or did he?

Cranking his neck around, Kalan looked into the back seat, seeing the black ripstop nylon bag he always carried. He had to trust that he had all the essentials in there, it looked like a flight was leaving Lincoln in just under five hours. There was another leaving in three.

He was probably two hours from the airport. It was cutting it too close to buy the first ticket, but hopefully he could buy it at the ticket counter if he made it to the terminal in time.

Kalan hit the gas.

The drive was tense and he dialed his mother's number only to swerve around another car. The other driver was just trying to pull into his lane, but Kalan had only barely missed getting hit. He couldn't be on the phone and drive. Not in this traffic.

He'd told Seline he would show up at her house this afternoon after her meeting. But he was in no shape to message her with his news, he thought as he pulled a quick lane change and swerved around a car that was probably going a respectable speed. His lead foot was going to get him pulled over, and his terror about his mother wouldn't play well when he was asked for his license. Kalan couldn't afford to be stopped, so he slowed down.

It was so hard to do.

He should message Seline. She'd likely still be in her meeting, but she'd see it when she got out.

He wanted to call his mother, but that would be stupid. His mother was in the hospital. Unless Deja or Adia had Mom's phone in hand and answered it, it would go to voice mail. He needed to call his sisters.

A blast from a nearby horn might or might not have been meant for him, but it was a signal that his speed had crept up too high again. Kalan lifted his foot from the pedal and forced a deep breath. It didn't work. Though he tried, his lungs simply wouldn't expand all the way.

He tried telling himself it wasn't *his* mother, it was just someone else's mother. He was fantastic with other people's emergencies ... his own? Clearly, not so much.

It took another twenty minutes just to get to the edge of Lincoln. There was an airport here, but the flights to Chicago that he might take today were out of Omaha. He had to keep going. His only other option was to drive to Chicago, and that would take much much longer.

As he passed the business tower where he and Seline had gotten stuck in the elevator together, traffic came to a near standstill.

He huffed out a breath, smacking his steering wheel. He was mad at the commuters, didn't they understand that he didn't need a drive through meal, or just to run an errand? He was facing a real emergency.

But the stop meant he could use his phone finally. With his foot heavy on the brake, he pulled up the scroll log to call Deja first. Seline would understand if she didn't get a message from him. But his sister needed to know he'd gotten her email.

He frowned.

Behind him, a horn honked, and he jerked his head up to realize the light had changed. Not that he got that far, just one more block before he was stopped by the next light. He looked at the phone again.

There were no calls from Deja. None from Adia either. But the email said she'd been trying to reach him ...

Maybe he had no calls logged because the phone had glitched and not even received the signal. He scrolled through his contacts, hitting the delicate button with a thumb that felt too fat for the job. Deja's line rang and rang and when her voicemail finally came on, he hung up.

Was Mom already in surgery?

He pulled up his email again, checking the time stamp. It had come in just before he'd seen it. Maybe by about twenty minutes. Something else had dinged on his phone and he'd checked all his notifications, so he wasn't that far behind.

Kalan pulled another block forward with the next light, but this one was going to change faster. He was further back from the intersection, but he should make it through. He punched the button for Adia and his youngest sister answered with surprise.

"Hey, K! Good to hear from you—"

"How's mom?" He'd cut her off which wasn't appropriate, but right now he didn't care.

"I don't know ..." There was a hint of question at the end of her sentence. And Kalan dove into the space even as he looked up at the light and watched the car in front of him pull forward. He tacked onto the sedan's bumper and inched forward.

"Is she in surgery?"

"Why would she be in surgery?" Adia only sounded confused. "What are you talking about?"

"Deja didn't get in touch with you?" His tone was too demanding, but he was trying not to have a heart attack of his own and find some way to get to Chicago. Had he moved too far away from his family? Maybe he had.

"About what?" Clearly, Adia hadn't heard from Deja yet.

"She emailed me that mom had another heart attack."

"*When?*" At least now, Adia was as concerned as he was. It felt both awful and comforting.

"I just got the email about thirty minutes ago? But I don't know when she had it." He huffed out a breath, wanting to explain that he wasn't mad at his sister but at everything else. "I'm in traffic trying to get to the airport."

"Let me call Deja and get back to you." With that, Adia, the youngest and ever the go-getter, promptly hung up.

Frowning at the phone, Kalan thought about swearing at it and at her for a moment. But he quickly realized that she'd made the smart move. He'd told her he was driving. She would take care of it. Adia could take care of anything.

His mother had raised three very capable adults.

He made it out the other side of town, into the long rolling landscape between Lincoln and Omaha. The home stretch. He could pull right into the airport from the freeway.

Kalan was looking over his shoulder and merging when his phone rang.

His head whipped back and forth, checking for cars and for the caller.

Deja.

He hit the green dot on his phone harder than necessary. "Hey! What's the news?"

"What's going on, K? There is no news."

He almost hit the brakes. Deja sounded like he was being crazy. "What? You emailed me."

"Bro, I haven't emailed you in a month. You've got Adia calling me repeatedly until I stepped out of my meeting to call you."

What?

He told her what he'd told Adia. "You emailed me that mom had another heart attack."

"No, I didn't. Mom is fine."

Just as she said it, his phone buzzed with a message to both him and Deja. –Mom is fine.

Adia must have called to check on their mother directly, because this was immediately followed by –K is batshit. No idea what he's talking about.

"Mom is fine?" He asked.

"Yeah," Deja managed to have the same tone as Adia's message did. "Sorry you had a scare, but I have to get back to my meeting."

He felt bad now that he'd pulled her out of her work. "You're not missing anything?"

"No, because I'm running this show. Everyone's waiting on me and I'm waiting on you." She offered only the smallest of pauses. "You good?"

"If Mom's good, I'm good. Sorry sis!" But she was already gone.

He was so confused.

He let the car follow along with traffic until he found an exit with a gas station and he pulled in. Had he misread the email?

Kalan parked the car and started tapping on the damn small phone again. No. He hadn't misread it. There it was. Then he frowned.

It didn't say "Mom had *another* heart attack," it said "Mom had a heart attack." Was it ...?

He tapped at the phone, pulling up a search and looking for the three-year old email from Deja. Kalan blinked.

He'd gotten the exact same email again.

Flipping back and forth he checked three times. It was the same one.

But how?

He rested his head against the headrest and closed his eyes. He needed to get his head on straight. It had certainly been spun round today by a stupid email glitch.

Huffing into the empty space of the car, Kalan watched as one of the people walking by tipped his head to check whether the strange man just sitting in his car was okay. He guessed he was okay.

As long as Mom was okay, he was good.

He tapped out a message to his sisters, thanking them both for taking the time to straighten him out. And for saving him the last minute airfare to Chicago over nothing.

His mother called him then. Of course, the girls had told Mom what a dipshit he was being. But the sound of her voice was soothing and he hadn't realized until he let go of the last of the tension that he'd still been carrying it.

"You got an email from Deja?" his mother asked, and he explained the whole thing for a third time.

"I think my phone resent me the same email from three years ago."

"You know I'm taking my meds. I have no intention of going through that again." She paused. "Why would your phone do that? Does it send you old emails often?"

"Never before this."

They chatted a little while and he realized he was overheated and must stink of stress sweat, but he headed into the gas station for a sandwich and a soda before turning around and aiming the car back toward Redemption.

This time, when he stopped at a light in Lincoln, his mother's words picked at his brain. *Why would his phone do that?*

He pulled up the email again, and when he opened the details he saw that it wasn't even from Deja. He frowned.

It was from a University of Nebraska .edu address. Had Seline emailed him and the system had swapped out an old email for the new one? He'd had glitches where the screen didn't change. But this was the old email, and everything else was lining up.

The light changed and he pulled forward.

The email was weird. And on a whim, he called the Redemption Library. Ivy Dean's cheerful voice answered the line and Kalan asked what she knew about wonky emails.

"I don't know much about email delivery glitches. Not off the top of my head, but hold on. Oh! Tell Seline her book came in."

"I will." He listened to her tapping on the keys and she said, "What specifically happened?"

"I'm sure it's nothing." He realized even as he said it that more ominous words might never have been spoken. But he explained everything about the email.

"Well, I'm glad your mother's okay!" He could almost hear

Ivy clutching her pearls. Not that she wore pearls, but there was something old school about her despite her young age.

"Me, too." He thanked her, but her information was that this wasn't any known glitch with his carrier. Before he hung up, Kalan had another idea. Since he had her on the phone and something about the email was bothering him. He needed to distract himself. "Hey, have you still been looking into Sanders' history?"

"I have." Her tone perked at his request about her research. She seemed to love having all the knowledge of the library at her fingertips. "I don't think I've really found anything else more of use, but I did track down another odd death and another property in the family. The property sold and a new family lives there. So it's not like he would have access to it and I didn't find other abandoned properties that would be useful."

They chatted a few moments longer and this time when he thanked her, Kalan actually managed to hang up. He was pulling up in front of Seline's house at last. Aside from him needing a shower, and not getting that new shirt, maybe the evening would be salvageable.

But her car wasn't there. Had her meeting run this long?

It shouldn't have.

Kalan didn't like the way it was adding up. Seline running late, not answering messages. Him getting sent out of town on a wild goose chase ... But maybe it was all just coincidence and growing paranoia.

He reached out to Sebastian. "Hey, man, is Seline with Maggie?"

"No, Maggie's in with her last clients of the day. She's been booked solid." But the question in Sebastian's voice told Kalan maybe he should worry. He pushed it down.

"Gotta go." He hung up on Sebastian as he threw open his car door.

He crossed the street and by the time he arrived at the

passenger side window, Verner and Rossi had both looked up from their freshly unwrapped burgers with questioning frowns on their faces.

"What do you need?" Verner asked him at the same time Rossi rolled her eyes and scolded him. "We aren't under cover if you're chatting at the car window."

"Seline's not home." The words gushed out.

"That's fine. We watch the house, too. We already checked the mailbox before we parked."

"I got a strange email from a university address. It sent me running out of town." *And where was she? Why hadn't she responded to his messages?* Between getting halfway to Omaha and back, it had been hours. "Seline should have been home long before this."

Leaning hard on the edge of the passenger window, he fought to get the words out. "I can't find her."

CHAPTER THIRTY-NINE

"Agh!" Seline called out, a cross between a yell and a groan as her head knocked against the hard surface above her. What she'd hit, she couldn't tell, but she didn't have time to figure it out. She was immediately jolted again. This time, she curled into a tight ball, cushioning her head with her arms.

Her first thought was that getting her head slammed around would only make her make poor decisions. And she didn't know where she was or what was happening, but she knew she was in trouble. The ominous thought permeated her brain, *there would be no room for bad decisions.*

The small space bounced again, the hit coming from her left hand side and popping her into the air. She bounced against what she quickly realized was the top of a car trunk, then slammed back down onto the rough carpet surface.

"Ooof!" She fought the urge to pull her arms down and leave her skull more exposed to the knocks. She had to protect her head.

Luckily, the ride became a little smoother after that, if anything about being locked in a trunk could be considered *smooth.*

But as she fought her way through whatever lingering haze clouded her brain, she knew what to do: Pull the latch or kick out a light.

The bumps and jostles kept coming, though they were smaller now, and she couldn't figure out what that meant. But it might mean she was running out of time. She would fare better if she left the trunk of her own accord rather than someone taking her out of it, so she reached up to feel for the latch.

When she found it in the center middle of the trunk, she grabbed it, ready to pop the back open, but she paused.

Someone had put her in this trunk and when she opened it, whoever was driving would know she was awake and getting away. She needed to be ready to pop out and hit the ground running.

That was assuming the driver was the only other person in the car with her. Another option was that the driver had no idea a person was in his trunk, but she didn't put much stock in that thought. In fact, she had a pretty damned good idea whose trunk she was locked inside and she was pissed about it.

If it was Sanders, he was going to kill her. Seline had gotten only the briefest look at the man in the parking garage before he grabbed her arm. Though she'd tried to wrench away—a pure reactionary move—she'd felt the prick at the side of her neck.

That fucker had drugged her and put her in a trunk!

She wasn't going to stay here. Moving her feet, she checked her mobility. She wasn't taped up. He must have thought she'd stay out for longer than she did. What she wouldn't give for that tracker right now, but she couldn't dwell on the things she didn't have. Maybe they could follow her phone signal.

Seline had to stay focused on the things she could do.

The bumps weren't too bad now. It didn't feel like the car was moving that fast, so now was the time and she would have to take her chances. She ran the scenario in her mind, her hand still clutching the emergency trunk latch far too tightly.

If he was going to chase after her, he'd have to slow the car down enough for him to get out. The car would have to come to a stop before he could do that, so she just had to get a head start. She could do that.

Three ...

Two ...

One.

She yanked hard on the pull tab and watched as the trunk swung open wide. The daylight hit her making her head snap back and her eyes squeeze closed in self preservation. She hadn't been prepared for the blinding brightness, but it didn't matter if she was prepared or not. This was William Treat Sanders, and he was going to carve her up while she was still alive.

She could feel the car beginning to swerve. He'd clearly seen the trunk fly up, probably blocking his view in the rearview mirror. It was now or never, so Seline swung her feet up and out over the back, watching the gravel pass underneath. Of course it was gravel. She'd most likely twist an ankle, but she'd run on it anyway.

She quickly shucked her shoes—stupid heels—but held onto them tightly. She was going barefoot.

Three ...

Two ...

Fait chier!

She jumped. Hitting the ground and curling into a ball, she managed to roll instead of taking the hit full on. But it still didn't feel great.

Behind her, she heard the tires grinding into the loose road as the car careened and slowed. With the trunk gaping wide, she couldn't see the driver at all, but she didn't need to. She was far enough back that, when the spinning of the tires spit the gravel back toward her, only a few pieces made it far enough to hit her.

The sting of them against her skin was motivation enough to get up and run.

She still held her high heels, so that was good. But she was on the run in stocking feet on gravel. *Too bad.* It still wasn't worse than facing Sanders, so she took off through the woods. Staying on the road would have been a death sentence.

Sanders probably knew the area well. She didn't. He had every advantage, but she had every will to live. Seline stumbled, stubbing her big toe on a thick root, but didn't care. Her feet sank into muddy spots, slipped over mossy patches, and took nicks and cuts as she ran. She barely felt any of it as she pushed forward, knowing that if he caught her, she was as good as dead.

"You bitch!" he bellowed, as if any of this was her fault.

Seline kept running. She heard him behind her, his heavy footsteps pounding in time to her thumping heart.

She heard the chirping of birds, as though they didn't understand what was happening on the ground. She heard twigs snap beneath her feet, and branches slapping and scraping at her clothes. She heard the car in the distance behind her.

Her feet kept moving as though with a mind of their own. She took a hard right, ducking between trees, hoping to get out of his line of sight. Why hadn't she worn a color that would blend better into the forest today? She didn't know. Surely her feet were cut by now, but she couldn't feel it. Her adrenaline was far too high, her breath soughing in and out of her lungs as she ran.

She could have thrown the shoes, but they were the only weapon she had. So she clutched them tight. Maggie said she'd used one of her heels against Geller. So Seline—whose brain was racing at sixty miles a minute—decided she could do the same.

She bolted forward, ducking between trees, listening as she plowed through the underbrush and, behind her, the heavy beat of Sanders' boots came closer and closer.

She looked again to the right. *Why could she hear the car?*

She could hear it because it was *on!* He had left the keys in the ignition!

If she got there first, she could get away. She cut to the right again, hoping to make a triangle back to where she'd started, but immediately she ducked left again. If she turned too sharply, she would give Sanders the advantage of realizing what she was doing and cutting her off. She couldn't afford any wrong moves. She had to lead him in a wide enough circle that he followed her.

Merde! Despite the adrenaline, she could feel her body tiring. How far had she come? But it didn't matter, she wasn't a runner. She might be getting tired, but she had to keep going.

Seline was confident she could hear him right behind her. Her own skin felt tight, her blood bitter with terror. *But surely he wasn't*, she told herself. She'd gotten a reasonable lead. She couldn't afford to turn around and look back, so she told herself she was far enough in front and she ran further, faster. She put on an extra burst of speed, leaping over fallen trees, and diving through bushes.

She stubbed her toe again and didn't even feel it, but gravity did. She tumbled forward, hands hitting the ground, the heels of the shoes she was somehow still gripping digging into the dirt because she refused to let go.

She tucked her shoulder and rolled gain. But though she stood back up and started running as quickly as she could, in that short time she'd seen him. William Treat Sanders was behind her, and far too close.

She couldn't outrun him. She didn't have the skills or the stamina. He was faster, in better shape, and that fucker had boots! It was not fair. But she didn't have to outrun him for long. If she could just get back to the car...

She followed the path, or what she thought was a path and was dumped onto the gravel road. This time, the car was just on her right and she turned to make her final bid for safety. But she almost stopped dead, realizing it was *her own car* waiting in the road. Door open, engine running. This asshole had kidnapped her in *her own car*.

How would they find her? How would they even know she was gone?

Her car wasn't abandoned somewhere. He'd cleaned up and made it look as if she'd simply left to run errands. Help wouldn't be coming until it was far too late.

Seline was going to have to save herself. Putting on an extra burst of speed, she pushed as fast as she could. Even as she heard the heavy thud of his boots, getting closer and closer behind her, she didn't bother to take the time to look back.

So it was a complete surprise when she was tackled to the ground. Her face was pressed into the gravel as he rolled, taking her with him. Heavy arms held her close, pulling her tightly against his chest. She couldn't see him, but she knew who and what he was, so Seline fought with everything she had. She screamed her loudest, fiercest shriek to the sky. She kicked with her legs, slapped with the shoes, as he grabbed each one and tossed it into the woods.

"Nooooo!" Now her scream was a word. He'd taken her only weapons. She was in a stupid pantsuit and the heels had been the only things he had left her.

"Get up, bitch." He dragged her up with him, her arms pinned at her side in his vicelike hug. Though she kicked with everything she had, her bruised heels did nothing against the thick fabric of his jeans. At best, she'd bruised him.

She leaned forward and slammed her head backward in a sudden burst of speed. But he must have seen it coming. Her blow didn't connect.

In her ear she could feel his warm breath as he laughed at her, the sound just making her furious. She couldn't even get a hold of him to dig her nails in anywhere. Sanders stood upright, hauling her backward as he headed toward the car.

In a last ditch effort, she let go of every bit of muscle tone. Dead weight was harder to carry. It worked! He grunted as she nearly slipped from his hands. *Yes!* she thought.

But he ducked down, the quick move wrapping his arms tighter and hauled her up even closer to him. His grip not only pinned her arms to her side now, but plausibly cracked her ribs, as he whispered, "You're not getting away, you little bitch."

He hauled her back to her own car. Though she fought like a hellcat, her blows did nothing while Sanders managed to grab her clothing and haul her around with it. It took a few moments and gave her a few fleeting shots of hope, before he managed a solid grip on the front of her suit and used it to slam her backward.

Seline's head smacked against the warm metal of the car and a wave of dizziness and nausea overtook her, as everything spun. She fought to surface into the real world. But even as she did, she felt the needle go into her neck again.

CHAPTER FORTY

Seline woke slowly. Her pounding skull was the driving force pulling her out of the blackness.

She was alone in the small room as light filtered in through windows on two walls. Pressing herself up with her hands against the dirty hardwood floor, she slowly dragged herself upright. If she'd felt like this on any normal day, she would have rolled over and gone back to sleep. But it was painfully obvious that this wasn't normal, and she had to save herself.

The memory of Sanders shoving her in the trunk for the second time as her limbs had gone heavy and dull spurred her into action. Whatever he was using on her, he was dosing her wrong. Maybe she simply wasn't susceptible to the medication he'd injected, because he clearly hadn't expected her to wake up in the trunk, and he probably didn't expect to come back to someone alert enough to fight him.

She had to take every piece of luck that she had, because nothing else was working.

How long had she been out?

Given the angle of the sun burning her eyes, it appeared

she'd been under for maybe even several hours. The other option was that it had been a full day and several hours, but she figured that was less likely because she wasn't hungry. That could be a fault of the adrenaline, or the drugs, though.

Slowly, she pushed her way to her feet. This time when she stood, her soles stung and screamed, fighting back against her desire to be upright. But her need to see out the windows more than overshadowed her need to stop the pain.

When she looked out, she saw fields beyond the windows and trees in the far distance. She could only see two directions. Aside from the lack of noise there was every possibility that there was a city behind her. But given what she knew of Sanders, she was far away from everyone.

Even as she tested the glass, wondering if she could break her way out, Seline heard a car in the driveway.

Her car? she wondered.

But that detail didn't matter right now. She could fight Sanders when he came in, or she could take a chance on surprising him. Without her heels and with no weapons at hand, Seline quickly decided her best chance was to let Sanders come in and find her curled up on the floor. Let him think she was still out cold.

So she padded softly back to the middle of the space. As she lowered herself to the floor, she heard the front door open several rooms away. *Another small house*, his preferred site for operation.

It was very similar to the one that Geller had taken Maggie to. But of course it was, that cabin had been another of Sanders' preferred killing spots. Lowering herself to her knees, Seline realized she was already at the 'secondary location.' Meaning she was as good as dead if he got to her.

As she curled onto her side, her feet thanked her for getting off of them. She looked down to see that they were swollen.

Harsh red cuts and dirt marred her skin, and her clothing was torn and stained. She must look an awful mess, but that was the least of her concerns.

She tried to remember the exact way she'd been curled on the floor, but who knew if she'd rolled around or stayed the way he'd last left her? She closed her eyes and shallowed out her breathing as best she could. Adrenaline raced through her system once more as the door creaked, right in front of her, but she couldn't even peek at him. If he saw, it might mean he killed her.

Sanders came in and nudged her with a toe. For a moment, she considered playing it as though she were waking; she almost groaned and rolled over. Thinking that if she offered a sign of life, if she looked to still be drugged, he might leave her be. But she very quickly had a second thought. She needed to look *fully* drugged. Let him think his medication was still in full effect.

So she stayed limp and fought to keep her breathing as slow as she could. She let him nudge her, offering only the slightest sound when he kicked at her side hard enough that she should have responded if she were awake. Seline was proud of herself for not giving it away. And she hated him even more.

It seemed to work. When he was convinced she wasn't awake, he knelt down to pick up her wrist and check her pulse. She could only pray it wasn't racing. But he didn't seem to respond to the quick staccato beat of her blood. Maybe he was bad at feeling the small changes beneath his fingertips, maybe he just felt enough to know that she was still alive and didn't care beyond that.

Though she wanted to yank her wrist away from him, she let her hand hang limp. This was her only chance.

She heard the tiny sounds that said he was shifting position. But she couldn't open her eyes to see. Seline kept playing possum because her life did depend on it. Above her, his voice offered a soft but clear, "All right," as he nudged her one more time.

Only then did she realize her mistake as she felt the needle plunge into her neck one more time.

CHAPTER FORTY-ONE

"It's okay man."

Kalan felt Luke's hands settle on his shoulders in a gesture that was meant to be comforting. But Kalan exploded, shaking off his friend and nearly knocking him backwards. "It's not okay."

There was nothing okay about this

Seline was missing. And he hadn't even gotten to take her out on a real date. As if that were the real problem here. He shook his head, but nothing cleared. If anything, his thoughts fogged more. He'd fallen crazy, head over heels in love with her. And, aside from looking deeply into her eyes a couple of times while they'd made love, he'd done exactly jack shit about it.

Now she was gone.

Verner and Rossi had set up camp in Seline's living room. They hadn't done this when Maggie disappeared. Then, they'd set up on the front lawn, but they quickly informed him that because Seline had not been taken from her home, it wasn't considered a crime scene, like Maggie's place had been. There wasn't any evidence here for him to destroy.

That was almost worse.

They were keeping her abduction quiet.

Quieter than the last time this had happened. The very thought of that made Kalan explode again. "Why is there a *this time?* Shouldn't you have learned better *last time?*"

Though his fury was directed at the two FBI agents, Sebastian and Maggie stood by, watching. Unlike Luke, they didn't try to comfort him. They knew better than anyone what this was like, what was at stake.

"I'm sorry Kalan," Maggie stepped forward, her hand reaching out but stopping just shy of touching his arm. Maybe she was afraid he'd direct his anger at her. She sounded like the words were ripped from her throat. "But I have to leave."

Lord, he thought, finally taking a good look at her. He'd missed every sign.

She was gripping Sebastian's hand in a way that looked like it might break bones. This whole situation was triggering the PTSD that she surely had from her own ordeal.

"Go," he told her, giving her permission to not be the supportive friend right now. He nodded at Sebastian to follow her. There wasn't much they could do anyway. The FBI had every piece of tech at their disposal ... *now.* After they'd failed to do everything they could when they should have.

Turning, Kalan looked again at the whiteboard that they'd wheeled in. Maybe he would see something he'd missed the first time, or the fifth. It was old school next to all the tech laid out on folding tables around Seline's living room. It all felt so wrong ... but he forced his focus to the black marker line.

Verner had laid out the order of events that they knew. And Kalan could see that Seline had arrived at Dr. Morales' office on time. At some point after that, Kalan's email had arrived, baiting him out of town.

Rossi had told him the professor who's email it had come

from had been out of his office at the time. On the keyboard, they'd found partial fingerprints that likely matched Sanders.

So the man had been at the university, near Seline, just before she went missing.

None of it was coincidence. Kalan knew that now.

Dr. Morales had already been interviewed and had given the FBI a time when Seline left the office. The administrative assistant had confirmed it.

Luckily, the school had cameras and they'd already confirmed that Seline's car left the school less than fifteen minutes after she left the chemistry department.

Somewhere between there and Redemption, she'd disappeared. And so had her car.

Every muscle clenched with the need to act. There was nowhere to go, no race to win to save her, not until they had at least an idea where she was. It was debilitating feeling so helpless. If her house had caught fire, he'd know what to do. If she was trapped in a grain silo, he could help save her. Hell, if she was stuck in an elevator, he could at least be useful. The thought brought a small, sad smile to his lips. But this?

He ran his hands across his head. He wanted to call his mother —bold and smart, she would either know the right thing to do, or the right thing to say. But there wasn't time. Besides, how did he tell her that he found the woman he wanted to be with? The one his mother had constantly asked him if he would ever find. Because in the same breath he'd have to tell her that he'd fucked up and lost her. That the mess he'd created just a few hours earlier had been a planned attempt to get him out of the picture.

Seline was gone.

"You can triangulate her cell phone, right?" He looked to Rossi, grateful that the FBI agents managed to stay busy, while still placating his needy requests. Maybe they'd been trained in how to handle angry and frightened family and friends.

"We can't triangulate phones like they do on TV, especially not out here where the towers are so far apart." She held up her tablet and showed him a map of Lincoln that he didn't quite understand. "Her phone's been off, anyway. Since thirteen minutes after she left the garage."

"She wouldn't have turned her phone off." He said it in a wooden tone, unable to conjure more emotion as they layered on evidence that she'd actually been taken by Sanders and wasn't just on the side of the road with a flat tire and a dead phone.

It was interesting, he thought, that they knew the times down to a minute, but had no idea where Sanders might have taken Seline.

Kalan remembered when Sanders had taken Balero, and how they'd counted down the fourteen hours he usually kept his victims alive. Balero had gotten longer than that. Maybe Seline would, too. But he didn't kid himself that she would come back from any of this.

Though Maggie seemed to have emerged relatively unscathed from her ordeal, she hadn't gone up against the likes of Sanders. And, as evidenced by her low key but clearly shaken exit, she was not exactly *unscathed* by it.

His brain was racing, and his mouth was spewing stupid idea after stupid idea. "So she stopped somewhere and ran into him? But where?"

"Somewhere within the fifteen minutes from when she left the garage to when the phone went dead," Verner answered, showing that she'd been paying attention to him, even if she didn't look like it.

"It wasn't between Lincoln and Redemption, though," Rossi told him, holding up the tablet. This time, instead of showing a tracking line on the map, it had now populated a series of dots, each labeled with a time.

He followed each one, trying to place a path. "It looks like she drove an odd path out of Lincoln."

"That's what it would appear."

"That's not like Seline."

"Dr. Morales said she'd basically offered Seline her job back. You don't think that would give her a few errands to run?"

"No." Kalan said it with a conviction that he wasn't confident was correct. But he was relatively certain that she'd said she was coming home afterward. That didn't mean she hadn't changed her mind and stopped to pick something up. "That wasn't part of the plan."

He felt as if he could finally contribute something of value. "This just doesn't look right."

He pointed at the tablet and the dots. Seline's phone pinged off the towers for the last time on the northwest side of Lincoln. "Where would she have been going?"

That wasn't on the road home.

"Who does she know out there?" Verner was interested, as if this might be helpful.

Kalan wracked his brain. "No one."

Though he wondered if he truly knew all of these things about Seline. But she'd said several times that she had a few friends in Lincoln, but that was it. "She has an extended cousin in Idaho, in Boise."

But she wouldn't be going *there*. Not when she'd just gotten her job back and expected to start again on Monday. She would have to drive across all of Nebraska and the bulk of Idaho to get to Boise.

"Look," Verner said, "Watson just sent updated cell tower data."

"I thought you couldn't triangulate her phone?"

Verner shook her head. "Not out in the boonies. But near the city, there are a lot more towers."

This time, there were twice as many dots and timestamps on

the map. Slowly, the three connected where she'd gone. This solidified that Seline had in fact taken a random series of turns for about ten minutes, and then headed out of town.

"There isn't even enough time to stop … if she was running errands," Kalan commented and both Verner and Rossi nodded their agreement.

The phone signal finally disappeared on a stretch of road with nothing on it. Verner pointed. "There are no stores here, no homes, just open road."

Kalan caught the meaning at the same time Rossi said the words. "He threw the phone out the window."

"Because Seline wouldn't have done that," Kalan added. "Which means he probably had her before the car left the parking garage."

Verner tapped at the screen and pulled up the footage from the university garage. "Maybe we can see something from the car leaving."

Seline had been gone for over five hours already, but Kalan told himself not to think of the time he'd wasted driving out of town. Whether Sanders' plan with the email had fully worked, Kalan didn't know, but he'd certainly stalled the person who'd eventually declared her missing. He'd bought himself at least a few more hours with that bullshit. Kalan fought the pit that formed in his stomach. How had he fallen for it?

"It's pretty good footage." Rossi's voice pulled him back to the job at hand. "They have cameras aimed on the cars both coming and going."

"So you're sure it's her car?" he asked.

"That's her plate," Verner pointed, and Kalan had to take her word. He'd not memorized the number.

Despite his self flagellation, he still looked at the image. "I don't see her in the car. The person in the driver's seat—" he pointed at the silhouette. "—That's not Seline."

"No. She's either low in the backseat or in the trunk." Verner said it as though it wasn't a horrific thought. The two agents looked at each other, but didn't say anything more.

And Kalan once again lost his cool.

"What?" he demanded, slapping his hands on the small folding table and nearly collapsing it. "What aren't you telling me?"

CHAPTER FORTY-TWO

S eline pushed herself to her hands once more. Her brain rolled through a thick fog of deja vu and pain. Her joints ached, her throat was dry, and this time she was hungry. Her anger fueled her to lift her head and get to her feet.

The sky beyond the window was dark. Probably it was later in the same night, though Seline admitted to the possibility that she was missing days. She took two steps toward the window before freezing in her tracks. Luckily, the floor had not creaked. The cold floor made her think that the place might be too old to have a raised foundation.

Slowly and carefully, she made her way to the window, though this time she didn't step directly to it. The only light in the room came through the window, as best she could tell without looking, it was from the moon. If it was a streetlight, she was in a different place than she thought. But she stayed tucked to one side and didn't step to the glass to look.

She was afraid that, if Sanders was out there, he would see her.

No sounds came except for the sounds of her own breathing and as she grew brave, she peeked around the window frame.

This time she saw no cars from either of the two lines of sight that she had. She'd heard nothing from the rest of the house. Nothing from outside; even the wind didn't rattle a branch or a window. It sounded as if there was no one in or outside the home.

Seline contemplated breaking out the window and escaping that way. Wasn't that what Maggie had done? And didn't it make sense? Two friends abducted by two friends? So crazy and so wrong but it didn't change the very serious issue that she could escape or she could die. Those were her only two options. Still peeking out into the night and scanning the landscape, Seline began to plot.

It made sense that her abduction was eerily reminiscent of Maggie's. The two men had shared techniques and plans and eventually even one of Sanders' sites. But hadn't Maggie said her windows had been nailed shut? Seline thought she could just lift this one and run, but she needed a backup in case she couldn't.

Sanders must have changed something about his methods, or he hadn't had time to prepare this place for her. Maybe that could work in her favor.

One option was to break the glass and climb through the window.

A second was to lift the sash and climb out.

But both would take time and be noisy and dangerous. She couldn't afford to get cut or twist her ankle. Her gut was already clenching and she could feel her blood sugar was low. She didn't have shoes on ... going out the window was a last resort, as it could cause far too much damage.

So she softly moved back to the other side of the room and placed her hand on the doorknob. Then she bit her lip and stilled everything including her breathing as she waited for it to swing open in her face.

When it didn't, she slowly began to turn the knob, on high

alert for any squeaks or clicks that would give her away. She took possibly a full minute to rotate the knob, until it stopped and told her that the latch was all the way back.

She let her breath out, not having realized she was holding it. The constant screaming of her feet from where she stood on cuts and bruises seemed to play as an appropriate backdrop for the screaming of her senses. If she didn't have her hand on the knob, it would have been shaking fiercely.

Taking another breath for fortitude and knowing this was possibly the only way she'd get out, Seline slowly creeped the door open. As she got a view into the hallway she found that all of the house was dark. She would never go to one of those American Halloween fun houses again. She was petrified something might jump out at her at any moment but, here, it wouldn't be a costumed player there for the scare. Here, she would find Sanders, or a large dog with fangs bared and gums dripping.

But she'd heard no dogs, and she hadn't heard Sanders either. So she took a step forward into the short hallway and immediately pressed herself against the wall on the left. Slowly, she leaned out and peeked around the corner.

It could easily be that she simply hadn't seen a car from the bedroom window because it was on this side of the house. Sanders himself could be sleeping in a chair in the front room, or in the room next to her.

Her head whipped back, her eyes straining in the dark of the short hallway. One of the rooms was probably a restroom. The other another bedroom, maybe, but she wasn't going to look. When neither door opened of its own accord, she turned back to the living room.

She was getting out.

This place didn't look as abandoned as the farm outside of Stromberg had. This place had furniture and the floor wasn't covered in dust. It looked as though someone was here regularly, plausibly the place Sanders was living.

When no one and nothing jumped out at her, she began to pad softly across the room, more than aware of the shadows and that the kitchen to her left most likely led to the back of the house. These small circular designs helped with airflow in the days before air conditioning, but now they let someone linger and hide. They offered the chance for Sanders to stay constantly one step ahead of her.

Her breath held tight and her heart pounding in her ears, Seline tiptoed softly across the room. The soles of her feet protested at every step. Her teeth clenched and sweat rolled down the middle of her back. But she didn't let herself stop. If she did, she might never start again.

When she reached the front door, she grabbed for the knob and found it locked. In fact, three bolts graced the side of the door, all of them flipped into position.

If Sanders wasn't here, and if she got out beyond that door, he would know she was gone from the moment he reached the door. His key would turn too easily and he would know all the bolts had been thrown.

Merde, Bon sang! Putain! She went mentally through every swear she knew but dared not speak them out loud.

The question was, was she alone? Was speed her friend here or was diligence?

CHAPTER FORTY-THREE

Seline gripped the doorknob almost too tightly. Her breath was shallow but somehow heavy as she tried desperately to make the decision. She realized then that it had already been made for her.

She wanted to go home. She wanted to curl up in bed next to Kalan and tell him how she really felt and let the chips fall where they may. She wanted so many things that depended on getting out of here.

Verner and Rossi had not been checking in regularly with new information about Sanders. Though they would likely have pulled out all the stops searching for her by now, the last Seline had heard, they had no idea where Sanders was operating from. And, she'd stopped swallowing those stupid trackers a few weeks ago.

She was going to have to save herself.

So she turned away and tiptoed her way through the kitchen. Now moving more quickly, she was convinced enough that he wasn't inside the house, and she didn't worry quite as much about him hearing her. Though diligence was her primary concern, speed was still a close second.

Quickly, she located a small back door out of the kitchen. This one had two bolts. And she was going to have to make a decision: which one did she think Sanders was using?

She remembered the first time she'd woken, she'd seen the parked car from her bedroom window. So chances were good, he was coming through this door. Then she should have gone out the front in the first place.

With that realization, she turned and ran. Aiming for the front door, she arrived almost fast enough to slam into it. But she skidded to a stop, her feet screaming in pain at the stupid move. If someone were coming up the walk, she should hear him ... right?

She didn't know. But she threw the bolts one after the other and tugged hard on the knob.

Though it twisted easily in her hands, the door did not open.

She yanked at it again and again and felt tears in her eyes before she managed to stop herself. Though the tears still threatened, it didn't matter. She had to get out. She was too smart to get stuck. Sanders himself might be smarter than her, but this stupid door wasn't.

So she took a deep breath, and looked up and down for something that held the door shut. She realized it might well be something bracing it from the outside. And at least there was another door to try. But as she looked, she saw a small brass flap at the top.

Yes! she thought. She'd seen these as a child. They were safety locks, so the door could only be opened from the inside and by a person tall enough to reach them. As a child, she'd not been able to reach the one her father installed on the front door, but now, as an adult, she was certainly tall enough.

She pushed up on the lock, felt the metal piece slide out of the grooves that held it and the door firmly in place, and watched this one flip open. This time, when she yanked the knob, the door swung open.

That was a mistake.

She should have opened it slowly. But as she scanned the long drive in front of her and found nothing, she put another bit of good news together.

That was the kind of lock that could only be locked from the inside. Which meant Sanders *was* coming in and out through the kitchen. She turned quickly, pulling the door closed behind her. Stepping out onto a small patio, she felt the ground shoot ice through her feet almost instantly. The cold night air was far chillier than she'd given credit for. She was going to freeze to death out here.

She could deal with warmth later, first she had to get away.

The small house sat in a large open yard.

This one had a cornfield out back, though whether anyone was actively maintaining it she didn't know enough to tell. There were trees in the distance in several directions, and she hoped they would provide cover once she got there.

Looking for the closest stand, her eyes flicked down the long driveway. Her suit was a pale pink and the moonlight caught it, making her shine like a pastel beacon.

Another mistake.

She was out in the open and anyone could see her. But getting away wasn't a mistake. And right now, there wasn't anyone around. So she crouched low, ignored the pain in her feet, and bolted for the trees.

Seline had covered half of the distance when she heard tires crunch on gravel. Her head whipped back and she saw the headlights swing toward her as the car came up the drive.

CHAPTER FORTY-FOUR

Kalan jolted around as he heard the front door open behind him.

In walked Ivy Dean, a huge bag thrown over her shoulder, heavy with whatever she'd brought to show them.

Today she wore a long sleeved t shirt and jeans. Sneakers graced her feet, as though she were ready to tackle anything. Not quite the prim librarian getup she usually wore.

"Ivy!" he said, the relief probably coming off him in waves strong enough to bowl her over.

But Ivy didn't waver. She turned and looked at him. "I'm here, the library's covered or closed. You have me and every resource I have. Let's find her."

Only then did he realize that a second woman trailed behind her. Taller than Ivy, though not tall, her hair glistened mahogany and something about her t-shirt said it was expensive. But her walk ... Kalan knew it from somewhere ...

He opened his mouth, but Ivy beat him to the punch. "Oh, this is Jo! She's new in town—"

"Jo Huston," the woman interrupted but made it smooth as glass. "Ivy said this might involve an SAR. I'm trained." She stuck out her hand and offered a firm, reassuring handshake. If she said "SAR" instead of "Search and Rescue" then she probably knew at least something.

Ivy really had brought all the resources.

He could have hugged her right then, but he was afraid if he did, he would crush the petite woman. Instead, the words "Thank you," gushed from his mouth.

Ivy, small and delicate, pushed her way into the room like a five star general taking over the battle. Pointing to a table that had only a singular laptop on it, she motioned for the space to be cleared for her. Jo and Kalan followed along and even the FBI agents did as she indicated. She probably dealt with school rooms full of unruly children.

She had that stern teacher face on as she set down her bag and began pulling out various books and maps. She reached in again, this time depositing a handful of USBs like playing jacks across the table.

"I gathered what I thought would be useful."

Verner and Rossi looked to each other, as if to say *who was this?* But didn't they already know that Ivy Dean was the head librarian?

It was Kalan who looked to them, his own stern expression learned from firefighting—the kind that said *you will stay behind the established line.* "Ivy helped us find the farmhouse. She's an excellent resource. Listen to her."

If he didn't repeat the last part out loud, he did in his head— several times. All he could think was *Listen.* If everyone put enough information together, they could find Sanders.

He watched as Ivy took over the room. Verner and Rossi had been operating back and forth, occasionally picking up a marker and adding something to the whiteboard or passing something back and forth. Kalan had literally been pacing with nothing to do. Ivy gave him action that he'd desperately needed.

"This and this—" Ivy pointed as she spoke and rolled out a

large map, letting her new helper anchor the corners. "These are the two previous locations that we know of. The ones where Sanders took his victims. One was where Merrit Geller took Maggie. The second one was found by us."

Oh, go Ivy! Kalan thought as she readily established her past successes.

"But what else do you have?" Verner wasn't beating around the bush. She'd already closed the door on two nosy-slash-helpful neighbors.

Ivy wasn't done. "Here are other places that I've found with my research these past weeks."

She reached into the bag again, and this time pulled out little pieces that looked like tiny chess pawns. She set one at each position she pointed to, and then pulled out another color and began placing other markers. "Here, between Thedford and Brownlee. He has a cousin who had a farm there." She dropped a marker. "And here—" she trailed a finger the other direction, "—northeast of Lincoln. Outside of Defiance, Sanders had a great-grandfather who maintained a farm until about fifteen years ago. This farm has since been sold."

Ivy dropped a marker there, too, then laid out three more of the pieces. She moved her finger off of the map and to the right. "Apologies, but here—almost to Des Moines ..." she touched bare tabletop, "He has a cousin and a second cousin. Here and here." She touched a third marker. "This is a great uncle."

Ivy pointed to one, then looked to Kalan. "This is the one who went to jail for the rape case." Then she turned back to the agents, who were following with rapt attention. "This was his farm, but it also sold."

"So these are all possibilities for where he could be now?" Verner waved her hand at the table, indicating the tiny markers.

"To a certain extent, yes," said Ivy. "However, I've followed the records and contacted the families where I could. We have the genealogy and the public records." She pointed to one of the last pawns. "This family here, near Des Moines, lives in that home. I reached out and—at least by what they were willing to tell me—they have had no contact with William Treat Sanders. The man, Daniel Swilling, remembered Sanders and said he didn't like his cousin when they were kids, and has cut off all contact as adults. This one was the same." She motioned to the other nearby pawn. "These two families remain close. So I think these two places are much less likely to be where Sanders is taking victims. Both contacts would have had to lie to me. This one's also closer to Kansas City, and I think it would be harder to get in and out with a body."

She looked to Verner and Kalan waited for a harsh question. When none came, Ivy plowed ahead. "Here," she pointed to a third marker. "The aunt and uncle are still alive. Here, here and here. These properties have been sold. I managed to get through to the owner at this one and tried to contact the others. But haven't made it through to any of these three. There's another one over here, though the relation may be too distant for Sanders to be taking advantage of it."

She pulled a stack of printed pages from the bag. "I also began looking at people who Sanders went to school with or lived with over the years. But I'll be honest, the spider map on that got far too complex, and I wasn't able to follow them up. However, I do have some information about who he was most in contact with. And I did manage to locate the names of people he'd worked for in the past. So I have his work history up until about … ten years ago."

Kalan could have kissed her right then. She'd done a good portion of the FBI's work for them. Or maybe they'd done it too. Either way, it gave them a starting point. If the FBI had canvassed all these places as well, the overlap would give them a clearer starting point.

Rossi immediately confirmed his thoughts. "We have eyes on these properties—" she pointed to Ivy's markers. "And these we'd ruled out. We also decided the cousins outside of Des Moines were unlikely bets."

"But," Verner stepped in. "We didn't know about these two. Do you have the addresses?"

"Absolutely," Ivy said with a fresh smile as she reached into her bag once again. She pulled out another small stack of pages. She had a printed document on each piece of land, copied and pasted material about the family, the physical address, and a picture of the property.

Kalan was just thinking, *Damn, she's good,* when one of them caught his eye. "Ivy? Can I have that one?"

But he didn't wait for her permission, just reached out and snatched the page from her hands, his eyes growing wide.

CHAPTER FORTY-FIVE

Seline peeled her suit jacket as quickly as she could, revealing her bare arms to the cold night air. She clutched the wad of fabric beneath her as she crushed herself to the ground and tried her hardest not to be seen in the headlights and not to breathe at all.

Her arms were pale. The shell she wore under her suit was a cream color, but hopefully less reflective than the pink had been. She still wore the pants and there was nothing she could do about her skin.

This was the moment when there was nothing to do but pray. It had to be Sanders. Who else would be here? She fought back tears at being caught again.

But she wasn't done yet, so she prayed the light didn't catch her. Prayed that he didn't think to look this direction. Prayed that he still thought she was in the house …

Luckily, the headlights of the car did not sweep over her. She squeezed her eyes shut, seeing only the red of light beyond her eyelids. And when the redness went dim, she opened them again to see the car had driven behind the house. He couldn't see her right now.

With that, she was up and running again.

Her feet pounded the cold ground, her heart beat heavily enough that he could likely hear her from the driveway. She chastised herself with each step.

She'd taken too long getting out of the house. She hadn't decided quickly enough which door to use. She'd taken nothing with her, just run, leaving her exposed out here in the dark and cold of night with nothing but a suit that was more likely to get her caught than anything else.

But she didn't hear him behind her—if she could hear anything over her own blood rushing through her senses. Hopefully she'd gained enough time by choosing the right exit. Maybe he was unlocking the side door and not realizing yet that she was already gone.

She thought all these things as her bare feet slapped against the cold ground, the low temperature the only thing stopping them now from stinging. Still, she could tell they were going numb. And that meant she would trip. Even as she thought about it, she sailed forward, not sure what she might have stubbed her toe on to make her go flying.

Hitting the ground hard, she fought to not let out a grunt or an "oof" that might give her away. Without any thought besides getting away, she pushed herself back upright and began running again. This time, instead of keeping her eyes on the trees, she kept them trained on the ground in front of her.

The jacket stayed clutched in her arms. It would have been more useful to hold the heat had she worn it, but it would also have been more reflective. It was a choice she had to make. She could hopefully get warm again later. She could not get uncaught again later.

Seline watched where she put her feet and ignored the gravel now embedded in her palms. She was so busy watching where she stepped, that she almost ran headlong into a tree. The sound of her breath drowned out everything else.

Relief washed through her at having reached the woods. *Maybe she could be safe here.* But she looked up and saw that it wasn't woods at all. The trees weren't the cover she'd thought they would be. Instead, they were just a thin line of trunks, only three or four deep. Likely, they'd been planted years ago to delineate a property line. But it wasn't a robust forest offering her protection.

In the night, she hadn't been able to see beyond the outline, but now as she stood here it became clear she was in between several open fields. Even the corn wasn't tall enough for someone of her height, and she dare not run in it with her feet already cut up. She might not be from Nebraska, but she'd learned pretty quickly that it wasn't soft and fluffy but hard and sharp.

She was screwed.

And, as she had that thought, she heard his voice bellow behind her.

Though it was in the distance, and it didn't sound like he'd found her yet, there was still nowhere to go. If he looked this direction, she would only be able to hide behind the meager trunks for so long. The colors she wore would likely give her away at first glance. If she ran through the field, she would probably catch the light and flash like a beacon. It would only be a matter of time before he caught her and dragged her back.

If she was lucky, he might kill her here in the open space tonight.

Though her heart was pounding and her adrenaline was the only thing keeping her going, Seline understood that she didn't have much more in reserve.

She didn't know when she'd last eaten. She should have drunk from the sink before she'd left the house, but she'd been far too scared. And now, her only cover was a few tall trees. There wasn't even ground cover here.

She heard him behind her again.

For the briefest moment, she closed her eyes, but quickly realized that only held her in one place until he saw her. And once he saw her he would find her.

Sanders was fed. He had shoes. And, she'd realized that while her need to stay alive was a vital one, his need to kill her seemed almost as vital.

Seline opened her eyes, and looked left, then right, and she saw nothing that would save her. Nothing that would help.

Behind her, his voice called her name, demanded her return, and bellowed into the dark night.

CHAPTER FORTY-SIX

Seline breathed heavily and clutched her wrists with loose fingers forming a circle around the trunk.

She might not make it.

Her blood sugar was low, lower than she could ever remember it being in the past. She was woozy and it was getting hard to hold on. She wasn't safe sitting here in the top of the tree for much longer. If she stayed, she'd pass out and fall down through the branches.

The wind was colder up this high, though the day should have warmed up by now, the chill of night hadn't truly left yet. She'd begun to not notice the cold anymore and she was smart enough to understand that that was the most dangerous time.

Pulling herself once again into a fetal position, she took stock.

Her feet were okay—not good, but okay. She'd taken off her shell and wrapped it around her feet, then pulled her jacket back on, needing to keep herself covered. It was the only way she'd stay warm enough to survive.

Luckily, the shell was silk, and it held the heat in well

enough for her feet to hurt. Which again, sucked but she recognized that at least for the good sign that it was.

Seline clutched the tree for probably several hours after the sun had come up. While Sanders had searched the property the night before, he'd walked right under her, high beam flashlight shining. Each time he passed by, she'd held her breath, knowing that he'd figure out that she'd climbed one of the trees.

If he saw her, she'd be done for.

But he hadn't.

In her favor, even the low branches had been high overhead. But she'd played volleyball in high school. Though she wasn't tall, her leap was still solid. Normally, it was a move she wouldn't have been able to pull off, but the terror of the situation had fueled her into not only grabbing the branch, but muscling her way up onto it. Once she was on the first branch, she'd been easily able to climb higher and higher. She'd climbed almost to the top of the tree.

Then, she'd hugged the trunk and curled into a ball, letting the needles of the fir obscure her. Though Sanders had quickly shone the light upward once, it had been merely a glance. And, while the other trees were starting to go bare, this pine had been her salvation.

If he'd seen her, he hadn't let on.

Now the daylight had come. She could see the house from where she sat. She had missed it when Sanders came out in the early light and began searching for her again. She'd dozed off and on and at one point had opened her eyes to see him coming along the back tree line as he searched for her. This time he looked at the ground periodically, maybe hoping to see signs of where she'd run the night before.

If he looked up even once, he would see her in all her pink glory.

Her already dry throat clenched the closer he got, and she hugged the tree tighter, confident he'd find an obvious trail from the night before. Her only thought had been escape, not covering her tracks. When he caught the mess she'd left as she looked around and then jumped to grab the branch, he would surely look up.

She'd clung tightly and prayed.

She'd held her breath.

He'd searched almost directly beneath her, and then he'd left.

She could only hope that she was covered enough that he hadn't seen her. That if he looked back, he wouldn't see a shock of pale pink up in the tree. At least the daylight was her friend. She'd sat motionless for who knew how long, until he went back to the house. Until he emerged, got in the car and drove away.

Now, she counted to sixty again.

As she hit her sixtieth sixty, she decided that an hour had passed—or at least close enough to it—since the car had left.

Counting was her only method of tracking the passage of time. And she was quite certain she was way off. But if it had been forty minutes, that was good enough. And if it had been an hour and a half, well, that too should be sufficient.

The problem was, it was now time to climb down the tree. And that meant untying her feet from the shell. She thought about taking off the jacket and putting the top back on underneath, but she teetered on the branch just a little.

She was only sitting, not yet moving and she wasn't stable at even that. She didn't have the energy to do all the maneuvering it took, and time was more of the essence. She tucked the silk into her waistband, her fingers sticking to it, covered in sap. The shell itself was dirty on the inside from everything that had clung to her feet. Every part of her was a mess. She probably had sap in her hair.

No, she was certain she did.

Seline had leaned against the tree during the night to get what sleep she could. She had sap and bark and fir needles and who knew what else stuck to her. But with a deep breath, she hugged the trunk now and threw her leg over the branch that had held her all night. Slowly, she lowered herself until her toes felt the next one beneath her. Though her feet were still cold, the silk of her sleeveless top had saved her.

With her hands on the branches near her waist, she slowly lowered herself, reaching one foot down and then another. Firs were at least excellent for climbing—if you could jump up to the bottom branch. And thank God, because she could not have navigated a more complex system.

When she reached the lowest branch. She looked around carefully, knowing she was still a beacon in her pale pink suit. But when she saw nothing, Seline swung down, dangling until she couldn't hold on any longer. She hit the ground with a thud and a sting that shot all the way up to her thighs.

But there was no time to nurse injuries. She walked three steps to the edge of the trees, and still saw no one.

This, she thought, was when her plan truly became dangerous. She didn't know if his home was wired with sensors or cameras. She hadn't checked. But last night when he searched for her, Sanders hadn't seemed to know which direction she'd run in. His search had been haphazard, circling the entire perimeter of the large property. Which meant that he hadn't watched a video to see where she had run.

Given the time she'd had to cover the last of the distance to the tree line once the car had pulled into the drive, he'd done exactly as she'd hoped. He'd unlocked the door at the kitchen and wandered into the house before he discovered she was missing.

Seline had to believe now that her luck would hold. It was her only hope. If she was right—and she wasn't missing any full days of time—she'd now been gone for almost twenty-four hours.

She had a short while to do what she could and there was nothing she could do about the luck part of it.

She simply had to pray that hers, as bad as it had been, held.

Once again, she closed her eyes for a moment, but knew she couldn't hold out that way. The days were much warmer than the nights, and that was in her favor. Her feet were still bare, but she took a moment and pulled the shell from her waist and began ripping it at the seams.

Tearing out the high quality stitches took more strength than she felt she had, but she got it done. When she had two separate scraps, she managed to tie them around her feet. The thin fabric wasn't much protection, but the warmth was good and it would keep things from poking into her skin. Lord knew, she'd pulled pine needles and small rocks out of her feet last night. But now, when nothing moved, she took her first tentative steps back toward the house.

CHAPTER FORTY-SEVEN

"Are you okay?"

The words came from Sebastian, who should have been on shift today.

"I'm fine," Kalan said, though he knew he was anything but.

He could only rate himself in comparison with Seline. Every time he thought about what she might be going through, his stomach churned and he nearly vomited.

Twenty four hours she'd been gone now.

There was every possibility she was already dead.

He was confident she'd been tortured by this point. Contrary to those horrible thoughts, Kalan was equally as confident that she was brilliant and would have figured out a way to get away.

If that was the case, then all they needed to do was go find her. But where?

He held to both his deepest fears and his greatest hopes simultaneously.

As for himself, he hadn't eaten. He'd barely slept, and he hadn't left the house, though Rossi had reminded him repeatedly that he needed to take care of himself.

"If you hope to be ready when we find Seline, you'll need to have sleep and food *before* we get the word."

The agents had all managed to catch naps and he resented every single one of them for their ability to sleep. He decided that his version of being ready included lying about everything.

So he lied now to Sebastian. "I'm fine."

His friend had returned without Maggie. Maggie had not come back to the house once in the time since she'd left. Kalan pushed the subject away from himself and asked about her now.

"She's all right," Sebastian said, but he said it with the kind of tone that let Kalan know that Maggie's *all right*, was also relative. "She's holding together. She took one of the pills her doctor gave her and managed to get some sleep last night."

Kalan nodded. He'd refused something similar, knowing that if he slept because he was medicated, he'd sleep hard. If something broke, he wouldn't have woken up to be there. Now, hours later, he wished he'd taken the medicine because nothing had broken.

The FBI passed information back and forth and said they would figure out where Seline was. Though he'd looked at the one picture Ivy had brought and thought he recognized it, nothing had happened. The FBI had diligently sent agents to the place to check it out, but they hadn't found her.

Kalan had listened as they alerted station after station to be on the lookout. They sent BOLOs to police officers, to the sheriffs who roamed a lot of the open range not populated by cities. They notified fire stations and EMTs. Everyone was on the lookout for Seline's car and for Seline herself. The police were watching the addresses that Ivy had brought in. Even the cousins outside of Des Moines had an agent on them despite the fact that they seemed the least likely source of trouble.

The FBI was being resourceful, but it hadn't changed anything. Nothing had popped.

No one had seen the car or Seline. No one had found a body, face down, floating at the edge of the water. At least, that was a good thing, he thought. But with nothing happening, Ivy had eventually gone home. Jo had followed her, both claiming they needed their own beds. Ivy said she would return to the library in the morning and then come by with whatever she learned. Kalan hoped to see her at any moment with whatever new information she had dug up.

The agents had even called the park ranger they'd talked to before. Leo Evans had checked the cabins himself to see if Sanders had in fact gone right back there, as Seline had once suggested. But he reported that all the cabins in the area were not only empty but completely untouched for some time.

Given that there was nothing for him to do here but wait and pace, there was clearly nothing for Sebastian to do either.

"You should go back and be with Maggie." Kalan pushed on Sebastian's shoulder, as if to shove his immovable friend out the door. "Nothing's happening here."

He hated saying that out loud. His throat was tight. His muscles clenched to the point where his nervous energy was the only thing that kept him upright and not curled in a fetal ball on the floor. There were no hoses to run. No fires to fight back. No burning buildings to rush into, or children or kittens to pull from under a bed.

He was utterly useless.

"I'll go," Sebastian said, "but only after you've eaten something."

Kalan would have fought back. He didn't feel like eating. He didn't want to eat and eating when Seline might not be able to eat at all felt like the worst betrayal of all. But he had gone up against Sebastian in the past and had not fared well. At this point he conceded that his friend was right, and that he had to be fueled and ready to run when they did find her. So he simply said, "Okay."

He followed Sebastian into the kitchen and watched as his friend pulled out the toaster and methodically handed over several slices of buttered toast. Though Kalan chewed and swallowed methodically, they tasted like nothing more than sawdust. When he was done, he looked to his friend, only to find that Sebastian had pulled pasta from the pantry along with a jar of sauce and had set water to boiling. Vegetables had been rejected from the fridge, but a bag had been pulled from the freezer.

Kalan didn't know how much time had passed before Sebastian put the heavily loaded plate in front of him. Sebastian was smart enough to fix himself a plate, too, understanding that if he sat and took his own meal, Kalan would only be forced to mimic him.

They ate in silence, until Kalan had cleared most of the food from in front of him, but not all of it. At Sebastian's raised eyebrow and soft nod, he realized his friend had overfilled the plate, knowing that Kalan would stop early. Kalan had been had.

Though he'd tasted none of the food, he found he was incredibly grateful to be taken care of. He could feel his body chemistry altering with the hit of carbs and vitamins.

"Hold on," Sebastian motioned with the plates he was now carrying into the kitchen to clean up. He returned with a second, full glass of cold water. "Drink all of this and then I'll go."

It was an easy enough task. *Easier than fighting*, Kalan thought as he gulped the water. Though his brain still churned, still wondered if Seline had water, if Seline had food, if Seline had *life*.

But he fulfilled the promise and saw his friend out the front door. The two men walked through the living room where FBI agents sat, a mild buzz permeating the air and telling them the agents were still working diligently. And that they had still achieved nothing for all their effort.

As the door clicked behind Sebastian, Kalan felt the click somewhere in his chest as well.

And he wondered if this was how it would always be. If Seline would always be gone, and if he would never find her ...

CHAPTER FORTY-EIGHT

Seline's heart pounded as she put her hand on the doorknob at the small house. She swallowed hard and prayed that the car had taken Sanders away and he hadn't returned. She twisted at the knob but it didn't give.

Seline furtively looked around, though it appeared no one had seen her—luckily not Sanders, and unfortunately not anyone else.

She headed around the side of the house, trying to avoid stepping on the gravel in the driveway. Her feet had only the torn silk of her old top to protect them, but it was unavoidable. The gravel and stone bit into already soft skin, and she found she was past caring. As she tried this door, the knob also didn't give. But this one had a panel of nine smaller panes of glass. That was all she needed to break in.

Shit, she thought. *She was going to have to do this.*

Clearly, Sanders had chosen this place for being out in the middle of nowhere, so she was unlikely to be seen. Sadly, the thing that meant no one would see her also meant *no one would see her...* Nebraska was known for big open spaces.

And she had to do this, because he *would* come back.

Seline looked around again. For the first time it occurred to her that his getting in the car and driving off was a ploy to draw her out. To make her brave enough to risk running across an open field. But she could run for a long time and not find anyone. Of that, she was certain.

Now her only question was, how long before he came back?

He most likely figured he could find her. But—exactly as she'd told Kalan and others—what if Sanders had gone back to the cabins? Because that would be the one place no one would look. So she had returned here—hopefully the one place Sanders wouldn't expect her.

So she could only hope that Sanders was out driving around searching anywhere but here. He would likely assume she'd gotten further than she actually had the night before. Or maybe he'd figured out that she'd found a hiding place. But wouldn't he expect her to keep moving far from here?

And if anyone else found her? Well, that should be her best chance of staying alive. In fact, she *needed* other people to find her. That was why she was here. So she unbuttoned the front of her suit jacket, which already made her look like a refugee from the Victoria's Secret modeling event and stood there in her bra. She wrapped her hand in her once expensive blazer and punched through the glass.

She paused only for long enough to flex her now-bruised fingers and listen for noise coming from inside. With the car away, she had to guess that Sanders was gone, too. After picking out the shards of glass that jutted into the hole she'd made, she reached inside and turned the knob.

She had a very short time period to do what she needed.

Seline followed the plan she'd made on the way over and threw open the pantry doors. Grabbing the first thing she saw— a box of Cheerios—she opened it and stuffed her hand inside and began eating for the first time in two days. Had anyone seen her, they would have guessed she was more horse than human, but she had zero fucks left to give. She stuffed another handful in as she next opened the fridge, the precious, nearly-stale cheerios still hugged tightly to her side.

There was no filtered water, but that wasn't surprising. A gallon of milk sat in the middle of mostly empty space and when she opened it her head snapped back. She wasn't that desperate yet, so she slapped open cabinets with no concern for noise and grabbed a large plastic cup from the mismatched pieces and poured herself water from the sink.

She listened happily as the water glugged from the glass and down her throat. But just as soon as she finished the whole thing and sighed with relief, her body rebelled. Her stomach seized and she barfed everything into the sink.

Tears formed in her eyes, she needed food. She had to keep it down, but it had been too long and she'd eaten too fast. So she braced her hands on the sink and waited through the heaves she didn't have the time for.

Slowly, her stomach untied itself, as she took in big gulps of only air this time. In and out. In and out. She told herself she'd be okay.

But she still had to eat and drink. So she poured more water and this time took it in sips. She ate just a small portion of cheerios as she rinsed out the sink because she would need it later, not because she was cleaning Sanders' shitbox.

Taking her big plastic cup of water and her box of Cheerios toward the back of the house, she slammed through the place. If Sanders was here, he'd already heard her and she stood no chance. And she didn't have time to be quiet. She quickly used the restroom and then found what she needed in the second bedroom: a closet full of clothing.

She ate another slow handful of Cheerios and managed to keep them down as she looked through what was available. If she hadn't just barfed up the only food she'd eaten in over a day, her stomach would have churned at the thought of putting on

Sanders' clothing. But she'd thought of no other options, so she pulled out an old t shirt and wondered if it had microscopic bloodstains on it from his previous victims. She was in no position to care.

Seline tugged it on over her head. Then she found a long sleeve shirt and pulled that on top. An old flannel lumberjack-type shirt came next, and she tied it around her waist. She found jeans and a belt and rolled them up so she could wear them, and she abandoned her once-favorite pink suit pants to the floor.

She rummaged through drawers, looking for socks and found several thick pairs. They would be too warm for the day, but overheating was the least of her problems. She also needed shoes and found a pair of old, worn hiking boots that looked to be her best bet. Sitting on the floor and eating another small dose of cheerios, she layered on three pairs of socks, shoved her feet down in the boots and wiggled her toes. They still felt as if there was too much room, but she didn't have time to complain or shop around. Lacing them as tightly as she could, she stood up and tested to see if the size wouldn't cause more harm than help. But they stayed in place and she figured she could run in them if she had to.

It would feel good to get away from Sanders using his own things.

She drank more water carefully to help her wash down the cereal. This time when she headed into the kitchen, she clumped her way through the house. Her feet, now cushioned by all the socks, didn't scream quite as loudly as they had before. Though she could still feel the cuts, and she was confident they would need medical attention, she could move more freely. But it made her think ...

Turning around, she headed into the bathroom where she found a box of band aids and a half-used tube of antibiotic ointment. She shoved them in her pockets and realized she needed a bag. There was nothing in the bathroom or bedroom

—no backpack, no duffel, no bags at all. She headed back into the kitchen, looking out the front window as she passed, afraid of seeing the car coming up the drive. She could run now if she needed to, but she wasn't anywhere near finished.

Luckily, there were a few old plastic bags shoved under the sink and she grabbed one. She put in the band aids, ointment, and headed back into the bedroom, throwing in a second pair of jeans and another long sleeved shirt. She refilled her plastic cup as she passed by the bathroom.

Now was the real work, she thought as she laid everything on the counter in the kitchen. She'd hauled a plastic jug from under the sink and she pulled the milk from the fridge. She needed just a few more things. She had to pull this off or they would never find her.

CHAPTER FORTY-NINE

This was taking far too much time, Seline thought as she ran toward a designated space in the yard behind the house, setting down the bag and the largest cups she'd found, full of water. She then left all the precious things she needed and headed back inside.

She wished she could have taken the gallon jug of milk and filled it with water, but she needed it for other things. She had plenty of food, but had found no safe containers for water— these cups were all she had for her escape. At least if she found more she could carry it.

She scurried inside, already moving better since the food had hit her system. She hadn't quite been ready to shock it with the twinkies she'd scrounged up, but they waited for her in the bag sitting at a distance in the back yard.

She'd left the side door open as there was no point in hiding her presence here. In a little while, hopefully many people would know someone was here. She moved through the place, room by room, waving a filthy old sheet pan she'd found and spreading the smell.

Before she'd run her things outside, she'd turned on the gas stovetop and blown out the pilot light. From what she'd seen, the gas was piped in from a tank on the far side of the property. That would do.

Now she looked over everything she'd prepared for this final piece of her plan.

The milk jug was now empty and relatively thoroughly cleaned. It would be perfect.

In the bathroom, she'd found rust remover and heavy duty tile cleaner. On the stove, Sanders' empty pots sat ruined, destroyed by her boiling down the toxic liquids she'd found. Now, as the smell of gas permeated the air, she poured the thickened and cooled liquids into the waiting jug.

While she'd waited for the cleaners to boil then cool, she'd pulled aluminum foil from under the sink and shredded it into small slivers. She had a good-sized pile and she wished she had a way to weigh it and see if it was too much or too little. But her abductor did not have a kitchen scale. She would have to guess.

There were no funnels in this kitchen so she'd created a paper one to help keep her new formula from sloshing. She couldn't afford to lose a drop.

Then she set the paper onto the counter, touching only the edges and not the soaked parts—she didn't have the time to treat a chemical burn right now. Seline plucked another piece of paper and rolled it into another quick funnel, tucking the edge and making it stay.

With a sharp prayer she held the jug—funnel and all—under the edge of the counter and scraped the shavings into the mouth. A few fluttered away, but she just started the clock ticking, and she couldn't afford to retrieve them.

She stepped into the living room, her breath held against the now strong odor of natural gas. She capped the jug and shook it once.

She lifted the cap briefly to vent it, then shook it a second time. She could feel the liquid inside begin to heat and she smiled to herself. As she shook it a third time, it became almost too warm to touch. But she needed to keep going.

She shook it hard, counting as she did. *Four. Five. Six.*

That would have to do. She set it carefully in the center of the living room, wishing she could have thrown it, but this concoction required ginger handling. The moment it touched the floor, she ran.

Slapping the kitchen door shut behind her she bolted for her things. Taking no time to stop and be careful, she leaned down as she went by and snatched them to her. The water sloshed a bit from both cups, a small leaf had fallen into one of them, but she couldn't worry about such things.

She ran another ten paces before the silence bothered her. She went another twenty before she became truly concerned. Another ten and she stopped.

Turning, she looked back. It should have happened already.

Had it been too weak, and nothing had happened?

She had matches tucked in the back pocket of Sanders' jeans —now hers—in case she had to go back and light the place by hand, but that would be far too dangerous to get close, and she hadn't yet figured out how to do it in a way that would be safe for her ... well, she *had* figured it out, she thought. It just didn't seem to be working.

Seline hurried farther and farther away until eventually she deemed herself safely away. Turning around again, she walked backwards for a few paces before deciding that was a wonderful way to back directly into Sanders.

Paranoid, she spun a rapid circle, scanning the whole area. But she saw no one. So she beelined for the trees again, though this time she aimed for a different place. If Sanders had actually managed to trace her footsteps, or follow any kinds of marking or trail she'd left the night before, then he would go where she had been.

But she was banking on the fact that no one would expect her to go back. Certainly not Sanders.

She was disappointed now. She'd wasted all that time to ruin his house. She'd destroyed all the food with the gas. She'd broken the window. He couldn't stay there anymore. But she'd also destroyed her only source of water and food. *It should have worked!*

She was almost to the treeline again, but this time, as she stepped into the shade of the firs, she heard a noise. It still wasn't the noise she had hoped for, it was tires on gravel.

Holding her breath again, every movement fight or flight, she ducked behind the nearest trunk, not wanting to move. At least she was no longer dressed in pale pink and she would blend in better if he did look this way.

Seline peeked around the edge and tipped her head to get a look at the car coming up the drive. It was the same one she'd seen the day before. Whatever he'd done with hers, she didn't know. She couldn't see the driver but had to assume this was Sanders again.

She took a chance and ducked farther back into the trees. Her eyes still on the car, she nearly bumped into a trunk and then she stepped into something soft. Looking down, she found her foot had sunk into relatively fresh soil.

It wasn't too recent, but not old work either.

She stepped back far enough to see the three foot by five foot shape. Her stomach rolled once again as she realized the churned dirt and almost neat, ninety degree corners left no doubt it was human work. *And,* she thought, *human sized.*

Seline leaped backward trying to get away, but stepped into another similar spot.

Were they graves? But Sanders left his bodies in the water. Didn't he?

But she didn't have time to think about that. She tucked herself out of sight again, ignoring the probability of dead bodies at her feet. Plucking the leaf from the cup, she sipped at the water and watched the car disappear behind the house.

Her plan hadn't worked.

If she was very lucky, Sanders would spark something when he walked inside. The whole place would blow, because that was what she needed. She could only wait and hope.

She heard the faint metal of the car door slamming, but on the heels of that noise came a larger, louder *Boom*.

Seline rocked back as she felt the air move around her. Surely, she wasn't close enough for a shockwave? She wondered as she watched in satisfaction.

The small building went up in a fireball.

CHAPTER FIFTY

Seline stood back, watching the fire as it ate the house.

She hoped Sanders had fried inside. She hoped he'd stepped into the kitchen and smelled the gas and that he'd been standing in the middle of the place as her homemade bomb exploded.

Watching, finally satisfied from the shadow of the trees, she saw pieces of the house floating back to the ground. Probably it was shingles, scraps of curtain or bedding, the lightweight materials that had been inside. The glass in the windows had blown outward on the initial blast, but nothing had reached as far as where she stood.

She was grateful she'd been smart enough to gather supplies for herself. Her stolen plastic grocery bag held food, clothes, and Sanders' two sharpest kitchen knives. Seline had been disappointed to find no guns in her search through the house. That was a damn shame, because if she had she simply could have shot him when he'd come home. She wouldn't have had to blow the place up.

If the car was undamaged and Sanders was dead, maybe she could drive it away from here. Just the thought was heavenly, but she couldn't head back toward the building until she was certain he was dead … and until the fires were put out. Probably the local firefighters would arrive well before she would get a chance to scope out the car.

She had her two cups of water, still mostly full and she hoped it would be enough to sustain her until somebody showed up. Because someone had to report that a nearby building had exploded. At the very least someone would catch it on a satellite image somewhere. She was certain that Sanders had taken her as far from any nearby civilization as possible, but he'd underestimated her will to live.

As she watched, a massive weight lifted from her shoulders —one she hadn't quite realized she was carrying. If anyone had asked her, Seline would have said *of course she was carrying a huge weight*. She knew she was in a life or death fight, but feeling the weight of it suddenly dissipate was headier than she'd anticipated.

Her knees threatened to give way, and she quickly wrapped one arm around the nearest trunk to steady herself. In her free hand, she managed to clutch both of the big plastic cups, suddenly realizing that if she dropped them, she'd be in maybe just as much trouble as before. Surely, she still hadn't drunk or eaten enough to make up for going almost thirty-six hours without food or water. But she was alive.

After several big, deep breaths, she reached down into the bag and pulled out one of the Twinkies. It wasn't even food, she was confident of that. A friend of hers had once discussed having a food-to-plastic scale on which an organic apple scored a 'one' and a Lego scored a 'ten.' Seline was pretty certain that her Twinkie ranked about a 9.8. But she'd never seen anything so heavenly in her whole life.

The loud crinkle of the wrapper startled her. Had her ears been ringing from the explosion? She hadn't been that close. Forcibly calming her nerves, she reminded herself that loud noises were problematic when Williams Sanders could hear her —but he couldn't hear her now.

So she crumpled the wrapper in her hand and ate the Twinkie. While she wanted to shove the whole thing into her mouth, she forced herself to take small bites and wondered if her stomach would accept it. It didn't matter. Nothing had ever tasted so good.

She had just popped the last bite in her mouth when she heard the voice bellow across the open land.

"You fucking bitch!"

CHAPTER FIFTY-ONE

"What did they say?" Kalan demanded an answer even as he jumped up from where he'd been dozing on the couch.

Clearly, he'd been sleeping like a firefighter: still listening with one ear, and ready to leap to action at a moment's notice.

Verner held the phone to her ear so Kalan had no idea what had roused him, but he must have heard something. Honestly, there'd been a lot of times people in the room had been on the phone, and *everyone* in the room had been able to hear both sides of the conversation. So it was a bitch that he couldn't hear whatever had triggered him awake now.

Verner waved her hand at him, as if to tell him it was nothing.

His heart was still beating heavily from jolting awake and his brain reminded him that Verner was probably right. So far *everything* had been nothing.

Him recognizing the house in the picture Ivy brought hadn't been right. It hadn't turned out to be the house he was thinking of. Though it did look like a house that Sanders would use, the police in the area had already rushed out to the place and interrupted the occupants—an older couple who had been watching TV. So some poor couple who had no connection to anything was now suffering because the FBI had rushed the house.

Other checks had all been a big bust, too. So Kalan forced himself to hang back until Verner hung up the phone. Then he asked, "What was it?"

Though it was probably another round of nothing, he wanted to know what *exact kind* of nothing it was. Because, sooner or later, some of these nothings had to add up to *something* they could use.

"A property out near Brownlee," Verner said, as though that were enough information.

Kalan pressed harder. "What about it?"

"There was an explosion."

Every cell in his body clicked into place. He was wide awake now. "The local authorities are checking it out. Right?"

"Of course, they are." Verner set the phone down on the folding table and leaned back over her laptop, as though Kalan's questions were of no consequence.

"No." Kalan tapped her shoulder and forced her to look up at him. "This is important. We need to go there, now."

And then he said what he had suddenly begun to *believe.* "Seline is there."

"They said it looks like a gas fire."

"Okay." He backed off for a moment but it didn't change his conviction. Then he turned back to Verner, this time his intensity caught Rossi's attention as well. "You're saying that one of the properties we were watching—a property with a known link to Sanders—just exploded."

"That doesn't mean your girlfriend's there," Verner told him, her expression not moving from the neutral setting it had been at for almost two days now.

"I think it does."

"No." Verner countered with such a blah tone that he almost backed off.

But there was more. "Someone turned on the gas and blew up the house. It's not a coincidence."

"It could have been an accident," Verner replied. "Gas leaks happen all the time, especially on these older properties."

"Right. But none of the other properties has blown up since Seline disappeared."

"True." But though Verner voiced agreement, she once again dismissed him and turned back to the laptop.

That was when it hit him. Verner and Rossi, and the rest of the FBI agents, were just doing their due diligence. Though they all desperately wanted to find Seline, they no longer believed they would find her alive.

He was looking for his girlfriend. They were looking for a body.

She'd passed the fourteen-hours-missing mark quite some time ago. In fact, far too long ago to have blown up a house just now.

Kalan swallowed hard, as if he could swallow down the idea that she was gone just as easily.

On the one hand, he told himself he should believe them, that they knew what they were doing. Despite their dismissal of his idea, they hadn't yet declared her dead, nor had they packed up their laptops, folded up their tables, and left him sitting here in her living room alone. They had not changed her status officially from "missing" to "missing presumed dead."

The other side of him fought back. They hadn't changed her status, but his hope cost them nothing. However, losing hope would cost him *everything*.

He plopped back down onto the couch and tried to be a good resident. He'd been fighting this for a full day, knowing that if he got too overheated or fought too hard, they could and would throw him out. It wasn't his home any more than it was theirs. They had jurisdiction. He did not.

He was only allowed to stay while he was being helpful, or at least while he remained out of their way. But then the phone rang again and Verner frowned a little as she answered. "Arson?"

Kalan's heart felt like it lifted in his chest. *He was right.*

Tapping Verner on the arm, he motioned to her phone, waving his hand and silently insisting that she put it on speaker. Though she rolled her eyes, she did it, and Kalan inserted himself into the conversation.

"Accelerant?"

"Doesn't look like it. I'm standing at the edge of the property, so I'm a good way off, but I know fire." The voice replied, though Kalan had no idea who he was now talking to.

"Can you tell the ignition source?" Kalan hoped his language was proving that he was the right person to handle the call—not Verner—when it came to arson. The firefighter outranked everyone here in that case.

"I'll know more when the team gets here. I was nearby, and I'm first on the scene. Honestly, it smells like a bomb."

Kalan heard the words in every fiber of his body. "Can you tell what kind?"

He was staring at Verner now. Though her expression was still firmly in the neutral zone, she was at least looking a little more curious.

"Smells like household cleaners but I can't tell more until I get close."

Yes! Kalan thought, relief flooding through his system as he handed the phone back to Verner.

"That's Seline," he said. "She made a chemical bomb."

Verner was now nodding along to whatever the other firefighter was saying.

But one of the other agents on the other side of the room

was looking at him like he was crazy. So Kalan turned around and nearly yelled, "She's a chemist!"

He jabbed his hand toward the back of the house. "She built her own laboratory in the back of the house. And one of Sanders houses just blew up with a bomb made from common household ingredients."

"Probably." Verner held her hand up to keep him from jumping to conclusions.

But he was jumping right off that cliff. "Seline was there and she's alive."

CHAPTER FIFTY-TWO

The water sloshed from the cups, as Seline bolted across the open field. She was down to a quarter of what she had started with.

She risked a pause to raise the cup to her mouth. It was a risk with Sanders still very alive and likely coming after her now. But she was burning energy fast, and it was better to drink the water than to lose it. She had no idea when she would find more.

The work boots were a godsend. Though the soles of her feet were still cranky and angry, she could move quickly. Her sure step was much faster than she had been moving the night before. She cut a straight line this time, no longer needing to avoid corn rows. Still, she could feel when she stepped on a sharp rock or a stalk that didn't give way, but this time she didn't have to worry that she'd injured herself further.

She'd tied the laces just a little too tight, anticipating a run—and that was paying off now. She was probably visible to anyone who looked this direction as the field had already died off a bit for autumn. The grass and the corn was low to the earth—not high enough to dive into to hide. The pale colors of wheat and corn made her jeans and the blue flannel shirt stand out. So she kept pushing forward.

Drinking while she ran was proving too difficult. So she stopped for a moment and glugged as much water as she could. Then she poured one cup into the other and used the empty one on top, hoping to keep as much of it as possible from sloshing out.

With her quick task accomplished, Seline took off again as fast as she could. It had been a calculated risk. Stopping gave Sanders a chance to catch up, however brief her break had been. Having a moment to breathe and having more water in her system gave her the opportunity to go for longer. She had no idea right now if her gamble would pay off.

She ran away from the house and not toward anything. There wasn't anything to run toward. Either the earth curved away before anything of value was on the horizon, or another line of trees had impeded her sight. Behind her, Sanders occasionally bellowed out that she was a bitch or that he was going to find her.

He at least seemed confident there was no one around to hear him.

She just wished she knew whether or not he had a gun. But if he had one, he hadn't yet fired it. Still, there was every possibility that he was simply waiting to get close enough before using it.

Seline might never know. There might be no warning; she might simply feel the sting of a bullet in her back as she went face down onto the hard ground. But until that happened, she would keep running.

She passed through another tree line and considered stopping and climbing again. But she now had the water and the bag of clothes and food. Stopping might be the right choice *if* she knew she could hide, but she didn't know that. She didn't dare look back, but she made another calculated guess—this time she estimated the distance between them by the volume of his voice, and she had to pray that she had a decent enough lead.

While she'd initially run hell for leather, she was now trying to regulate her pace. This was a long game and, if she could run until he was tired, she might get away.

He was older, though probably still in good shape. One of the times he'd passed her before he'd been jogging.

Fuck, she thought, wishing suddenly that she, too, was a jogger. But it didn't matter, it was too late now.

As she passed through the tree line—again only a small handful of trunks deep—she finally spotted a blip on the horizon. With a slight shift in direction, she aimed toward it. Whatever it was, it was the only thing out here.

Seline didn't know how long she ran, but it wasn't that far before she was able to make out the peak of a roof and the pale color of what was probably once white siding.

It was a house!

Even as she dashed toward it with everything she had, she wondered: Did she dare lead Sanders to someone else? Would he then slaughter them all? Or would the homeowners defend her?

At the very least, she thought, they might not be home. But a home out here may very well have a gun or something else she could blow up. She decided to try her luck with whomever might be there.

With her eyes on the prize and her hope the thing fueling her, Seline aimed toward the tiny house and ran with everything she had.

CHAPTER FIFTY-THREE

No! Seline screamed in her own head.

No one was home.

She'd hoped for a miracle, that the owners would hear her pounding on the door and take her in and she'd be safe—finally. But she'd wasted time knocking and gone hoarse yelling and all for no one.

Giving up on help, she'd broken the glass in the door, just like at Sanders place. She'd wrapped her hand in the spare shirt, broke the little window, and then reached in and turned the lock. She was an old pro at breaking and entering now.

Her heart sank. She'd done all that work to blow up the other house, to bring everyone there, and now she was too far away. Sanders had pushed her from the one chance at rescue that she had. She was sad and angry and about to start shaking.

Though it would be easier to give up, she hadn't come this far to sit on the porch and cry. So she walked her way inside and checked the place out. They could forgive her later.

Somehow, the home held no more weapons she could use than the kitchen knives she'd passed. On her rush through the place, she'd found a gun safe. Exactly as she suspected, the home out in the middle of nowhere definitely housed gun owners. But the safe was doing exactly as it was supposed to do—keeping her out.

Though this place was lived in, Seline couldn't find a damn phone either. That would have been her second best option after a gun. But the owners appeared not to have a landline. That meant maybe there was a cell tower nearby, but since Seline had no cell phone it would do her no good until she found one.

She wanted to scream and beat her fist on the wall. But it was too late to wallow in her bad luck. Instead, she searched the house, keeping an eye to the windows and staying low, in case Sanders showed up. She didn't want to be seen.

Listening for him, she grabbed one of the knives—the only weapon at hand—and checked every drawer and closet. The house yielded nothing of value.

When she'd looked everywhere she could and come up with nothing, she moved into the short central hallway. Though she could see the front door, it had no windows and she wasn't visible. With her back to the wall and the knife firmly in her clenched fist, she tried to eat or at least drink some water.

Maybe he hadn't found her. Maybe she'd gotten away.

Seline didn't know how long she sat there like that, but the tension slowly ebbed from her bones. She could only sustain that level of fear for so long. She breathed deeply and, though she still waited for the sharp retort of a bullet or a crash as he breached the door, nothing came.

Was she safe?

Just when enough time had passed that she'd started to believe he wouldn't find her, the front doorknob rattled.

Seline's chest clenched hard at once again being thwarted. Sanders had found her. *Could nothing work in her damn favor?*

"Bitch! I know you're in there!"

Any hope that it was the homeowner disappeared in a puff of smoke. Sanders had caught up, and she had only a few options. But Seline was already on her feet.

She could try to get out the back door before Sanders made it around to the side. But even if she made it, she could run but he would be right behind her.

Another option was to go out the window from one of these back rooms. As the door rattled and he raged behind her, she pushed against the sash, but it didn't want to lift. It appeared to have been painted shut.

And that meant maybe her best chance was to stand and fight.

She told herself it had taken him a while to find her. While he'd been hunting, she'd been resting. She was ready. Standing in the back room, she dropped her precious bag at her feet.

With the large kitchen knife clutched close, she waited. It was maybe two seconds of eternity later that she realized she was holding it wrong. She turned the blade outward and changed her grip so that her thumb was over the end, giving her more force. She'd not practiced like this—why would she?—but she'd seen that this was the better way to go into a knife fight.

After another moment when nothing happened, she reached down and got the second smaller knife. Was there anywhere on her that she could keep it?

The smaller one might be easier to wield and having a second weapon at hand wouldn't hurt. She stuck it in her back pocket, thinking it just might injure her. But a cut on her ass was better than not having a knife if she needed it.

Gripping the large blade with two hands now, she plastered herself to the wall behind the corner and waited. She couldn't afford to peek down the hallway and give herself away, so she breathed shallowly and listened hard.

She heard nothing.

272

He wouldn't have left.

For a moment, everything stood still, and then the shadow passed the window.

Her guts leapt into her throat as she saw Sanders' face appear.

CHAPTER FIFTY-FOUR

S anders looked at her through the glass and held her gaze as he grinned.

In that moment, Seline knew she was as good as dead. Had she not been held motionless with fear, she would have shuddered at the ice that gripped its fingers down her spine and along every nerve ending.

But he just stared, as if knowing the worst thing he could do was terrorize her. Sanders didn't raise a gun and shoot her through the window. Instead, he nodded and passed by, heading around the side of the house.

She felt the flare of conviction that she wouldn't die easily.

As soon as he was out of sight, she ran. She needed another hiding place. One he couldn't see from outside. She searched frantically through the living room but found nothing well enough hidden.

The bathroom! It wouldn't have windows he could peer into!

She could hear him outside as she raced back down the short hallway, wondering if he was watching her disorganized search. But she pushed the door mostly closed and got a smart idea.

Good.

She dared to set down the knife for a moment and unscrewed the cap of the bottle of cleaner she'd found under the sink.

Then she waited, jug in one hand, knife in the other.

She waited until she heard him come through the side door, using the path she'd already made. She heard the softest of footsteps as he crossed through the living area. Only when she heard him in the hallway, did she slap the door wide open.

He was further away than she'd anticipated, but he lunged for her anyway.

She ran toward him—hopefully not what he was expecting—and she arced her arm upward, managing to aim the open top of the jug at his face. The caustic bathroom cleaner caught him in the eyes and his open mouth.

Yes! she thought.

But though he bellowed in rage and clawed at his own eyes in pain, he was now directly in her way.

She hadn't thought this through well enough. As fast as her brain had been racing, as many plans as she'd considered and rejected, she'd somehow managed to trap herself.

Oh, well, she thought. She'd come this far. If the only way out was *through*, then she'd go through him.

She'd just burned his eyes badly enough that he'd never see again. So she dropped the jug, already rushing him as she had heard it hit the ground. This time she raised the knife. Her primal scream echoed off the walls and she knew she was going to kill him.

But as she went to drive the blade into his chest, his hands closed over her wrist.

Seline fought back with everything she had, though it wasn't worth much. She kicked out but missed contact. She planted her right foot and rammed her left knee up and tried to nail him in the groin.

Sanders avoided everything she threw.

White hot pain seared her wrist as he twisted it, forcing her to let go of the knife. In a move she'd not anticipated, the knife did not fall to the ground, but wound up in his hand.

Ducking and lunging was the only thing that saved her from taking the knife directly through her heart. But he stabbed it downward into her side. The blaze of hot pain bloomed through her side and she could feel the warmth of her own blood seeping out.

Shock was likely the only thing keeping her upright.

With a sneer, Sanders stepped back. His eyes were red and puffy, his mouth drooling, looking—finally—less like a man and more like the hideous creature that he was. But his expression said that he knew that he'd won.

In that moment, Seline had a blinding flash of clarity. *She was as good as dead.*

Her only hope now was to take Sanders with her.

She bolted toward him, ignoring the pain shooting through her right side, from her toes to her shoulder. With each step, Sanders watched her approach, the confident grin remaining in place.

At the last possible moment, Seline reached into her back pocket and pulled out the steak knife. This time she did manage to take him by surprise as she plunged into his chest.

It went in much easier than she had expected. In the adrenaline-fueled haze of the moment, she saw that she'd punched it in sideways. *Had she been smart enough to weave it between his ribs?*

It didn't matter. His face contorted in pain.

Had she hit his heart? She didn't know.

Her head pounded, and noise came from all sides. Her ears rang with wavering high pitched wails underlaid with a gravelly static. It was probably the sound her body made as she gave up on this life.

Sanders bellowed again.

She had the kitchen knife sticking out of her torso, but he now had a steak knife sticking out of his chest. She felt a moment of satisfaction at that.

This time, he didn't lunge for her. Instead, he turned away and ran.

Her last thought before she collapsed onto the floor was that somehow the bastard was still alive.

CHAPTER FIFTY-FIVE

Kalan ran past the still burning remains of the exploded home, his feet pounding the hard earth as his eyes darted in every direction.

While much of the house still stood, there was nothing he could check. Firefighters had arrived before he and the agents had, and they'd already turned water to the blaze. He knew better than to get in their way.

Kalan only hoped they could see enough to know that no one was inside.

The FBI agents had their guns drawn, but Kalan's hands were empty.

They hadn't wanted to bring him, but he'd simply followed them out to the driveway and climbed in the backseat of Verner and Rossi's old sedan.

Though Rossi had demanded, "You can't be here." Kalan only answered, "okay," and proceeded to buckle himself in. He watched as the two women in the front seat looked to each other and simply gave up before peeling out of the driveway.

Now, he and Verner and Rossi ran around one side of the house, as Watson and Decker squealed to a stop behind them.

Kalan veered around the car the explosion had overturned. And once again, Kalan thought, *Way to go, Seline!*

"Car's clear!" Decker called.

"Blood?" Rossi yelled back.

"No. I don't think anyone was in it when it flipped. The doors are all still closed."

Kalan heard the conversation as though the others were at some great distance, until Watson declared, "I'm going to do a search for body parts."

With that, he felt his stomach clench. His feet stopped and he would have toppled over had he not had way too much practice running and changing direction suddenly.

But he headed back to the house, getting as close as he dared, and this time he joined the conversation. "Seline's not in there."

Watson, at least, took him seriously. "Why not?"

"The bomb. She made it and she wouldn't have blown herself up. She would have blown up Sanders."

"Then I'm looking for Sanders," Watson told him, and he turned back to the open space, wondering where Seline had gone. There were fields and sky in all directions. She might have gone through the fields or crossed the road they'd driven in on. He had no idea, and he turned a full circle praying for a clue.

It was only moments later that Verner hollered. "This way! I think I've got a trail."

But right as she said it, just as he felt the relief of having a direction, Rossi also called out, "I've got a trail!"

The two agents were pointing in different enough directions that Kalan was forced to choose.

Either might lead to Seline. If he chose wrong, he wouldn't be there when they found her.

But there was no time to linger, so he followed Verner, who'd already taken off at an alarmingly fast pace. He followed her simply because he was slightly closer to her than to Rossi.

Decker took off from the yard, leaving the house behind to

follow them, but Verner waved him back. "Go with Rossi. I've got this guy."

He might be only *this guy*, Kalan thought, but he was the guy who was going to do everything to save Seline.

They didn't move as fast as he would like. Verner had to stop periodically and check to see if she still had eyes on a trail. It seemed it would go cold—though, honestly, Kalan had no idea what they were looking for. And he was entirely at the mercy of her best guess for which direction to aim.

Verner would stop, look around, and then declare, "I think it's there." And they would take off again, until they hit whatever point in the distance she had seen and the painstaking process would begin again.

The whole time, he wondered what might be happening to Seline.

They halted again in the middle of a cornfield, and this time when Verner looked up, she said, "It looks like the trail leads directly to that house."

That house was still standing, and Kalan was confident that if Seline had seen it, she would have run for it. She hadn't blown it up, too, so she might still be inside.

When he and Verner finally reached the house, it was almost eerily silent.

This time, Verner treated him like an agent. She motioned to him with two fingers indicating that he go one way while she went the other. She, of course, still had her gun drawn, and he was still empty handed.

There were no trees close to the house. No fallen branches he could pick up to use for a club. But he made a note to himself to grab the first weapon that he could.

Heading around the side of the house, Kalan nearly smacked into the man standing on wavering feet. He had blood on his hands and more dripping down his chest. His face was red and swollen, his mouth wide as he gulped for air. The sound he made was wrong—almost inhuman—and it took Kalan a full second to realize that he was looking directly at William Treat Sanders.

The man was damaged, possibly on his last legs, but he stepped forward toward Kalan. And while it had taken Kalan a moment to recognize Sanders, Sanders recognized him in a heartbeat. The red mouth pulled into a cruel smile and—though it was difficult to understand the words—Sanders' meaning was clear.

"She's dead."

With his own scream of rage, Kalan rushed at him. He pushed with two hands, sending Sanders stumbling backwards. It didn't matter how much the killer fought back, whatever Seline had done to him, he was too weak to have any effect.

Quickly, Kalan recognized that at least some of the blood was from a puncture wound, and the knife that caused it was still sticking out of Sanders' chest.

Wrapping his own hand firmly around the handle, Kalan defied every medical protocol he knew and yanked the blade out. Sanders screamed in pain.

But Kalan didn't give him enough time to cut off the sound before he plunged it in again and again.

CHAPTER FIFTY-SIX

As soon as Sanders' head rolled to the side and the breath seeped out of his body, Kalan let go of the knife.

Pushing himself off of the body, he ran screaming into the house.

Verner had taken no time to alert him that she'd found Seline, she simply knelt over the woman he loved as the agent shouted into her phone.

"I need medical here immediately. Severe trauma, knife wound, torso, severe blood loss."

It wasn't at all what an EMT would say, not quite the language that Kalan was used to on medical scenes. And he wasn't as fully trained as some of the others—not a firefighter-paramedic—but he knew enough.

He didn't ask, just pushed Verner out of the way, peeled his shirt, and wrapped the blade sticking out of Seline's side. He had to anchor it. The less it moved, the safer she would be.

He put his hand on her hip and motioned Verner to hold Seline's shoulder.

"Don't move, baby. Don't move. We've got you." He crooned the words, working to hold very still.

He didn't need to keep Seline still. She didn't move at all, and that scared the shit out of him. He wasn't sure if she was still conscious, and with his free hand he kept two fingers on her pulse, petrified each time he couldn't feel it.

The EMTs were too far out and she was losing blood far too fast.

He moved his hand from her hip to her side, trying to apply pressure as best he could without moving the knife at all. Had it hit a kidney? He didn't know. It had certainly sliced her up.

His brain ran through all the horrid scenarios. The blade could have nicked something vital. She might lose something necessary, and even if she didn't, he knew that sepsis was a risk. Who knew where the knife had been before it had been plunged into her side?

She roused for a moment, and he felt the slight movement under his hand. "Don't move, baby."

"He got away." Seline murmured the words, as she fought for consciousness.

Kalan told her the one thing that might help. "No baby. He's dead."

He almost said, *I killed him*, but instead, he whispered the words, "You got him, Seline. You got him."

Then, as she faded into unconsciousness again, he yelled to Verner. *"Where's the damn ambulance?"*

CHAPTER FIFTY-SEVEN

S eline put a hand to her side as she slowly levered herself off the couch.

"You're not supposed to be doing that!" Kalan chastised her as he jumped out of the chair to hold onto her arm.

He tugged at her, as though to help her lower back to the seat she was trying so desperately to leave. She had been on the couch for too long.

"I have to go *somewhere else*. And the *doctor—*" she emphasized the title, "—said I could walk a little bit each day and that I should."

She didn't fault Kalan, he was just being overly careful. But it had been two weeks.

"For twelve days now, we've known I'm going to make a full recovery." She tugged a little and he let her arm go.

"Okay," he conceded, backing away a little bit. Both hands were in the air, pale palms facing her, but he trailed along as though she might topple at any moment. "Where are you going?"

"To the kitchen." She fought not to sigh and roll her eyes at him. He'd taken yet more time off of work to be her nursemaid since she'd gotten home.

"How about ..." he countered, "you go to the dining room, and I will bring you whatever you need from the kitchen."

"Fine." But she waved him away. And then, as he watched her take a few more steps, she waved him away again, until he finally headed into the kitchen.

She might be slow, but she was good. She had not only survived Sanders, she'd helped take him out.

She had hazy memories of the fight and everything after. From the ambulance ride, she had vague recollections of Kalan telling the EMTs that she had not nicked a kidney. She'd asked him later how he'd known, and he'd only said, "Because you weren't already dead."

Apparently, kidneys bled out fast.

They'd had an ongoing argument about who had killed Sanders. Seline said it was Kalan. Kalan said it was Seline—that while he might have plunged the blade in for the final time, the man was already on his last legs. He'd already been burned with a caustic solution and stabbed in the chest. The killer would have died anyway even if Kalan hadn't gotten to him. Kalan insisted that he had just finished the job a little quicker.

She'd had two surgeries repairing the damage from the blade. Her feet had been treated for cuts and a minor infection. She'd been rehydrated by IV and pumped full of antibiotics and painkillers. But she had been home for four days now.

And, as she sat at her own dining room table, she realized there was something she needed to do.

Her snippets of memory included Kalan holding her hand in the ambulance. And then again in the hospital. She'd passed in and out of consciousness, but the one thing that remained the same was his soft voice whispering, "I love you."

He returned with a glass of milk and a bowl of cocoa puffs. He knew better than to bring her Cheerios and had, in fact, thrown out the box that she'd had in the pantry. He set the junk food in front of her before he returned with his own bowl.

Her cereal was going to get soggy, but this was definitely more important.

He'd said nothing about his feelings in any of the time she'd been truly awake. Now she was healthy enough that she could get around her house by herself if she needed to. So she said, "I remember some things you said in the ambulance and in between my surgeries."

Though he'd already managed to get two bites into his mouth, the spoon stopped at her words. He set it down and looked at her carefully as if knowing where she was headed. His words were cautious. "What do you remember?"

Taking a deep breath for fortitude, Seline regretting it immediately as she felt a pull from her side. *Nope.* Not quite ready for that yet. But she still needed to do this. "You said you loved me."

He nodded, not denying any of it. She would have breathed a sigh of relief, if not for the wound she was still healing from. But he didn't deny it.

Well, it hadn't been her imagination then. *Next step.* "Did you mean it?"

He didn't respond right away and she rushed to fill in the empty space. "It's okay. I understand if it was a spur of the moment thing."

"It wasn't. It did mean it."

"But you haven't said it again ..." She let the words trail off, so he could fill in the blanks.

"Once we knew you were going to make it, my feelings didn't seem like the kind of thing to burden you with. You need to heal. This could wait."

She nodded. "Well, I'm out of the woods now." They'd had so many interesting conversations.

He told her that he'd known the second the report came in

about the house blowing up, that it was her. She'd told him that that had been her plan. That she believed no one could find her unless there was something to draw them. Her goal had been to be seen, but Sanders had survived the blast and she'd run so far she hadn't expected to be found.

They'd talked about her job. He'd contacted Dr. Morales with the updates, and her boss had even visited her in the hospital, reassuring her that her job was safe whenever she was ready to come back. She hadn't even pushed her back on her tenure track and Seline had held it together until the department chair left the room. Then Kalan had found her crying. She'd told him all of it.

The job was her safety net. She'd told him about leaving her home to search for an opportunity like this. And he'd told her about another case of arson they'd had in town. How his fellow firefighter, Luke Hernandez, was getting squirrely about it.

Then he'd told her about how the department was getting a new firefighter—each shift got an extra person. A-shift was getting some guy named Joe. They'd all been stunned when Jo had turned out to be Joely. Seline had laughed at him, but it made her side hurt.

They'd talked about everything and anything ... except this.

"If you're ready to hear it," he said, softly reaching out to take her hand, "then you should know that I'm head over heels in love with you. And I think I have been since that day we got stuck in the elevator."

Seline smiled. At least that didn't hurt. She'd doubted him along the way, wondered if all of his feelings had been based in the heady trouble swirling around her. He was such a hero, but she hadn't wanted to be the woman he rescued.

Now, with everything behind them, her doubts fled.

She turned his hand over and laced her fingers through his, dark and light making a perfect pattern. She looked him in the eyes to leave no doubt and said, "I love you, too."

CHAPTER FIFTY-EIGHT

Jo Huston shut the door of her BMW and her heart sank. She'd screwed up. Again.

She'd parked in the firefighters lot behind the department the last time she was here, to meet the crew. Then, she'd been too nervous to notice. She'd gone inside, met the guys on A-shift—who were open-mouth stunned that Jo wasn't a male—and left.

But this time, she wasn't as nervous. This time she was staying to work her first shift and as she looked around the lot, she saw her silver BMW stuck out like a sore thumb. Aside from one nice sports car, hers was the only one that said 'money.' And of course it was. *What was she thinking?*

She had too many strikes against her; she couldn't afford to not fit in here. She was a woman, she came from a wealthy family, and … she had that history. If she was smart, she would have bought herself a Camry or something.

If she was lucky, no one would notice and she would have two days to get something else.

"Nice M-series there, JoJo!"

Crap. She let out an aggravated sigh as she hit the lock. It beeped loud enough to make sure that every head turned her direction. Shift change—everyone was here.

As she looked up, Jo saw the grin and the mustache. Conrad Phillips. C-shift. Asshole.

Should she call back, "My name's not JoJo"? No. That would only provoke him. Instead, she offered a sweet smile. "You like it? What are you driving, Connie?"

If they were playing the "stupid names game" she could at least fire back.

His lips tightened and she kept a neutral expression. She was glad she wasn't on shift with him and she told herself it was good to know where the hits were going to come from.

She stood next to her silver performance model, watching as he crossed the lot. Every time she came in, she'd pass him, so she wouldn't give an inch now, even though she wanted to go inside and start her shift.

A-shift had to be better than Conrad Phillips, didn't they?

Aside from acting like fools that Jo was a woman, they'd been fine. Two of them had treated her with kid gloves and two had dismissed her. But the chief was nice, and she knew she'd have to prove herself like anyone else.

As long as they let her.

Phillips took his sweet time getting in the car, so she started to walk away. But, as he backed up, he went too fast and stopped just inches shy of her bumper ... and her legs.

Fuck him.

She had her bag in one hand, just like everyone else in the lot, so she used her free one to slap the trunk of his old Camry. Maybe she wouldn't get one, after all. "Hey! I hope they don't let you drive the rigs."

She grinned, though it was forced and not funny at all.

He flipped her off as he peeled away.

Day One.

She kept her head down and walked through the open back

doors with the other firefighters coming onto shift. She'd tried to memorize their names.

Sebastian Kane, the blond surfer-looking guy, was polishing the already-shiny bumper of the ladder truck. Kalan Smith was at his locker, his nearly bald head reaching the top edge, black skin moving with a strength and efficiency she admired. Ronan ... *something-Irish* came out the door and grinned at her. He was the happy-go-lucky one on the crew. They told her he made the coffee and she wasn't to touch the pot.

"Hey, Jo!" he called out, "Chief wants you in his office."

She frowned. Jesus, she'd just walked in. "What could I have possibly done wrong already?"

She'd tried to say it as a joke, but it tugged at her guts. She couldn't fuck this up.

"I think it's something with paperwork?" But Ronan ... *Kelly!* was already walking past her.

Jo tried to hide her sigh as she walked into the chief's office. But another man sat with his back to her. His khaki shirt and olive green pants told her he wasn't another firefighter.

Chief Taggert stood up from his seat, "Jo! I wanted to introduce you to—"

The man stood up, too, and Jo couldn't help the words that fell from her mouth. "Leo Evans."

"You two know each other?"

"She came with Ivy to help find Seline," was all Leo said.

Jo guessed that everyone here was on a first name basis. It already felt weird.

Taggert motioned them both to sit. "Evans is our local search leader. When something happens, you'll be working with him."

Jo nodded. Of course, he was. She'd made the mistake of telling Evans she was search trained and he'd brushed her off back at Seline Marchand's house. Jo had let it slide, *not her monkeys, not her circus.* Though it sounded as if Taggert was now telling her it *was* her circus.

He turned to Leo. "Huston here is one of the top USAR trainees from Dallas."

Leo Evans only nodded slightly. "We don't even have USAR out here."

Urban Search And Rescue wasn't going to help her much in the wilds of Nebraska. To her credit, she hadn't expected to leave Dallas ... or get forced out, as it were.

She just smiled tightly and let the chief handle it.

"Her chief said she's the best. And USAR is still SAR. We need her."

Thank you! she thought. Chief was right, all Search and Rescue was tied together. She wasn't bringing a useless skill to the table.

"Okay," was the only reply Leo Evans gave. He clearly wasn't thrilled to have her here, but Jo had faced worse.

The chief stood up then, a smile on his face as if he'd missed every bit of tension eating up the space in the tiny room. "I just wanted you to meet each other before it was an emergency situation! Mission accomplished."

With his self-congratulation done, he walked past them into the main room and bellowed, "A-shift!"

"That's my call." She motioned over her shoulder as she stood. "Nice to meet you again."

She would *try*, at least.

Leo Evans stood, too. His brown hair and green eyes should have been ordinary. His nose had a small crook, his mouth was neither wide nor thin. He shouldn't have been a heartthrob, but even with that less-than-neutral expression on his face, something about him grabbed her.

He reached out and shook her hand. Just a formality, she knew. Then he walked away, leaving her wondering why she felt as if she should remember him from somewhere ...

Thank you for reading! I love romances with real love and believable characters, and I hope you found all that in these pages. I want to fall in love right along with the characters, and I do, while I'm writing it.

About Savannah

I started writing when I was eight--I hand wrote an 80-page novella that I believed to be (adult) romantic suspense. I'm proud to say, I've gotten a lot better since then. I've grown up to be a nerd at heart! I love neuroscience and people watching, and if you look, you'll find some of that in each Savannah Kade book. Most days you'll find me in my office, looking out my window at a handful of the neighbor's cows, or watching my dogs or my cat roam the backyard.

Follow me, find me, ask me questions! I would love to hear from you.
www.SavannahKade.com
Savannah@SavannahKade.com